THE KILLING GROUND

The shout of "Airlock drill" woke Bran from sleep. He thought of making speed by omitting socks and underwear, but decided that Butcher Korbeith might take the omission as an excuse for having him killed. On the Butcher's ship, a cadet's first space trip was an all-or-nothing final exam; if you screwed up, they spaced you out the airlock.

Downship as fast as he dared go, he was eighth to reach the airlock deck. Quickly they all lined up. The guard checked off his list, and Korbeith began to stalk along the rank.

As he neared, Bran felt sweat gather at crotch and armpits, and begin to slither down his skin. *I never thought I could wish to be back at the Slaughterhouse!* In his mind a resolve formed. If Korbeith jabbed that great, knobby thumb at him, he would immediately, without thought, take his best shot at killing the man. No matter what happened then, if he could take the Butcher with him, that would have to do. *Sometimes to survive you have to become a monster. . . .*

STAR REBEL

F. M. Busby

BANTAM BOOKS
TORONTO · NEW YORK · LONDON · SYDNEY

To Robert and Ginny,
with much gratitude

STAR REBEL
A Bantam Book / February 1984

ISBN 0-553-23852-3

Bantam Books are published by Bantam Books, Inc. Its trademark,
consisting of the words "Bantam Books" and the portrayal of a
rooster, is Registered in U.S. Patent and Trademark Office and in
other countries. Marca Registrada. Bantam Books, Inc., 666 Fifth
Avenue, New York, New York 10103.

1

The Boy

Near to his thirteenth birthday, Bran Tregare lost his home, his family and his surname, which had been Moray.

Some of the reasons he didn't know or understand, but a few he did. His family, headed by his mother Liesel Hulzein, lived at an Australian outpost, in exile from the Hulzein Establishment's North American headquarters. An exile part disgrace and part sanctuary, caused by the fact that Bran and his sister Sparline had a father, the tall young man Hawkman Moray. Whereas their mother Liesel and her implacable older sister Erika, not to mention Bran's grandmother Renalle Hulzein, had none.

They were not illegitimate, those women, but parthenogenetic. Heidele Hulzein had conceived and birthed her daughter Renalle using micro-genetic techniques and no male whatsoever. "Not cloning," Bran's mother once explained, "but the melding of two gametes from the same person." And Renalle's daughters, Erika and Liesel, also carried the continuation of Heidele's original genes, and no others.

And there, or so Bran's father said, lay the problem. The tall, dark man, so obviously junior in age to his wife, told his children, "Renalle and Erika have faith only in their own genes. They won't admit that without an inmixture from time to time, the pattern can deteriorate." Sparline asked why it would, and Hawkman talked about cellular entropy, how a few genes or chromosomes always went wrong. With simpler organisms it wasn't too serious. His white grin transformed his dark face. "But humans are too complex to survive much of a defect rate. So that's why sexual reproduction, with the most

1

vigorous gametes producing new mixes, works best for us. Your aunt and grandmother don't see it that way."

Bran nodded. At twelve he knew a little about sex. He'd know more, he thought, except that Sparline had caught him trying to learn some things with Sheylah, the cook's daughter, and ran and told. He knew she'd do that, so he ran too. Sheylah yelled after him in anger, but he kept going anyway.

Even so, his parents called him in, with Sparline as witness, for inquiry. He wasn't sure whether he was "before the mast" or only "on the carpet," but neither was much fun. Sparline grinned with triumph, getting back at Bran for the bird nest thing the week before, but all that happened was Bran being asked some questions about his own body. The answers were simple. Yes, lately sometimes that part stood up and felt very good. And no, he hadn't actually done anything about it, with Sheylah or with anyone else. His parents nodded to each other. Liesel said, "Before you do, come talk with one of us."

Hawkman added, "And especially, don't mess with the help."

That was all there was to it. Sparline looked disappointed. Though usually they got along well, on some levels there was a kind of running contest. This time, Bran thought, she hadn't won as big as she'd expected to.

Later, with Hawkman telling family problems, she and Bran listened quietly. Aunt Erika, it seemed, hadn't had great luck with gene-replicating herself. "Two miscarriages and a still-born monster, before she managed your cousin Frieda. And that one's flawed." Which, he said, was why the children's own mother Liesel, after two self-fertilization misfires of her own, had defied Hulzein custom. "Came out here to run this boondocks operation, and—"

"And you and Mama fell in love and got married!" Sparline, Bran noted, had to get in *her* two cents' worth.

Hawkman laughed. "Not exactly. For genetic reasons, Liesel chose me; it's no secret. *Later* she paid me the high compliment of keeping me around for my own sake." But ancient history or not, their parents' genuine affection was apparent to both children. Suddenly, counting back, Bran realized that when he'd been born his mother had been thirty-two, and his father only sixteen.

Hawkman was still talking. "To the Hulzein Establishment—Renalle and Erika—you kids are a slap in the face. Their dynasty doesn't include two-parent children." He ruffled

Bran's hair. "Let alone a male child. That's why we live here quietly, using my name, rather than flaunting ourselves at local Hulzein HQ." His eyes slitted. "The fact is, you're safer here. And yet—"

"And yet we mustn't disturb the balance." Bran turned to see that his mother had entered the room. "Against UET's tyranny in North America there's only three forces still effective. And with the New Mafia driven into hiding nearly as bad as the Underground itsel, the Hulzein Establishment is the *only* opposition that dares show its head."

Hawkman grinned. "So that's why we, here, keep ours down."

Bran knew his share of recent history. Both the official version ("*that* pile of crap," Liesel called it), and some dissenting material from the family library and two parents who would answer questions. The official stuff mostly began with New Year One, right after the United Energy and Transport conglomerate won the governing bid from the Synthetic Foods Combine and took control of North America. And immediately began building Total Welfare centers and filling them with "clients." A more accurate term, said Liesel, would be government-owned slaves.

It was also in NY One that star travel had begun. "But UET didn't invent it," said Hawkman, "no matter what they claim now. Do you know about the Shrakken?"

Bran did. "Sure. There's some old fax sheets in the library. Telling how they traveled more than a hundred light-years to get here. Pictures too, but faded." He remembered the tall, hairless aliens with their triangular eyes and inverted-V mouths. "And they walk on their toes, like a dog on its hind legs."

"But what *about* them?" Sparline asked.

Liesel snorted. "According to UET, the poor things fell prey to some Earthly disease or other. What really happened was, as soon as UET's Committee Police were sure the Shrakken didn't have faster-than-light communications, they pumped that ship full of cyanide gas one night—no more Shrakken. So UET had the ship, and their labs could analyze and copy it."

"So now," said Hawkman, "UET has interstellar travel, and their Space Academy has a bigger job than training pilots for asteroid mining."

Then he changed the subject, telling something of how

things used to be. Years before UET achieved power and proclaimed New Year One there had been a time when elections involved voting by the citizenry rather than corporate bidding, and when North America hadn't been all one political unit. But the continent's largest segment, the United States of America, facing economic collapse, moved to the corporate system. "Otherwise," Hawkman said, "we might have gone under. I've never been sure the country chose right." He shrugged. "But of course 'perhaps' applies only to the future, never to the past."

He continued his story. The first two corporate elections, each closely fought, were won by Communications, Inc., and some measure of stability was restored. Then the Synthetic Foods combine made a landslide win, and capitalized on it by annexing Canada, Mexico, and most of Central America. In a new semblance of stability, SynFood held power for four elective terms. But United Energy and Transport had other ideas. "In the sixth corporate election," Hawkman concluded, "the deciding factor was UET's assassination section. We now know them as the Committee Police. And more and more nowadays, their power seems to be permanent."

UET didn't have it all gravy, though. True, with starships as weapons, North America need no longer accept forced immigration from freely breeding Third World countries. But at home, the Underground, loosely descended from the previous century's Counterculture, sometimes made dire examples of those who misused power too flagrantly. And the New Mafia, driven back from almost respectability (in one corporate election the group had even entered a bid) to shadow-legal status, now concentrated on blackmail and extortion from the powerful. "Oh, it's a right mess," Liesel said.

The third thorn in UET's side was quite different: the Hulzein Establishment's legal superstructure carried a long tradition of spotless escutcheon and pristine standing. "The underside of it, though," said Hawkman, "is trickier, and always has been. For every asset that shows on paper, your grandmother Renalle keeps ten that *don't* show, working for her."

"If we're to confuse the children," Liesel put in, "add that Hulzeins seldom make a move that serves only one purpose." As near as Bran could tell, his mother spoke in total sincerity.

What it boiled down to, the boy decided, was that his aunt and grandmother never gave an inch to *anybody*, whether it was UET or a Hulzein defecting from the parthenogenetic ideal. No one knew if the marauders who had tried to kill Bran and Sparline, and who did burn the house, came from either Erika or UET. The new house was better fortified, and fireproof. Hulzein money paid for it, and no argument on the matter reached the children's ears.

Once only, Bran saw his aunt Erika in person. She invited Liesel to a conference in North America, and Bran went along. That was Liesel's idea, but the deciding wasn't so simple. Renalle, the matriarch, wouldn't be present. "She's in Israel," Liesel reported, "trying to wangle an Establishment branch there. Not much chance, I'd think. I expect the Hulzeins have some Jewish ancestry, but no political or religious ties to offer. And strict neutrality is the only safe way to keep UET's hands off a country."

Lying on a sofa, stretched out at his great length, Hawkman asked, "Will you attend Erika's conference alone?"

Liesel smiled. "I can't take *you*; you'd be a red flag to Erika's bull. And Sparline's too young to risk. Bran though—" Her eyes narrowed. "I think our son's cornered the family's devious streak." She turned to the boy. "How'd you like to go see Hulzeins on their own home ground?" Puzzled but interested, he nodded. "Then assuming we disguise you well, can you forget we're mother and son, and be only my serving-boy? Every minute, day and night, for the next two weeks?"

For only a moment, he thought. "Yes, I can."

"Yes, *what*?"

"Yes, Madame Hulzein!" He suppressed the grin that would have come, because it didn't fit the part he had to play.

His mother smiled. Hawkman nodded. Sparline still seemed dubious. And next day she looked at him—with his curly black hair bleached and dyed red, plastered flat, and cut straight across in front—and couldn't hold her laughter. "Old sad *horseface*!" Well, the mirror told him she was right, and the serving-boy's voluminous gold-trimmed costume, hardly cut for anyone of active ways, didn't help much either. But Bran did want to go on this journey, so he put up with everything and made no complaint.

Neither did he protest the crash course, administered by his mother's chief-of-maids. Bran had seen Alexa Duggan's stern ways with the lesser help, of course, but without really noticing. All his ten years he had been one of Alexa's employers, not a menial. The change jolted him. At first he couldn't take it seriously when she threatened him with a caning if his work did not improve (calling him "Jerrin," the name assumed for this role). His weak smile drew a harsher frown; he decided not to test the matter. The third day, after he'd slept two nights in the cubby off Alexa's room, she said, "If you mind your ways, Jerrin, and pay heed, perhaps you won't disgrace us after all."

Only Alexa on the journey would know who Bran really was. Except for his mother, of course. The other servants and the four guards came from Liesel's official headquarters. Even if they had seen Bran as himself, they'd hardly recognize him as Jerrin.

The hard part was his parents ignoring everything about him except "Jerrin"—but he knew they had to. He didn't see Sparline at all, and decided that she couldn't be expected to keep his role straight.

Early one morning the party left. Loading a small mountain of gear, the dozen or so boarded four pogiecopters and flew for several hours across bare, reddish land to the nearest commercial port. Then a suborbital SST across the Pacific to North America. Nobody said exactly where, and Bran knew better than to ask. They were met by squat groundcars, two armed guards to each car, the cars and guards all wearing Erika Hulzein's monogram crest. Bran had seen it on letterheads in his mother's study.

He didn't know how long they rode. He slept most of the way. When Alexa shook him awake their car was stopped. Getting out, he met chill air. A dark, overcast night was lit by floodlights that showed the front of a large timber-beamed lodge. Shivering as he walked, he was glad to reach the warmth inside.

Sheer luxury overwhelmed him. Later he recalled few details, only that this place made his own well-appointed home look like an Outback trail cabin.

He did notice that the lodge was a weaponed fortress. A platoon of tanks might have cracked it, but nothing less. Of course UET's bombs could breach even the underground sanctuaries he saw next day. But as Hawkman explained later, back home, Erika's installation sat at the outskirts of a fair-sized city. "They'd have to be pretty desperate," he said, "to blow half the town."

Four days, the conference lasted. Mostly, young Bran was

stuck with servants' quarters and company; he cared not greatly for either. Jimmy Kazich, an older youth in Erika's retinue, liked to mimic Bran's slight accent. "Sye soomthin' fer us in Orstreyelian, won'tcher?"

Somehow shamed, and no longer willing to be, Bran faced the other. "Orl right. Oop yoors!" Exaggerating Jimmy's own parody, and waiting. Not for long; Kazich slapped him. Shock brought tears, but no sound. Hand cupped to his slapped cheek, Bran shuffled forward, and as the larger boy leaned to grin at closer range, slammed the heel of his hand to Jimmy's nose. As hard as he could, bringing blood and yells, and suddenly the room full of adults. *"What happened?"*

If an older girl, sixteen maybe, hadn't kept insisting that Jimmy struck first, Bran would have had the caning Alexa once threatened. Not from her, but from her counterpart on Erika's staff. As it went, though, he escaped with a scolding.

One thing about it: Jimmy Kazich didn't bother him again.

The conference dealt with strengthening the Hulzein branch in Argentina: whether, how much, and *how*. "Erika wants an ace in the hole," Liesel told Bran when the two were alone briefly, "a backup hideout. Our mother resists the idea, so while she's away, Erika wants to push it through." Pleased to be confided in, Bran nodded as though he understood.

He kept hoping to get a look at Erika Hulzein's gene-replicated daughter, his cousin Frieda, who was a year his senior, but no opportunity occurred. With no chance to question his mother, finally Bran asked Alexa Duggan where Frieda was.

The woman shook her head. "She's sickly, poor child. Had a horrible fever a few weeks ago, and the treatments, what I've heard, even worse. She's out of intensive care now, but still bedridden." Then Duggan realized that Bran had broken his Jerrin role, and scowled at him. "Get on with you, young Jerrin. Haven't you chores to do, besides pestering me about your betters?"

So Bran scuttled off with an armful of clothes for the launderers. Duggan wasn't so bad, after all!

The visit ended with a banquet, and on this occasion Liesel's servants were themselves served, at a smaller table to one side. Before that, in the vacant end of the large room a series of unarmed combat bouts occurred. Erika Hulzein stood to

announce them and Bran got his first good look at her. She
looked like his mother and yet she didn't; Liesel's features
were rounded, Erika's cut more sharply. Liesel's grey-flecked
brown braids formed a crown; Erika's iron-grey hair hung
straight, to chin-length. Erika stood half a decimeter the
taller—but blade-thin, she probably weighed a few kilos less.
And the edge to Erika's voice was one that Liesel used only
rarely. All in all, Bran's aunt impressed him more than was
comfortable.

Now, paired in combat, her trained athletes showed their
skills. Graceful, and at first harmless-looking, but in the third
match a young woman came up pale, cradling a broken arm.
And after that, more injuries occurred. Neither Erika nor the
contestants seemed to be surprised.

Eight bouts, then a pause for appetizers and wine—which
Erika did not sample. Then in four contests the eight winners
reduced their number by half; all losers not in need of medical
aid went to a table at the far side and got a belated start on the
banquet. Another rest period, another elimination series,
leaving only two persons undefeated. And one of the losers
had to be carried off.

Momentarily distracted by his salad—those crinkly char-
treuse tendrils *had* to be from off Earth—Bran looked up to
see the two finalists ready for combat. Both were male: one
brawny and built thick like a bear, the other slim and moving
catlike. Their styles differed. The bear lunged and smote,
while the cat evaded and flicked punishing blows that seemed
effortless. At the end the bear lay prone, panting, bleeding
slightly but not dangerously, and the cat stalked out in no
hurry at all.

Liesel cleared her throat. "Very impressive, Erika. You train
your people well." She gestured, and a servitor refilled her
wine glass. "And is that all of it?"

With a quick headshake, Erika said, "One more stint. Soon
now." And when the last victor returned, Erika stood and
threw off her ornate gown. Under it she wore only brief,
skintight fighting togs. "Now," she said, "we'll see." And she
rounded the table to meet the man who moved like a cat.

He bowed to her. "Madame." Her answer was too quiet for
others' hearing. Then, as in some strange dance, their
movements joined. Fascinated, young Bran watched.

Some of the earlier bouts had been highly skilled, but this
was like magic! Strikes and evasions, swift grace of attack and

reprisal—sharp crack of a savage blow finding its mark, thump when defensive move sapped most of the force.

Suddenly, at the arena's marked-off edge, the cat had Erika trapped—and made his ultimate assault. Bran's eyes almost shut, but not quite, because he *couldn't* miss an instant of this, no matter what. The man's foot like a dagger, his arm slashing—but then, her leap perfectly timed, Erika seemed to *float* over the thrusts. Missing, he sprawled. She came down astraddle, fingers at his throat. He gasped, "Madame! I yield."

Erika Hulzein laughed, and patted her opponent gently. "You came close, Felipe, to making *me* yield." She stood, and gave him a hand up. "Well, it will come; I'm fifty-one and getting no younger." He tried to speak but she overrode him. "But when it does, my prize pupil, rest assured it won't be easy!" Bowing once more, the catlike man went to sit at the athletes' table. Calmly, Erika resumed her gown and her own seat. "And now, colleagues, let us dine." As near as Bran could see, she hadn't even worked up a sweat.

Not until the homeward suborbital flight did Bran find a chance to talk with his mother. "The way Aunt Erika fought . . . can I learn it?"

"Sure. You're a little young for combat work, though. What's your rush?"

He thought. "If anyone else can do it, maybe I need to."

Liesel nodded. " All right. We don't have the grade of instructors Erika has, let alone anyone like *her*. But what we do have, you're welcome to."

So once home he began training. He was small and skinny, and his coordination had a way to go yet, but he'd always had fast reflexes, and more strength than his slight build indicated. The Hulzein combat methods borrowed from several schools: The misdirection of the "gentle way" blended well with karate's emphasis on putting all one's *mind* into a blow or kick. And there was more, not the least being an overall conditioning program. He ran until he couldn't run any more, and then he kept going anyway. He climbed, he jumped, he swam— staying under water longer than he'd have believed possible at the start.

After a time, the boy began to run up against some of his natural limitations. He realized that although he could become very good at these skills he would never achieve the absolute top rankings. But by then he was more than capable of dealing with the likes of Jimmy Kazich.

Since the type is not rare, especially in that age group's schoolyards, he sometimes proved it.

At twelve Bran was small for his age. Sparline, a year younger, had two centimeters on him and probably three kilos, none of it excess bulk. Maybe girls did get their growth earlier, but Bran didn't have to like it. And if she picked on him he had to let her win. She hadn't done any combat training so if he used his with her, he'd hurt her for sure. It got pretty tiresome.

So one day he up and told her. Wide-eyed, she said, "You *let* me win?" He nodded. She reached, but only to hug him. "All right, Bran. I won't pick fights any more." And she didn't.

What she did was start lessons herself. Bran's instructor supervised several sessions before putting the siblings on their own. "And stay with practice rules, nothing all-out," the woman said. Bran knew what she meant. Against an adult instructor he could go full force because he simply wasn't strong enough to injure anyone both grown and trained. But with anyone near his own size and age, "practice rules" meant doing a move hard enough to prove it, but not to injure.

All right, Bran knew how to follow instructions. The worst Sparline suffered was a few bruises; at her age they healed quickly.

Nearing thirteen, Bran felt on the verge of something. He was still short—less than sixteen decimeters, to his father's twenty. But Hawkman said, "We Morays bloom late." So Bran waited. It wasn't as though he had any choice.

Besides being larger, the other boys in combat training showed signs of body hair where Bran had only fuzz. He supposed the difference shouldn't bother him, but it did anyway. Maybe that was why, when he threw a competitor in practice, he put extra effort into the throw. It didn't help his feelings much.

Still, he told himself, his mother stood honcho over this part of the Hulzein Establishment—and whether aunt Erika or grandma Renalle liked it or not, he was Liesel's co-heir.

But in a few brief moves, even that comfort vanished.

* * *

There was a morning of early sudden wakings and much confusion. Liesel was in the comm room, beating fist into palm: "They did it; UET's killed my mother!" Bran found the group—his parents, a few top aides, and Sparline—by following the sounds of commotion. Liesel paced, raging, while Hawkman talked at the overseas console. Pausing, he turned to say, "Long-term sabotage, Liesel. Ringers infiltrated. If Renalle could have laid hands on one of those experimental truth-field installations, UET couldn't have wormed in." Low-voiced, he talked again with the console, then reported, "They slagged the citadel's power plant, put all the central-powered weapons out of action. Only portables left, in the way of energy guns, to fight the sappers blasting in." Taut-faced, he shrugged. "You once said, Liesel, it'd take a regiment of tanks to invade that place. Well, that's what they used."

Hours later (and still no breakfast), the comm console went dead. Hawkman's far-end informant had escaped UET's holocaust in an aircar and reached a hidden ground-to-satellite terminal. Apparently UET had caught up to that person.

Gripping each of her children by a shoulder, Liesel sighed. "Well, you heard. UET's Committee Police jackals didn't take your grandmother easily. She was eighty-six, and nowhere near to wearing out." Incredibly, Liesel smiled. "Their own self-glorifying newscasters say she died firing a Mark-XVII two-hander, with a full squad of dead Police to mark the spot. And they only got her by coming down through stone shielding with a laser!"

In his mother's grasp, Bran stood taller. "I can't even aim a Mark-XVII yet, without resting it on something. But some-day . . ."

Suddenly, she hugged him.

Three uneasy days later, Liesel called family council. "I needed to know what's left of the Establishment and what's gone. Now I do know." She spread her hands. "In North America we're wiped out. But Renalle didn't keep all her nest eggs in the one citadel, and UET didn't catch Erika. She's managed to shift a great proportion of the assets, and many key personnel, to her Argentine branch. Totally outside UET's grasp."

Liesel didn't look as relieved as her words might indicate. Hawkman said, "So, then—the recent terrible reverses aside, Liesel—what's bothering you?"

She shook her head. "Erika isn't answering or returning my calls. And the message her aide relays to me is a very old one." She shrugged. "Don't call us; we'll call you."

Bran knew how time zones affect calling schedules, and the Argentine problem worried him so he tried to monitor it. Still, one day he reached the comm room to find his mother and her sister already involved in a long-distance yelling match. Viewscreen circuit this time, and except for gaunter face and whiter hair, aunt Erika hadn't changed much. The yelling, though: "—your mongrel brats, Liesel, will *never* come to power among Hulzeins. Oh, I'll see to that! And—"

"Erika!" If Liesel wanted to talk, Bran knew no one could stop her. "I'm not *asking* for power. Surely we can discuss these matters and settle them to our mutual satisfaction. I don't—"

Erika Hulzein's voice was high and harsh. "You don't tell me what to do, Liesel. You never did and you never will! What you'll do is come here in . . . oh, three days from now . . . and I'll offer you a settlement and you'll take it!" The screen blanked.

In the sudden quiet Hawkman spoke softly. "You'll go?" Fuming, breathing fast and deeply, Liesel nodded.

Obviously trying to relax, she began pacing. "How did it get this bad between us? When we were little children . . . so close and loving, Erika and me . . . and mother too! Erika always looked after me, protected me. And later we stayed close. How—"

Still quiet, Hawkman's voice. "You heard what she said."

"Sure. Of course. It's the children. Like mother, Erika's still totally devoted to the parthenogenetic principle; she still thinks it's workable indefinitely. Well, I decided it wasn't, and I have two healthy kids. And Erika has poor, sickly Frieda."

She paused in her motion and stood still. "Peace take us, that's it! After Erika the partho dynasty depends all on Frieda. Who likely isn't up to it. Leaving me, and then Bran and Sparline." She snorted. "No wonder Erika's birthing porcupines. I—"

"And you still intend to go there?"

"Yes, Hawkman. Erika won't hurt me."

"She's not entirely sane just now, you realize. Keep that in mind and try not to provoke her."

"And you keep in mind that you're talking to a Hulzein!" But her tone and expression showed no ill humor. "Which is the devil of it. I'm up against another one." She frowned. "I *think* Erika could share power with me if I had a one-parent daughter. I'm not certain but I think so. In this case, though, sharing would be an attack on her dynastic principles . . . which come all the way from our grandmother Heidele who started the whole thing."

Liesel shrugged. "Well, I'll just have to convince her that I'm no threat to either one. And believe me, Hawkman, I won't lose track of that need. Or of my temper, either."

"You'll go with only a nominal retinue then?" When she nodded, Hawkman said, "All right. But one other thing needs to be done. Until we have assurance that Erika isn't going to strike out at us—on behalf of her dynastic principles, I mean— we must put Bran into hiding, out of her reach, because he's the one she sees as a threat.

"And I think I know how to do it."

"It's simple enough," Hawkman explained, "with a little computer-tap fiddling. We give him a slightly different identity and slip him into the entrance quota for the Space Academy."

Liesel frowned. "Safe from Erika's hands, but in UET's?"

"As a trainee, a cadet. And—"

"Do I have to use a phony name *again?*"

Hawkman shook his head. "Not entirely. You'll be simply Bran Tregare, not Moray, and that's the beauty of it, because your middle name comes from an old friend of mine, Sean Tregare. His wife was Alexa Duggan's sister Lisbeth. Sean and Lis both died in the Artificial Plague, when you were a baby." For a moment, old pain tightened his mouth. "But now—"

"Sure," said Liesel. "Feed into the computer net that Bran's their son; run that datum through all his records—schools, all of it. Perfectly natural that he'd be taken in by his aunt. And—" Now she smiled. "If I remember right, Sean Tregare held North American citizenship, so Bran can claim the same thing."

At first puzzled, even frightened by his father's proposal, now the boy began to feel excitement. "What you're saying—I could train to captain a *starship?*"

Liesel gave a laugh. "By contagion, Hawkman, you're assimilating Hulzein ways! Every move to serve more than one purpose." She turned to Bran. "We don't know it'll come to that. For now, the point is hiding you from Erika's inflamed temper, and it might be you won't find the Academy all that pleasant. If it's a bad situation, then when it's safe to do so, we'll pull you out." She paused. "Alexa, of course, should be our communications link. But if all goes well with you there, Bran, it would not be a bad idea at all for the Hulzein Establishment to have a hook into UET's space fleet."

Hawkman's grin crinkled his face. "For one thing, it would show Erika that mongrel brats might be damned useful allies."

Sometimes, Bran thought, being a Hulzein was a lot of *work*.

Liesel and a moderate entourage left one morning to visit Erika's Argentine base. Before boarding the copter she found brief time to hug and kiss her children. To Bran she said, "I know this is a drastic change for you to handle so fast. But we've established credentials for Alexa . . . to exchange messages with you at the Academy. Just be careful what you put in yours."

"Keep my cover, yes. And with aunt Erika, *you* be careful."

"I always do." Then she climbed aboard and the craft lifted.

Later that day, Bran left his home. Waiting to enter the same kind of air vehicle his mother had used, he traded handshakes and then a surprisingly fierce hug with his father, and an embrace and kiss with Sparline. His sister was crying—and suddenly so was he. Well, nothing wrong with that, except that somehow he thought such things wouldn't be approved at the Academy.

The trip wasn't much different from the one he'd had to Erika's headquarters. Pogiecopter, suborbital SST over the ocean, then from the port a groundcar—this time driven by a uniformed cadet, a large, older youth with a livid scar down his right cheek. Still sleepy from his dozing on the SST, Bran hardly noticed the winding road the car took, through dark stretches punctuated by occasional bursts of glaring light. Then the sky at one side began to lighten. Unable to determine the time difference from his point of departure, Bran realized he was seeing dawn begin.

The car pulled up before a gate, the only break in heavy wire fencing that reached three meters above ground. The gate opened; the car went in. Now Bran saw the great grey slab of concrete. A building with no windows, like pictures he'd seen of Total Welfare Centers except those had a bit of blue to their coloring. The car stopped beside a door to the slab. The driver jumped out and motioned Bran out also. The door opened. Bran walked inside and he heard the door close.

Another young man met him. "You're who?" Bran told him. "Oh, a snotty, huh? New, *and* late. By an hour,' *Mister* Tregare."

"I—the suborbital plane—hey, I just *rode* it, is all."

"*Smart* snotty, too! You first-timers are all alike." The bigger youth stepped forward. "You have to *learn*, don't you?"

Bran avoided the first blow, shucking his gear to give him mobility, but the second numbed his face and sent him sprawling.

"Welcome to the Slaughterhouse, snotty!"

2

The Slaughterhouse

Scrambling up into a crouch, one hand braced against the floor, Bran paused. The big stubble-headed bully was shuffling forward, and Bran recognized the move. "Don't kick me!" But the words came out a barked order, not a plea. This one was too big for him to fight, and somehow he knew that even if he won, he'd lose here. But still . . .

The other stopped moving, then laughed. "All right . . . You're new, so I'll tell you. In here, don't fight unless you're told to. But you take a punch pretty well." He held out a hand. "Come on, get up. I'll show you to your cadre section. You'll have time for breakfast and a haircut, after you draw your issue . . . before the commandant interviews you." As Bran picked up his things and turned to follow, the large youth said, "I'm curious. Just what did you think you'd do if I *did* kick you?"

Put your foot on backwards! "Oh, I dunno," Bran said. He was Hulzein enough to realize that it's foolish to tell *everything* you know.

And already he knew something about UET's Space Academy.

The older boy took him to a ten-bed squad room, where seven cadets of about Bran's own age were dressing or using the room's adjacent sanitary facilities. "Three bunks vacant," his guide said, "so take your pick," then left. Bran did so, and chose a vacant locker also, to stow his gear. Then he stood, waiting, expecting some sign of acknowledgment from the room's incumbent residents. But no such thing happened, and soon the seven, ignoring Bran entirely, moved to leave the room. Bewildered, he lunged to the doorway and stood barring it. "What *is* this? My name is Bran Tregare and I'm assigned here. Don't you give your new people decent help or greeting?"

The skinny, freckle-splotched boy at the front of the group made a placating gesture. "Sure we do. But you have to speak up first. Come on. Breakfast may not be good, but it's hot."

In the large, crowded mess hall, Bran found the prediction correct.

Now he knew that to learn anything he had to ask. After breakfast he learned that he also had to know *who* to ask, for when he put a question to a uniformed adult, the woman whipped a backhand slap across his mouth and told him "Don't try to jump levels, snotty!"

So it took him longer than he expected to find where to draw his grey-green jumpsuit and uniform, and where to get the haircut that left only stubble on his knobby skull. So naturally he was late for his interview with the commandant.

As he waited in the outer office, Bran tried to run through the altered "facts" he needed to remember. Parentage, sure. Age, upped one year because otherwise he'd be about three months too young. Surname, he'd practiced and wouldn't fluff it. Anything else?

Too late to think more; he was summoned. And walked in to face fat, scarred, cigar-chewing Colonel Harold Arbogast. He expected the man to look up from the papers on his desk. When it didn't happen, Bran cleared his throat and said, "Cadet Bran Tregare reporting, sir."

Now Arbogast looked at him, pouched bloodshot eyes under bushy, straggling eyebrows. Around the wet cigar the heavy mouth twisted. "Reporting late, you mean."

"Yes, sir." *Excuses don't work here.*

"You know how to salute, don't you?"

"Not yet, sir."

Right answer, for now the cigar came out. With it, the colonel pointed at Bran, and the mouth formed something that was probably meant to be a smile. "Let's check your credentials," and rapid-fire he asked questions. Just as fast, Bran gave the answers. Finally Arbogast nodded. "I see you're in Cadre D, Squad 8. Too late for you to make morning drills, even if you'd been here on time. Well, that'll give you time to get your shots this morning, and read the Regs. Ask for a copy on your way out."

"Yes, sir." Arbogast was looking down again, so Bran turned to leave.

"Just a minute, cadet." Bran swung back. "With the Academy Regulations, I can save you a little time. The main thing is that everything your superiors tell you to do, you do. And nothing else. Got that?"

Sure, whatever is not compulsory, is forbidden. Bran had read about that, somewhere. He didn't say it out loud, though.

And now it seemed he was truly free to go. In the outer office he asked for and was given a copy of the Academy Regs, and directions to the infirmary, where he received various inoculations. Some hurt more than others, and by the time he got back to his empty squad room he was feeling a little light-headed. He figured he'd better read the Regs though, anyway.

It was pretty much the way Arbogast had said. There were separate buildings for each of the four cadres that made up the Southwest Quadrangle, and off-duty you stayed with your own. There was a definite hierarchy of seniority among cadets. One's superior was automatically right, and there was no appeal. Insubordination was a dire offense, and severity of punishment was pretty much up to the discretion of the higher-ranking offendee.

After reading carefully about halfway through, Bran skimmed the rest of the pamphlet. Already he thought he had the idea. *For a while, I can stand this place. But I hope they get me out soon.*

If one of his squadmates, looking harassed as well as bushed, hadn't stopped by the room on his way to lunch, Bran would have missed that meal; the shots had made him doze a little. Lunch was better than breakfast but not by much. Then Bran went with his squad out to the large central drill area, where each cadre trained in its own quadrant. The afternoon's subject was a series of marching maneuvers in formation, an art form as old as armies, and at first Bran thought it a harmless enough pastime. But then an instructor shouted someone's name and ran to intercept that person, giving the young man a slashing blow across the ribs with what appeared to be some kind of riding crop. More incidents of the same kind began to happen. Bewildered, Bran lost step on a Squads Right, heard his name called, and felt the quirt's burn across his right shoulder.

Instinct made him crouch and start to turn—to see last night's bully hefting the short whip, grinning, ready to strike again. So he turned back, sprang to regain place and step in the group. Counting cadence under his breath, he left the whip behind.

If the marching drill was bad, the calisthenics were worse. Bran was wiry and strong for his size, but never before had he been worked to exhaustion and then kicked or struck to force him to continue. Through a haze of fatigue he realized they weren't picking on *him*. Everyone got the same treatment. He saw one boy collapse and fail to rise no matter what was done to him. An instructor grabbed a foot and dragged the cadet off, out of the way. Gasping for breath, pausing a moment while no one seemed to notice him, Bran gathered strength for the next ordeal. And eventually the session came to an end. The squads marched back into the cadre building—with ten minutes to shower and change before dinner.

In the mess line, some were stopped and sent to another serving station at the room's far side. Facing Bran, the arbiter looked at a list and said, "Out there today, you stunk! But it's your first day, so I'll give you a break and not send you over to the bread-and-water line, this time. You get a real meal; enjoy it."

Maybe dinner was better than lunch, maybe not. Bran was too tired to know, and feverish, semi-nauseous. He concentrated on getting the food down and keeping it there, because he knew he was going to need it.

The following days didn't get any better, but somehow Bran managed to cope. He didn't exactly get used to the Academy's deliberate cruelty, but increasingly he learned to take the unremitting parts for granted; it was the new stuff that got to him, and always there *were* new outrages.

One evening after dinner he was unexpectedly penalized for some infraction he hadn't noticed at the time. "Tregare! Five laps around the drill field. Right now." On a full stomach, naturally, but no point in arguing; Bran went outside in the evening chill and did the five laps. He didn't hurry them a lot, though, and returned to his squad room at a leisurely pace. Only when he opened the room's door did he realize something was wrong there. "What the *hell?*"

The newest boy, who had come in only two days earlier, was spreadeagled face down and naked, with a larger cadet holding

him there, raping him. Screwing him. Boogering him. As he
yelled, and the others in the room stood back, white-faced,
watching.

Bran shook his head. "What you think you're *doing?* You
can't—" Two boys held him back. Then the rapist was done,
and that one, an upperclassman from two floors up, came over
to Bran.

Bran's arms were held and he couldn't stop that bigger youth
from cupping a palm around his jaw. "I can't *what*, snotty? Tell
me, huh? Can't come back here tomorrow maybe, and do
you?"

Nothing in Bran's whole life had scared him this badly. He
knew that in the room or in the entire Academy he would find
no help. *All right, damn it!* He jerked his head back from the
hand's grip, then lunged to bite its reaching edge. He drew
blood, and took a backhand across the face for his trouble. But
now he was pretty sure his voice wouldn't tremble. So he said,
keeping it slow, "You could, yes. But unless you killed me,
you'd never be safe again." Sheer bluff and he knew it, so he
held the other's gaze until that gaze turned away. Good thing,
too—Bran's eyes were starting to water with the strain.

The big one shrugged. "Oh, turn him loose. You know
better'n to jump me, don't you? I was kidding, anyway. You're
not the type." And pulling his clothes together, he walked out.

The others tried to talk to Bran then but he wouldn't answer.
Nor would he look at the naked one crying on the floor. He
took his shoes off and climbed into bed without undressing
further. He lay a long time, tensed, until the rest of the squad
also went to bed and turned the light out. Much later, hearing
their sleeping breaths, he found himself crying. He kept it
quiet.

Every day he checked the comm room for messages from
Alexa. For eleven days the visits were fruitless, but on the
twelfth the orderly said, "Tregare, Bran, you say?" Bran
nodded. "You know anybody in Australia?"

"Sure. I lived there." The sour-faced man seemed to want
something more, so Bran added, "I was expecting word from
my aunt. Ms. Alexa Duggan." And he gave the address.

The way the man looked at the flimsy he held, he might
have been trying to memorize it. Finally he handed it over. "I
guess it's for you, all right."

The orderly's grade of courtesy rated no thanks, but Bran

gave him some, anyway. After all, he'd be dealing with the slob again. He took the message and walked the long corridor to the building's "inside" exit. Late afternoon sun warmed him as he sat on a bench facing the now vacant drill field.

Then he read the message. What it said on the face of it was idle chatter, nothing important. Just in case, though, he read it that way first. Then he counted the letters in the first three words, which gave him the three digits of the code sequence Alexa had used. And then he read the real message.

It didn't say much either. Liesel was still in Argentina, and her own reports, telefaxed or direct on viewscreen circuits, were largely noncommittal.

Well, sometimes things did take a while. . . .

The next few days, not much new happened. In a tentative way, Bran became friends with the skinny, freckled boy who had first spoken to him. Jargy Hoad, his name was, and Jargy carried an air of irreverent independence that appealed to Bran. The other six in the room—the raped boy had simply vanished, transferred to another cadre without notice to his squad mates—the other six didn't impress Bran Tregare much, though four of them were second-year, not snotties. He could keep them straight in his mind because Ellsworth was fat, Donegan had buck teeth, Ahmad was black and said he was Muslim, Dale talked a lot and never said much, Pringle was just the opposite, and Hastings could do one-arm pushups. Jargy, though, was fun to be around, to talk to. To conspire with.

At first, all the two did was sneak extras out of mess at dinner, deciding who should swipe what in order to put together a late-night snack. They hid the stuff in shrubbery near their closest building exit, and went outside for the snacking: first, because they couldn't steal enough to feed the whole room; second, if they didn't share, someone would probably snitch; and third, share or not, Jargy said Dale would snitch anyway. "Reason he talks so much," said young Hoad, "is to cover what he's thinking."

Maybe so, maybe not, thought Bran—but Jargy's advice made sense.

There weren't any more rapes in Squad room 8. Between them, Jargy and Bran figured out how to stop those; Jargy told the rest of the squad. "What we do is, we get in the way a lot, and somebody opens the door so the whole floor can hear. Right, Bran?"

"Right." Staring at Dale, "Anybody goes to shut that door, or doesn't help stop one of those prongers, gets beat on a lot." It wasn't Bran's usual way of talking, but you had to learn things.

And one night the same upperclassman as before—his name was Channery—either drunk or on drugs, came barging in and hollered, "You're for me!" reaching for Ellsworth. Jargy yelled for everybody to move in, and pretty soon the older cadet found he couldn't scare the interference away. He cursed a certain amount, and left. A little later, when Bran and Jargy went out for their stolen snack, they brought some back, waking Ellsworth to share it.

And from then on, Ellsworth joined the mess-raiding crew.

The Academy setup wasn't all that complicated, but since nobody told you much unless you asked, Bran found it took him quite a while to put even the most basic facts together. For instance, normal cadre strength was about a thousand, so this four-cadre campus (one of six such, he was told) should have held roughly four thousand cadets. But for some reason the whole place, not just Squad 8's room, was nearly twenty percent under quota. Somehow that datum gave Bran a vague unease. But alongside the real hell of the place, not enough to keep him worried.

The three classes of cadets were (unofficially) snotties, middies, and uppers; the official designations were for the records and nobody except officers used them much. Between cadets and Academy officers were a few graduates who hadn't been assigned space duty yet; the Regs called them graduate instructors but the cadets, speaking among themselves, called them "mules." Those young men commanded sub-cadres, groups of squads, something on the order of a hundred cadets. The mule overseeing the contingent that included Bran was a thin, intense youth who was having moderate luck at growing a mustache. His name was Jimar Peralta, and he had no mercy on cadets who made his contingent look bad. Never cross that one, Bran decided, unless you really need to!

Peralta wasn't all bad, though. Some of the upperclassmen—such as Channery—liked to pull really dirty, degrading tricks on snotties and middies, in the way of punishment. Channery's fat buddy, Guelph, once punished the last cadet to finish in a five-lap race by tying him to a post and leaving him there for two days. He could eat or drink, but he couldn't leave. Then, stinking and wet, the boy was chased around the drill field three times while Guelph's squad cut at him with their little whips.

Maybe Jimar Peralta didn't hear about that incident. The one he came in on—that Bran saw—was a run-the-gauntlet bit. Channery liked putting snotties through the gauntlet. The way it worked, you stripped to the waist while all the squads in your area lined up to whale hell out of you with their belts. Bran had it happen once and didn't want it again. Luckily he was a fast runner and fell only once. So he wound up hurting, but not really *hurt*.

One time, though, late in the afternoon Jargy Hoad tripped and fell during a race with everybody carrying full packs, and came in a woeful last. It was Channery who assigned the gauntlet, and stationed himself about halfway along the double line. Jargy was pale, looking desperate as he ran. Bran swung his belt in a deliberate miss. Jargy wasn't doing too bad; he ducked some swings and took the hits pretty well. Then Channery stepped out, blocking Jargy's run, and smashed Jargy across the face with the *buckle* end of his belt. You weren't, Bran knew, supposed to do that—but Channery did it, and grinned as Jargy got up to his knees and held both hands to his bleeding mouth.

The hell with the rules! And Bran was going for Channery, blind rage driving him, when a hand grabbed his shoulder and threw him to one side. Levering himself up, he saw that Jimar Peralta had Channery by the throat. "*Muerto*, you should be!"

Gasping, Channery tried to speak. "I don't understand."

"You stupid cockroach . . . sadist idiot! You put bad marks on the record of *my* unit, I'll have your balls on toast—and you'll serve them up!" The angry man shook his head. "More seriously, if you do such a thing again, *you and I* will duel with these belts. And I will have your face off your skull in two minutes!" Glaring, Peralta looked around. "Unit dismissed!" Channery slunk away. With a little extra time before dinner, Bran accompanied Jargy to the infirmary, where his lip was stitched.

The next day Channery was missing. Transferred or discharged, Bran didn't know. Or care much, either.

What he couldn't understand was where the Slaughterhouse drew the line between routine brutalities and unacceptable ones. Lisping a little with his swollen lip, Jargy tried to explain. "It's the way the colonel says to everybody, on our first day. Anything you're *told* to do is all right, but nothing else is."

"Oh? Then how about Channery's little rape games?"

Hoad looked uncomfortable. "Rotten, yeah. But he always waited until he was senior cadet on duty in the unit. And you try to snitch on a guy that ranks you—his word against ours, it would've been. No contest."

So Bran learned a little more about the way the system worked.

Jargy also had some thoughts about what made Peralta tick. "He's ambitious like nobody else I ever saw; he wants rank, and power. I came in at half-term last year so I saw him operate as an upper before he graduated. You know he wound up as cadet colonel, in charge of all four of our cadres?"

Bran whistled. For the moment, he'd forgotten how badly he wanted *out* of this place. "You mean, by the time *we* graduate, he'll be an admiral or something?"

Headshake. "Not that fast. But if he isn't close to commanding his own ship by then, my guess is he'll Escape."

Bran had heard the term, always stressed a little. Now he asked what it meant, and Jargy told him. "UET's losing ships. One of my dad's cousins went into the Underground, and we used to see him once in a while." Hoad laughed. "Late at night, usually, and disguised never twice the same."

"Anyway, he said UET first thought there was something dangerous in space—black holes or aliens or something—but then some of these lost ships turned up raiding UET colonies. For supplies and people, both. Cousin Larry claimed these Escaped Ships were setting up their own colonies, on planets UET never heard of. The Hidden Worlds, he called 'em."

"You think he's right, Jargy?"

Shrug. "How would I know?" But it was something to think about.

Every time Bran thought he'd adjusted to whatever the Slaughterhouse could throw at him, it came up with something worse. He'd been there nearly two months, stretching hope between weekly message from Alexa Duggan—messages that only said she had no real news for him—when one afternoon Peralta summoned his unit to join a full cadre formation. For a moment the taut mask slipped and he looked human as he said, "They're starting the free-for-all season early this time. I hope none of you are chosen." And aside, Bran barely heard him mutter, "Goddamn waste of good talent!"

With all four cadres in tight formation surrounding the drill field's center, Colonel Arbogast himself waddled to climb a small stand that held public-address equipment. The colonel began, "All right, men! We have a challenge from cadre C, for the honor and rations-differentials of your respective groups. Two men per cadre into the arena—and this one's to the death, so no snotties allowed. Losing cadre goes on bread and water, as usual, for a month or until next challenge, whichever comes first." He turned to his adjutant. "Draw the names, captain."

Standing next to Jargy Hoad, Bran nudged and whispered. "What *is* this?"

"What the man says . . . eight-man free-for-all, until somebody gets killed." He gave a half-sob. "Jeez! I hope I'm still a snotty, on the record!"

This is insane! But Bran kept asking. "What kind of fighting? What weapons? What rules?"

Jargy stifled a hysterical laugh. "No weapons. They go out there naked and try to kill each other. Only two rules: you lay off the eyes and balls, because blind guys and eunuchs aren't much good to the space fleet."

"How about dead ones?"

"I guess they don't care about that."

The fight was more horrible than Bran could have imagined. At first the boys were hesitant, but then their respective officers shouted some things Bran could not hear clearly, and he saw how their feelings changed to desperation and their actions to reckless abandon. Bran especially watched Ellsworth, the middie from his own squad room, and bit his knuckles when he saw Ellsworth caught and cruelly thrown, to rise with one arm hanging limp and twisted, then fall again. But the boy's next attacker, leaping in to grab the throat, caught a hard-driven heel at his own larynx and dropped, rolling over to hands and knees but unable to rise again as his face purpled and he collapsed. And shortly died.

Bran wanted to look away but he couldn't. He'd never seen anybody die before. Then Jargy's elbow nudged his ribs. "Wake up, Tregare! We're supposed to sing the goddamn 'Victory Song' now. If you don't remember the words, fake it."

*   *   *

Next day at parade, Peralta told the unit that it was time to get into free-for-all practice. "Snotties rules, though, for everybody—bouts go to first disablement, only." The idea still didn't strike Bran as much fun. In fact he found himself shivering with fear as he waited for his first bout. The fact that Peralta didn't seem to approve of the whole matter was no help at all.

To avoid friends ganging up on strangers, the combats were set up among cadets from different squads. So that beginners would not inadvertently break the "eyes and balls" rules, the young combatants wore skimpy protective gear in those areas.

Nonetheless, the time came that Bran found himself in an arena with seven enemies. And until one of the eight was ruled disabled, the other seven could do damn near *anything* to him! Except deliberately kill him, of course, but accidental death didn't sound like such a great idea either. Nor did "disablement." Even sedated and with the dislocated shoulder strapped back into place, Ellsworth had with his moaning kept the whole squad room awake most of one night. And whether the injured boy had slept at all then, Bran couldn't be sure.

Now, moving and shifting with the other seven, trying for positions of advantage, Bran missed the sleep *he* hadn't got. The edge was off his timing. His first feint missed its purpose and he didn't dodge the counterblow cleanly; it stung him.

Suddenly Bran was scared. He knew he couldn't afford to be; it could freeze him, make him helpless. But he was anyway. The sweat of action went cold on his skin. His breathing came shallow. A kick rammed at his face, and missed only because the kicker was clumsy. Moving as if through water or mud, Bran backed away.

All right now, dammit! He drew a deep, shuddering breath and shouted, "Hai!" The boy coming toward him, startled, veered to one side, and Bran caught him with a neck chop. Not hard enough to drop him but the fellow did stagger for a moment.

Not the next one, though. A blow caught Bran's shoulder and spun him. He dropped and rolled, coming up to face that boy. He suddenly realized that he, Bran, was near to being the smallest of the eight combatants.

So the hell with it; he attacked. Right at the biggest kid,

because this move had to be feint and bluff, and then off to the side where he put a good solid throw on someone he caught standing flatfooted. The boy got up, though, and Bran danced back away.

Now his moves were working. He struck and twisted and tripped and kicked and threw, and nobody was stopping him much, except that there were just too damned many of them and he wasn't *winning*.

Panting, his throat felt raw; much more of this he couldn't take. What was wrong? Then he realized—all his training had been to *stop* an opponent, to register a defeat the other would have to accept. But that wasn't what *this* was all about! His training hadn't been to injure people deliberately. But now—

The big kid was back. Two others, smaller, flanked him. So Bran had succeeded—if that was the word for it—in uniting three against him. Vision glazing, he felt his eyes narrow to slits as he chose his move. Shouting again, he leaped to kick both feet at the big one's chest, because he wanted someone he could get a good solid bounce off—sidewise almost, in a diving tackle at the shins of one of the flankers. And as he and that one landed in a heap, Bran heard the other's knee pop like a dry stick.

He got up; his opponent could only lie there and shriek pain. First disablement—the bout was over.

In the mess hall when the afternoon finally ended, Bran forced his dinner down. Not much later, back at the squad room, he threw it up again. Jargy tried to help him but no one could. "You did what you had to, Bran. That's how it is, here."

Coughing, wiping away the tears of nausea, Bran said, "Sure. Stupid is how. Rotten is how. Pure total shit." He shook his head. "You know what time it is?" Jargy told him, and he stood up and wiped his face on a towel. "I have to go check something."

He got to the comm room just before the message desk closed. Tonight the orderly was a woman, neither young nor old, who was the friendliest of the lot who worked there. When he came trotting in, breathing a little fast from the run, she smiled at him. "Well, now. Just in time, young Tregare. And I have one for you." She handed him the slim packet, and he paused to thank her—not only for reasons of policy but because he had truly come to like her.

He went outside to the bench where now, by ritual, he read

all of Alexa's messages. Slowly, not expecting much news, he
opened the envelope and read the surface text. Nothing there,
so he studied the code group and reread from that standpoint.
And then he sat frozen.

Because, give or take a phrasing or two, it said: "Erika gave
an ultimatum. All of your mother's group have to get off Earth
immediately. There's a money settlement which is not too
unfair, but Liesel stays off Earth forever. We have to get
everything together and board a ship on the 15th of the month
which is less than a week from now. Liesel and Hawkman are
making every effort to get you free of the Academy so that you
can join us, so be ready. We all hope to see you soon. Earth
isn't the *only* place to live."

Bran blinked, and wondered why he had no tears. Because
the message made perfect sense, but there was one thing
wrong with it.

It was dated two weeks ago.

3

"Only One Latrine . . ."

STUCK here! It couldn't be that way—but it was. His parents wouldn't have left him here—but they had. He tried to get his mind to function, to come up with some kind of answer, but it wouldn't. Maybe crying would have let out some of the hurt, but he couldn't even do that.

He tried to think, but no thought came to him—only the dull ache at his solar plexus, as though he'd been kicked there. Maybe if he could talk to somebody. But he couldn't—not even to Jargy, for Jargy didn't know who Bran's parents were, or that he'd had any hope of escape from the Slaughterhouse where Jargy didn't. No, he'd better not tell anyone about that stuff, it would only bring scorn onto him.

Blank-minded again, he sat while memory pictures tormented him: good things at home, people he loved. He shook his head: all that was gone. Then recall gave him Jargy's face being cut by Channery's belt buckle, the purple-faced death of the boy Ellsworth had kicked, and finally twisted-face screaming after Bran himself had scored "first disablement" on a stranger's knee.

It was intolerable, all of it. Bran stood. He didn't know how he could help his own condition but there was one thing he had to do.

Quiet-voiced and blank-faced, Bran asked his questions. The clerk in Active Files, two offices away from Colonel Arbogast, seemed glad of someone to talk to. "You have a message for Cadet-captain Channery? All I know is, he's over in Cadre H now, in the next quadrangle but one." He pointed, and Bran said, yes, he knew where it was. He didn't, for sure,

29

but it shouldn't be hard to find. The clerk smiled a little. "Your best bet is, write the message down and I'll see it's forwarded."

Bran shook his head. "I'm to deliver it in person." And after a little waffling the clerk wrote him a temporary pass, to get him into the proper quadrangle.

A half hour or so later, in lingering dusk, Bran knocked on the door of Channery's quarters. Outlined against light from indoors, Channery held the door open and said, "Yeah?"

Standing in dimness, Bran said, "I have a message for you."

"Well, come the hell in, then!"

"I'm not authorized. Just to hand it to you." He stood there, and slowly Channery emerged. When he was within reach, Bran swung the belt, and again, and twice more after Channery fell to his knees, yelling, trying to shield face with hands, while between his fingers blood spurted.

Bran heard running footsteps, people coming to see what the yells were about. He took one more satisfying look at the blood, and turned and ran.

He made one wrong turn, though; just short of his own cadre-group area, he was caught. With blood on the buckle of the belt he still carried.

The hearing held by Colonel Arbogast wasn't like any court trial Bran had ever heard of; what it consisted of was denunciation and sentencing. Channery, his face swathed in bandages, sat on the witness stand and, with a Major Forsythe (or something like that) feeding him leading questions, did most of the talking. According to Channery, Bran Tregare had been nothing but trouble from the day he arrived at the Academy. In spite of himself, Bran was fascinated by some of the incidents Channery made up out of whole cloth: his arrival didn't find Channery raping some kid; instead Bran was beating the kid up for no reason and Channery stopped him. And of course Channery hadn't barged in drunk, later, to try another rape. Oh, no—he had intervened to stop Bran Tregare from molesting one of his squad mates. Rape wasn't specified in that instance, but it was sure as hell hinted pretty strong.

Sitting in the dock, Bran's feelings flared through rage to amusement to despair: what chance *was* there for him? After a time he simply quit hearing what was said. Until Arbogast's hoarse voice told him to stand for sentencing.

He stood; the colonel said, "I don't understand boys like you. You came here well-recommended. *Why* did you do these things?" He gestured toward Channery, and even now, Bran couldn't help but be glad that he'd carved *that* bastard up a little, with his belt. At least he'd paid back for Jargy. . . .

But to Colonel Arbogast's question he had no answer. Why had he sought out Channery and ambushed him? Because this place left him no sanity, and when he found he had no escape from it, *he had to hit back*. And Channery was the only person he knew who really deserved it.

But he couldn't say any of that; to anyone else it would make no sense. Nor, probably, would what he did find himself shouting: "Because Cadet-captain Channery is a cruel bully, and a boogering rapist, and a goddamned liar!"

Even before two cadet guards flung him back into his seat and held him there, Arbogast's face told him he had lost. The colonel, himself standing now, spoke in a voice that shook with rage. "You'd like me to throw you out of here, wouldn't you, you little sneak? Even if it's into Total Welfare, and that's where I'd put you! But it won't be so easy, Tregare. I've made men out of worse worms than you are—and I will this time, too." Regaining some semblance of calm, the man said, "I was going to let you off with ten days' ordinary detention. But your outburst, your attempt to traduce your superior officer the cadet-captain—I think, Tregare, you rate the special cell." He turned to the guards. "Take him there, strip him, throw him in, and set the controls. Ten days ought to do it, I should think."

The cell looked no different from the others. Each was a cube, roughly a meter in each dimension, made of heavy wire mesh and sitting over a drainage sink. The guards took Bran's clothes and shoved him inside and slammed the door. There was no room to lie down, except curled around on one side; neither was there a comfortable way to sit. In either case, his weight lay on the wire mesh. Suddenly he knew what other cadets had meant when they referred to punishment as "waffle ass."

Well, there wasn't much he could do about it, only try to shift his position a lot. That part wasn't too difficult because the place was so cold that he couldn't sleep, anyway. Maybe fatter guys could doze naked in what Bran estimated at sixteen-Celsius, but Bran couldn't. So for long hours he lay and shifted and shivered, and leaked and crapped, and had no way to

clean himself, and more and more felt thirst and hunger with
no relief, until finally his fatigue was too much and he dozed.

SHOCK! He came awake, arms and legs flailing, bruising
himself against the cage's roughness. For moments he couldn't
figure what had happened. Then he knew. Electrical shock,
they'd used; the wire mesh must be in two insulated parts.
GodDAMN!

Then he saw a kind of shallow bowl in the cage beside him.
It was only about half-full; his awakening convulsions had
spilled the rest of its contents. But—they would *have* to feed
him, wouldn't they? So he smelled, then tasted what was left
in the bowl. It wasn't good exactly, but he could eat it. So he
did.

The unpredictable pattern never changed. As long as Bran
could stay awake, he was neither electrically shocked nor fed.
When he slept, they jolted him the hell awake and fed him the
pig slop.

They had one more trick in reserve. Once when he dozed,
he was jarred awake not by voltage but by a slanting blast of icy
water. After his first yell, and his attempt to curl up away from
the deluge, he decided he'd better take advantage of it. He
turned this way and that to scrub himself as clean as he could.
When, abruptly, the flow ended, he crouched with teeth
chattering and wished for some way to dry himself. The
evaporative process chilled him horribly, but eventually he
was, for the most part, dry. His hair, short though it was, took a
while longer.

But at least the torrent had washed both himself and the
cell's floor mesh free of the stink of feces.

At this waking, though, he hadn't been fed. His hunger kept
him from sleep, so did the extra chill. But finally he did lose
consciousness, was jolted back to it, and ate again.

The only new trouble was that the blast of cold water had
been one blow too many against his body's powers of resistance. Whatever combinations of cold or flu virus he'd been
harboring, now they struck. Chills and fever shook him, along
with diarrhea and a grade of nausea that had him vomiting
before he could finish a bowl of slops.

A point came when he simply lay, partly conscious, and tried
to ignore the shocks. And then he passed out totally, and no
longer had to try.

When he next woke, he was in a hospital bed, with an IV

tube in his arm. Whether he'd lasted the colonel's ten days, he didn't know and didn't care. At any rate, he'd survived the special cell. This time, anyway.

The infirmary wasn't in the business of coddling patients. The first nurse to find Bran awake pulled the IV and slapped a band-aid on the puncture. There was a glass of water beside the bed; it was up to Bran to sit up and reach it, and a little later, at midday, he found that the same rules applied to lunch. A tray was set on the side table; he could either cope with it or go hungry. Shakily in both cases, he managed. Spilling a little, but not much. Lying back again, afterward, he slept more comfortably.

What woke him was the need to urinate. He looked around for the button that would summon a nurse; Bran had never been sick in a hospital before, but had visited them. No such button here, though; well, in the Slaughterhouse, that figured. So he clambered up out of bed, and leaned over to the wall, and carefully edged his way, bracing his weight as best he could, out of the room and along the corridor. For once his luck was in; he turned to the right and the john was only a few meters away. Once relieved, for a moment he paused: why make two trips if one would do? But his bowels seemed totally quiescent. All right; he made his painful hobble back to the room and his own bed. And quickly slept again.

Next day, Bran was visited by Jargy Hoad. "Hey, Bran—I'm glad you're all right!"

"Who says I am?" Bran's voice came out sulky, but he had to grin.

"Brought you something." Jargy held out a honeycone. "Better eat it right away; it's starting to melt." Dubiously, wondering if he *could* eat, Bran took it. But the first bite was delicious; his difficulty was trying to eat slowly enough to enjoy the taste of all of it. Meanwhile Jargy kept talking. "You're a hero, kind of . . . you know that? Eight days in that hell-hole . . . not quite the record, but you're close. Peralta came in the squad room and told us that." Jargy paused, then said, "But the big thing—by three or four days in the special cell, most cadets break down and start yelling, begging to be let out. Peralta says you never did, at all. Not even once."

Embarrassed, Bran shrugged. "Never thought to." He considered the idea, and added, "No point in it. They wouldn't let you out anyway." He frowned. "Nobody ever makes it the full ten days?"

"Not so far. Maybe next time you will."

Bran could see Jargy was kidding, but still he shivered. "I'd just as soon let somebody else set that record."

The honeycone was gone now; Bran wished there'd been two of them. Belatedly he thanked Jargy, then asked, "You hear anything? How long before I go back to regular duty?"

"You don't, exactly. One thing, classes started again, this week. Here." He lifted a book bag to the bedside stand. "I brought these, so you can read and catch up. The first two weeks you're out of here—or until the medics okay you for general duty—you're on classwork only."

Surprised, Bran said, "Somebody in this place has a heart?"

"It makes the colonel mad as hell probably, but once a cadet hits this infirmary, the medics have the say-so."

Something to remember, Bran thought. One for our side.

Restless after Hoad's short visit ended, Bran looked at some of the books. Parts of the math he knew already, but by no means all. The introductory course on spaceships, starting simply with construction layout and later—he flipped to the back of the book, to see how advanced it got—winding up with elementary drive room procedures and control functions, fascinated him. When a nurse brought his dinner he was still reading, and continued until another told him to cut the lights and get some sleep. Then he lay thinking of what he'd read. *A ship. I want a ship!*

Sooner than he expected, Bran was released from the infirmary. As Jargy had said, for two weeks he faced only classroom work, and because Bran's prior education was a little spotty, that two weeks with some free study time was a godsend to him. When once again he was also scheduled for physical drills, for some days he had a hard time of it. Eventually his stamina rebuilt itself, and he began to learn to live with chronic fatigue as the normal order of things. Along with fear and resentment, of course.

He'd never given much thought to the abstract concepts of bravery and cowardice. Some things scared him and some didn't, and he knew that with other people the things could be different, both ways. And mainly, the point was that if something scared you, don't let the bastards *know* it. But the Slaughterhouse stretched that point a lot.

What really got to him were the free-for-alls. A week later he was back to drill status, one was called: for middies and uppers, and so to the death. No one from Bran's squad room was tapped this time, but still the watching was bad. The kill came when a squat, bandy-legged middie from Cadre C had the head of an opponent locked, the victim standing behind, and made what started to be an ordinary wrestling throw. But the Cadre C ape, instead of letting go, clenched arms more tightly around the other's neck and twisted to one side. Both fell in a heap, but no spectator missed the sound of cracking vertebrae.

Only a few days later came a similar tourney for snotties, and again, no one Bran knew personally got the call. He stood, hands clenched, hoping to see some minor injury that would qualify as first-disablement. But the deciding blow was a kick to the abdomen—the attacker's foot sinking totally out of sight—and the loser died of a ruptured spleen before the medics arrived. They took good care of the kicker's sprained toe, though.

That night, Bran's nightmares began.

He was going to lunch but he couldn't find the mess hall. Pretty soon he knew he'd be late for drill, so he forgot about eating and headed for the quadrangle. It started getting dark and he knew he was late, so he began running. But his legs would hardly move at all; he could barely totter along. He looked for the way to the drill field, but there was some construction in his path. He had to go around, and then to climb over a lot of half-built structures and scaffolding. When he got to the top of it, he could see the drill field, but nearly a hundred meters below—a sheer drop. So he'd have to go back down and find a new way to get there, but when he began his return he couldn't locate any way out of the maze. He was underground now and couldn't find any familiar landmarks at all. The narrow passage was knee-deep in mud and something was behind him. He tried to run, and again his legs seemed almost paralyzed. Finally he saw light ahead, and *pushed* with one leg and then the other, and came to—

The special cell! With no choice, he entered it. . . .

* * *

And woke to hear himself making a soft, shrill whine. Sweat bathed him. He sat up, looked around in dim light until he was oriented, then lay back, feeling his pulse and breathing slowly return to normal.

Jeez! It had been three or four years since a dream fooled him that way; he'd learned to spot them, and break loose from the bad ones, when he was nine or ten. And he knew that the business of never being able to run in dreams was because he would *really* be trying to move the legs and the bedclothes wouldn't let him. Hawkman had explained that part, and Bran had tested it and proved it by sleeping coverless in warm weather.

But *this* one—! The rest of that night, he only half-dozed. The next was no better: He was in the mess hall and there was one egg too many on his tray so he had to run a gauntlet to his table. Channery and Jargy Hoad and Ellsworth and Colonel Arbogast were all swinging the buckle ends of belts at him and if he spilled his tray . . . He woke, not quite screaming because he was biting down hard on a mouthful of his right-hand knuckles.

Whatever had started didn't seem to want to stop. He dreamed of free-for-alls; sometimes he was injured horribly and sometimes the horror was a ghastly thing he'd done to someone else. He tore someone's head apart and then found his opponent had been Jargy Hoad. Once he won some kind of drill contest, and his prize was to be raped by Channery, who opened his trousers to reveal a jagged belt buckle. As Colonel Argobast chuckled . . .

It was the tension and fatigue, he decided, that gave the nightmares such power over him, so that he couldn't see they weren't real and wake up by normal effort of will.

The knowledge didn't help much. The damned things continued, and only eased off over a period of weeks.

At first he could keep them into nighttime, but after a while they invaded his days; of a sudden he would find himself wet with sweating from fear—from something that was said, or purely from memory of some deadly bout. He hated himself for what he considered to be his weakness. Some nights he woke up crying and only hoped no one had heard. He felt all too close to breaking, and knew that in this place he could not *afford* to break.

So the next time a snotties' bash was announced, Bran did the unthinkable: he volunteered for it. He lay awake the night before, dreading, and went through the next day and out into the arena feeling not alive but wooden, now and then wondering if he were simply and terminally stupid.

Four cadres, eight combatants: Bran's team mate was a new kid and looked as scared as Bran felt. No help there! But Bran had already chosen his tactic: two hands are stronger than one. So while the others were weaving and shifting cautiously, he made a great war whoop and charged. He made feints, kicks, and hand chops as he went—but these were only to clear path to his chosen target, who stood frozen. Bran grabbed a handshake hold with both hands, swung to turn under the other's arm for a standard wrestling throw—and then simply didn't let go. Between the dislocated shoulder and the ruined elbow, first disablement was clear enough.

With only a few twinges of conscience, that night he slept well.

What Bran liked about the math courses was applying the methods to spaceship operations, such as communication navigation. Yeah, probably the latter should be called "astrogation," but it wasn't. And the way the ships chewed time, up near light speed: the relativity stuff fascinated him. On his desk calculator, if he entered a velocity as a decimal fraction of c, he could get the time-ratio (one-over-the-square-root-of-one-minus-vee-squared) by punching seven keys. Or, going the other way, from ratio to vee, the same.

Then one day the class was doing some trig, and suddenly it came to Bran that with trig functions he could do it even faster. Enter vee and then hit: Arc. Sin. cos. 1/x. *Four* moves, and again, the same in reverse. He didn't tell anybody, and later when the instructor had the class do a chart of t_o/t from zero to c in 0.1c steps, he finished in two-thirds the time of the next fastest student. The instructor was impressed.

It paid to do well in classwork, because the lowest scorers on any exam got to run the gauntlet. Nobody liked to beat his own classmates, so the system was for classes to trade victims for the ordeals. Across cadres, sometimes.

Bran was no genius, but being half Hulzein he had to be bright, and Hawkman was no slouch, either. The boy knew his IQ figures qualified him for nearly any kind of training a university could offer. In the Space Academy program, only once throughout his first term did he have to run the gauntlet. That time he was fogged from lack of sleep and misread the crucial high points question.

Jargy Hoad had it rougher. It wasn't that he was dumb, but that here *nobody* was dumb, so someone had to drag bottom. Jargy endured four gauntlets that term—about average.

The trouble was, you never knew when they were going to call one of those damned free-for-alls. There was no regular schedule to them. Bran wasn't sure whether a predictable pattern would be easier to live with or not. He decided it would, because then you wouldn't have to be scared *all* the time, and could start psyching up when the time approached.

And there was no knowing how they picked the poor bastards who had to fight. Scholarship had nothing to do with it, nor skill on the drill field. But somehow Bran knew the "draw" was a farce. Once he muttered as much, and Peralta heard him and told him he'd do well not to talk that way. So he shut up.

But it seemed that Bran's unheard-of volunteering for a bout had gained him considerable respite from further ones. Time after time the "draw" missed him. Not his squad mates, though.

Ellsworth caught it, bragged that he'd repeat his earlier triumph, but was whipsawed by two Cadre B men and limped on crutches for a month or so. At least he wasn't the one killed. Neither was Donegan, whose front teeth were no longer buck, but artificial. Jargy had an easy one. On a muddy day he tripped and slid past the entire confrontation. By the time he got up, the action had moved away from him. All he had to do was watch.

Hastings, the strong man, managed by dint of vicious defense, black Ahmad by grace and quickness. The quiet Pringle went berserk and chased all seven opponents— including his supposed ally—out of the ring. When the one he'd rabbit punched couldn't get up for awhile, the umpires counted it as disablement. Mouthy Dale tried a spectacular leap-kick, missed, and cracked two of his own vertebrae when he landed. He was invalided out of the Slaughterhouse. Jargy Hoad said, "Some guys just get lucky."

Near the last day of his snotty year, Bran got tagged again. That night and next morning he couldn't keep his food down. Taking Ellsworth's example to heart ("Never try to repeat," the

fat youth had said later. "They'll be watching for it."), Bran
tried a different tactic. When the fight began, he yelled and
charged, made chops and kicks far short of any goal, jumped
back, yelled some more, and charged again. What he was
being was a threat and a distraction. At no time did he engage
in actual combat. He made one leap-kick, a deliberate miss,
sprawled and rolled, thinking to entice the opponent to come
after him. But while they circled, feinted, and taunted each
other, someone else wrapped the match up with a neck chop.

Well, at least no *real* disablement, in that bout.

With the end of that term's classes, ship training began. Not
in space, of course, but in two old, long-grounded hulks—the
Il Duce and the *Caesar*—that stood like towers behind the
Cadre H barracks. But just being *in* a ship gave Bran a strange,
thrilled feeling.

The *Caesar* had been an armed ship. Bran was glad to be
assigned to it rather than to the unarmed *Duce*. Of course the
six turrets were now empty of projectors, just as the drive
room no longer held a Nielson cube. But the controls—at the
pilots' chairs, turrets, or drive room—connected to computer
simulations and gave proper indications on the instruments.
Peralta said, the first day his groups were allowed on the
Caesar, "Don't consider these simulations as toys. Treat it all
as real. If you do, you'll learn how to handle a ship." Bran
believed him.

Ships, except for being armed or not, were pretty well
standardized, from Control at top to the drive room and
landing legs at bottom. In between, as you climbed, came
space for cargo and supplies, crew's quarters, the galley
complex, and officers' quarters. Well, it wasn't quite that
simple. For instance, the drive room didn't occupy its full
vertical section of the ship, but was itself surrounded by cargo
holds. And quarters were stratified, with ratings living topside
of unrated crew, and control officers occupying the deck above
engineering officers.

Total ship's complement was usually about one hundred,
give or take a few. So Peralta's subgroup made a good
simulation.

Even if the ship hadn't fascinated Bran, the change from
sadistic drills and calisthenic ordeals would have been wel-

come. Onship the cadets were first shown through the various
sections, given study assignments on each aspect, and then put
to practical test. Faced with the different types of control
simulations, Bran found that his skills varied. When the first
ten-day results were posted, he rated: Navigation, Very Good.
Communications Control, Excellent. Weaponry, Fair. Drive
Room Operation, Fair to Good. Overall Capability, Good to
Very Good.

Those results were a little misleading. Bran found drive
room work so easy as to be totally boring. Deliberately he had
made a poor showing there. Because if ever he did get onto a
ship, he wanted to be riding up front, not down with the
Nielson cube.

His weaponry rating bothered him. To be a control officer he
needed to be fairly expert at a turret. And right now, he wasn't.

It shouldn't, he felt, be all that difficult for him. A projector
consisted of two lasers that operated above the UV band and
converged to give a heterodyne frequency in the peak infra-
red. "Tune it right, and you could boil tungsten in less than a
second," one instructor said. The trouble was, the things
weren't tunable. What you did was, take about four shots for
ranging-in. These wouldn't be in peak heat range—but your
next five or six shots, before the heating of circuit components
drifted your heterodyne-freq *past* top performance—were
deadly.

A gunner's controls were really quite simple. The ship's
computer picked a target for you—then you had only two
choices to make. One was to get your beam-convergence on
target, which meant moving a lever toward either of your two
range lights, to extinguish it if it lit up. Any time both lights
were out and your heterodyne was near to peak heat, your
projector fired.

The other control was an override foot pedal, which doubled
your combined range-heterodyne tolerance for allowing fire.
"And that," said one instructor, adjusting the eye patch that
interrupted her face-splitting scar, "is the main reason for
having human gunners at all. Of course you use override to get
off your warm-up shots. When you're testing on sims, shots on
override give only half credit."

Bran knew what she meant. On test runs, any time your
shot was a damaging hit, a central viewscreen lit up with a dot.
At a run's end, the computer spit out a tab indicating what
percentage of time you'd had effective energy on target—that

you *could* have had—according to what the simulation had your target doing. Like changing course or pulling a quick accel or decel to evade. But hits made by using override counted only half.

But the point of having override at all, Bran learned, was that in a really tight spot, people can try to guess right and computers can't.

Bran's problem with gunnery didn't take him too long to figure out. Only thing was, he didn't know how to fix it. The ratings were simple: Fair was a 30-40% average on the sims; Good was 40-50 and Very Good 50-60. In Weapons he hadn't heard of any Excellent ratings. Which didn't mean there weren't any . . .

But he needed at least a Good, to get branched into Control Officers' training, and so far he was averaging a lousy 38. The thing was, his coordination was too ragged, and that was because he was running on the thin edge of fatigue. The damned nightmares cut into his sleep too much, and they wouldn't stop.

It had been over a month since the most recent free-for-all, but he couldn't keep from dreading and expecting the next one, any day. And he'd had to run a gauntlet, for coming last in a gunnery competition, and somebody's belt-end had caught him across the right eye and left him seeing blurry for a couple of days. No buckle, but the leather was bad enough. Even after his vision cleared, he had to squint through the swelling, to see much.

By now, though, at night he did not cry. He merely hated.

But Bran was, after all, an heir of the Hulzein Establishment. So eventually he began to think back, if only in desperation, to sayings he'd heard from his mother Liesel Hulzein and his father Hawkman Moray. And remembered something Liesel had said: "About so-called insoluble problems. First you find the logic. Then you find the handle on it. And then you twist it."

So once again Bran volunteered for a snotties' free-for-all, and made a great lot of attention-drawing commotion while doing his best to avoid any real action. As soon as he saw a disablement happen, he took a wild dive at a rather passive opponent and wound up with the both of them bruised enough to be excused from the rougher stuff for a time. Bran didn't know about the other guy, but he made sure to land with one arm on a sharp rock in the ring, gashing himself enough to bleed a reasonable amount.

Blood didn't scare Bran. He'd seen plenty of his own, having had the usual quota of silly childish accidents—which tend to happen to kids whose confidence exceeds their knowledge. His aim now was to get loose from the physical harassment by way of injury, and from the nightmares by way of temporary freedom from all the goddamned physical *hazing*. ("Whatever works," said Liesel Hulzein.)

So now he was free of mandatory combats and from calisthenic risks. He had time available for studies and his mind was clear—for the moment—of the usual dread. He'd learned the hard way to avoid thinking too far ahead, in this place. So he settled down and brought his gunnery average from a lousy 38 to a quite respectable 54. Which put him into the Control Officers curriculum.

For now—things being the way they were—that was good enough.

The term was ending. Pretty soon there'd be the summer session, and then Bran would be a middie, not a snotty. The graduation ceremonies for the uppers came on a sweltering day. Putting on his dress uniform for the first time since an all-cadres parade, he began sweating before he had his jacket buttoned.

All the way across their own quadrangle and the next, going to the main parade ground, the cadres marched at attention, loudspeakers blaring music at them. From the first time he'd heard it, Bran had hated the Academy's official march, "UET Forever," and now the sound of it made him grit his teeth.

Eventually all the cadres formed up. Now, thought Bran, maybe the show would get on the road! No such luck. Two cadres abreast, the entire Academy complement raised dust marching the full field perimeter, to pass in review before Colonel Arbogast.

Bran was in Cadre D's right-hand file, third in line behind Ellsworth, his squad leader, so that not too much dust was kicked up where he had to breathe it. He winced for Jargy Hoad, bringing up the rear as lance-corporal. But soon, heat and all, dust and hated marching song, the rhythm of the march got to Bran. In a sort of hypnosis without conscious effort, he went through his paces.

To his right, just ahead, a motion caught his eye—a motion that didn't fit the rhythmic pattern. He almost lost step himself, but caught the beat and recovered. Now he watched, to see what had distracted him, and for the first time noticed that the cadre beside him was H, and that leading it was Channery. And Channery wasn't doing too well.

He was limping, for one thing—his paces hesitant, not firm, and sometimes off rhythm. His balance didn't look too good either. And now as the columns turned, the final wheeling before the march past Arbogast's reviewing stand, Bran saw Channery's face. That it was red and sweating was no surprise, but as Bran watched, the face twitched and twisted into agonized grimace, fought its way toward standard parade blankness, then writhed again. One thing for certain: Channery had troubles. *Well, it couldn't happen to a nicer guy!*

Weaving noticeably but staying on his feet, Channery made it through the interminable graduation ceremonies. A couple of times Colonel Arbogast paused and stared at the cadet-captain, making the colonel's rambling tirade all that much longer. But it had to end sometime and finally it did. With shirt and undershorts sticking solidly to him, and sweat running down his arms and legs, Bran set his mind to lasting out the grim march back to barracks.

Channery, staggering and hardly keeping step at all, made less than fifty yards of the departure. One foot tripped on the other and he fell. The first ranks of his cadre stepped over him and then Bran was past and could see no more—whether anyone stepped on Channery, or who dragged him away.

Back at quarters, Bran, Jargy Hoad and Ellsworth were first into the showers. They ran the water fully cold and allowed no one to change that setting. Coming out of the shower, hearing others squabble over the water temperature and not caring, Bran didn't bother with a towel; evaporation in the hot room dried him soon enough. Then he lay on his bunk, trying to relax, and was half-dozing when Jargy poked at him and said, "Chow time, Bran." Once in the mess hall, he had better appetite than he'd expected, and afterward he and Jargy walked around the shady borders of the quadrangle, taking it easy and not saying much.

When they returned to the squad room, they found a party going.

* * *

Jimar Peralta wasn't exactly drunk, but sober wasn't the word, either. Still in dress uniform—or again, more likely, for his garb showed no sweat stains or other signs of the day's ordeal—the graduate instructor sat on a vacant bunk and waved greetings to Bran and Jargy. "Got my posting today, cadets!" He tipped up the beer he was working on, and pointed to two cases that sat alongside the bunk. "So I'm standing drinks for all my squads." He scowled and grinned at the same time. "Just remember—give your juniors a treat when *you* ship out."

Caught by Peralta's gaze, Bran said, "Sure; I've heard about that," and nodded. "First time I've seen it, though."

Wave of hand. "Then drink up, snotty! Oops—you're not one now, are you, Tregare? *Middie*, I meant. All right?"

Bran grinned, and took a beer. He looked around; he and Jargy were running late at this party; everyone else already had a start. Well, that was all right; he had no intention of getting tanked. But a small friendly load couldn't hurt anything at all. . . .

He raised the plastic can. "Thanks, Mr. Peralta. Here's to you and space."

"I accept . . . with pleasure." For a moment Peralta looked around vaguely, then again he put his attention to Tregare. "Hey! Something I heard, might tickle you a little bit. Since you did special-cell time for assaulting cadet-captain Channery."

Suddenly Bran felt chilled—was he to be punished *again?* But Peralta's expression, a little slack, was still pleasant. He said, "Y'know why Channery looked so bad today, and finally couldn't make it?" Bran shook his head; he didn't look to see how anyone else responded. And Peralta laughed, then hiccupped once before he said, "Somebody in his cadre filled his boots with water and put 'em in the freezer! He didn't find out until about five minutes to making formation—too late to fix anything. He had to borrow! Somebody else's *old* boots."

Bran couldn't see why the idea was so funny that Peralta couldn't talk for laughing. He waited, then asked. "Well," said Peralta, "the whole lot must have been in on it. Because the only boots Channery could lay hands on—or feet into . . ."

More laughter. Bran waited, and Peralta said, "Anybody here ever try to march five miles, in boots three sizes too small?"

All that came to Bran's mind was that he hoped the Slaughterhouse didn't hear about this and use it as a new way of punishment.

Bran had never drunk much alcohol at any one time. At home he'd been accustomed to a little wine at dinner or a cold beer to ease the heat of summer outdoor hiking. The few times during his first term here that beer had been smuggled into the squad room, it had been a matter of one or two cans per cadet, barely enough to feel the effects at all. Now, though, when Peralta's two cases were gone, somehow another two were delivered. Bran himself was on his fourth can, and his head felt strange—partly dizzy, partly godlike, and all mixed together.

One thing came clear to him, though: he had to take a leak. So he stood, feeling a slight imbalance, and went for the john. But the door was locked. He stood and he stood, and finally it opened. Ahmad came out. Bran went inside, wondering why Ahmad had closed off the group facility but not caring much. He relieved himself of a great lot of secondhand beer. As the flow splashed in the receptacle he heard singing from the squad room, and when he rejoined the group, Peralta said, "Once more now!" And the group sang:

"When I was a boy at UET,
Twice a day they maybe let you pee.
Sometime later, when we were men,
They told us we could hold it twice as long again.
So *that* is the reason, you can plainly see,
Why there's only one latrine in all of UET
Yes, *that* is the reason, you can plainly see,
Why there's only one latrine in all of UET!"

"Yay!" shouted Jimar Peralta, and lay back on the bunk where he sat, kicking both feet into the air—but not spilling a drop of his beer. Then he sat up, blinked, and said, "That's something you don't sing when there's any brass around. It's a verse of the Underground fight song, mind you. I learned it in a tavern, over the wall one time in my middie year—and don't ask me how to do that, because if you can't work it for yourselves you don't deserve to know." Again he blinked. "That's all of that."

To Bran's left, Hastings said, "I know that tune. It's from Gilbert and Solomon."

"That's *Sullivan*." Bran's tone sounded disgusted. But Hastings nodded assent—no argument.

Bran opened another beer. He was past his limit, but he was tracking and felt good. And this was term's end, Peralta was buying, and the hell with it! He started a song he'd heard Hawkman sing: "Cocaine Bill and Morphine Sue, walkin' down the avenue, two by two . . ." But nobody else knew enough of it to keep it going. Peralta had the first two verses, and Pringle knew the fourth, but Donegan had a different version, and pretty soon Bran lost his way in his own song, and gave up.

The singing ran down. Bran took another leak, no locked doors this time, and came back to open his fifth or sixth beer. Somebody was looking over to him. Jimar Peralta, who said, "Tregare? You make it through this hellhole. I want to see you in space." Bran accepted the offered handshake. Peralta stood. "Sorry . . . must go, gentlemen and snotties, if any. I will see you—" Suddenly he leaped, landed on his toes and stood arched, taut, like a matador evading the bull's rush and turning to attack. "—in space. *If* any of you make it that far!"

Head buzzing with mild disorientation, Bran sat while the others talked and sang, joked, argued—once Ellsworth and Ahmad almost but not quite came to fighting. He would just as soon have gone to sleep but he wasn't sleepy. So he sat, sipping beer that became more and more warm and stale, while one by one the roommates put themselves to bed. Some undressed, some not, but finally there was Bran, sitting in dim light, needing to work up the energy to shuck his clothes and sack out.

He was unlacing the first shoe when the intercom chimed; quickly he went to answer. "Yes? Bran Tregare, Squad 8, Cadre D."

A chuckle. Then, "Peralta here. Did I leave the personnel folder in your room? Please look for it."

One look; on the vacant bunk where the man had sat was the folder. "Yes, it's here."

"Good. Could you bring it to me? I'll phone down to pass you through the guardpoints."

"Sure. Of course. Right away." Bran retied his shoe, picked up Peralta's folder and set out on the trek through two quadrangles to deliver it. The journey was uneventful. He was back to quarters within the half hour, and again began to undress.

But when he lay in bed he could not immediately relax into sleep. Because he hadn't been able to resist the temptation to look into the personnel folder, before he took it to Peralta.

Most of the contents were routine, and Bran looked mostly at the entries for his own squad. But after each official summary of a cadet's standing, Peralta had added his own notes. He rated Ellsworth: "Adequate, but not much more." Jargy Hoad: "Good officer material perhaps, but too easy-going as yet." Hastings: "Sturdy chap, but this one is a rating, not an officer." Donegan: "Successful graduation not predicted." Ahmad: "A good one, I think."

And then, following some other remarks, Tregare: "If this boy survives, put him on an armed ship. Gunnery scores aren't everything; he may be the deadliest of the lot."

4

The Killings

With most of the graduating uppers posted out, either to space or to other groundside facilities, the Slaughterhouse seemed half-empty. Not for long, though. During the next weekend, Cadre B was dispersed among the other cadre buildings, while its own was occupied by an all-female cadre. "Oh, sure," Ellsworth said. "Every summer they shut down the women's section, move them in here. Saves money, I guess."

Seeing them on the drill field, Bran didn't find stubble-headed girls all that attractive. Still he was glad that no free-for-alls were demanded—combat drills, sure, but with practice rules in force, so nobody had to hurt anybody.

One day he put a throw on a freckle-faced redhead, shorter than himself but chunky, letting her down as easily as he could. When he helped her up she came upright slowly, and said, "Do you ever walk around the drill field, evenings? I do, sometimes."

Wondering if she meant what he thought she meant, he looked at her. "Tonight, I could."

She nodded. "Two hours after mess. Northwest corner." So, Bran decided, he had himself a date.

In the squad room after dinner, Bran felt uncomfortable. With their two new roommates from Cadre B, there was plenty to talk about, but tonight Bran couldn't seem to join in. More than a half hour before his scheduled rendezvous, he left the room and went outdoors. Then he didn't know what to do with himself. He'd feel funny showing up this early, to sit and wait a long time.

So he walked the field's perimeter, the long way around, taking it slow and easy. As he neared the tree-darkened corner the girl had specified, he saw her approaching from the other direction. As they met, she took his hand and steered them deeper into the shadows. Then she kissed him—and Sheylah the head cook's daughter had never kissed like *that*.

"Don't wait!" she said, and without quite knowing how it all happened, Bran found himself wriggling on the grass with her, their clothes off and discarded, him trying to find where it was supposed to *go*. For a moment he thought he heard a whish of shrubbery; then a whipstroke lashed his shoulder.

"All right, cadets! Up!" *He knew that voice*, and now as they obeyed, it said, "I don't know who you are, missy, and I don't want to. Pick up your clothes and get going. No—out *that* way, where it's darker. When you're out of sight from here, you can get dressed."

Bran watched, as in the dimness the redhead collected her clothes and scuttled away. Then he turned to the interloper, who had stepped back so that faint light lit her face. It was the gunnery instructor with the scarred face and the eyepatch. She was smiling.

"Why—?" He realized he didn't know what to ask. "Who—?"

She stepped forward. "You know me. Murphy. Maybe you never got the name." Low-voiced, she chuckled. "I see you picked your weapon scores up, some."

"Yes." Naked, he felt vulnerable, but the dark helped. He said, "Why are you here? I mean, what business—?" Crazy, to challenge an instructor, he knew—but dammit, what business of *hers*?

Murphy cleared her throat. "I don't know your chubby little friend but I do know *you*, Tregare, so watch your manners."

"Yes. Sure. You let her go. What happens to me?"

"You'll see." Incredibly, Murphy was taking off her clothes.

At thirteen he had never come before. It was close to tearing him in half and it lasted most of forever. When he knew himself again he was lying with his neck and head across Murphy's bosom, his face cuddled against her scarred cheek and her arms around him. "Your first time, it would be? Are you all right now?"

"Yes." And yes. But still he needed to know. "Why?"

Her laugh carried a brittle edge. "If you plowed that little ginch, likely as not you'd knock her up. You know what happens then? She gets Welfared—Total Welfare and no way out." She paused. "Me, now: I get off-base privileges, so my right thigh itches with a contraceptive implant. No problem."

"But—"

"Not charity for you, young Tregare. Believe it or never, kid, I used to be a good-looking female. But combat's a tough game. And it's funny, how losing an eye and picking up a red gully down the face takes a girl off the market."

Abruptly she pushed him off and away, and stood. As she dressed hurriedly, she said, "We don't owe each other anything; you don't have to know me. I—"

Half-dressed, he moved to her and held her. "Hey, Murphy . . . don't! You've been *good* to me. I—"

Hugging, her hand stroked down his back and side. "Sure, kid. You'd try. But if I was staying around here, I wouldn't have done this. Tuesday I transfer out . . . never mind where. So you can feel fine about good ol' Murphy, without ever having to see me again in daylight." She kissed him hard, then walked away fast.

He couldn't decide, the next day or two, how he felt about it all, with Murphy. Because he had no way to know how he was *supposed* to feel, and now he realized that he'd always depended, to some extent, on other people's ideas to guide him.

And one morning, waking up thinking and having no good ideas at all, he said to himself the hell with it. From now on, Bran Tregare would take his best shot at steering his own head. As to Murphy—well, what was wrong with just plain gratitude?

That day was one of ordinary ship drills, and that night, well before dawn, a great *whump* woke him. With no way to know what had happened, gradually he dozed off again. Not until after normal rising and breakfast did he learn what the *whump* was all about. In the mess were three persons in Space Service uniforms, and the mess attendant who slopped food onto Bran's tray said, "See those three? They brought the scout-ship."

So then Bran knew what was happening, a little. Scoutships were small spacecraft that berthed twelve and approxed a trillion-mile range, rest to rest. From light to zerch, maybe four times the distance in close to the same time. Real starships, or armed ones anyway, carried two scouts each. They could be combat auxiliaries or emergency lifecraft— supplied to feed six people six months. What happened after that, the manuals didn't say.

But Bran felt excitement. For the scoutship's presence meant that finally the Slaughterhouse would take some cadets into *space*.

Not all, though, and even after more scouts came, so that there were a dozen assembled, Bran despaired of his chances. Especially when the first two lifted carrying picked squads, chosen for performance. But then the system changed; personnel were tagged individually, by no method Bran could figure out, and his name came up for the tenth scout.

He packed his kit, going by the list on the handout sheet, the night before lift-off. And, considering, slept surprisingly well.

The scoutship, which carried no name but only a number, was a much-simplified miniature of the *Caesar*. Drive occupied all volume below the airlock. In ascending order, then, came the supplies hold, sleeping quarters with twelve acceleration couches, and the forward area which combined a mini-galley and control facilities with what passed for "social space."

And while it might not have been strictly true that there was only one latrine in all of U.E.T., there was only one on the good ship SX-2517. Everyone had better stay healthy!

Control was cramped by the addition of seats so that the entire complement could watch the viewscreens and monitors, and hear the lecture comments of scout commander Pell Quinlan and his aide, Janith Reggs. Quinlan was a tall, slim young man with tawny hair and a complexion that nearly matched it; he spoke in what might have been called an urgent drawl. Reggs was older, maybe close to thirty, a quiet woman with a round face, carrying a noticeable few pounds more than her best weight. But while Quinlan outranked her, Bran observed that when Reggs said anything, the man listened.

Everyone strapped in, watching the front screen: Quinlan said, "Now!" and his hands played across the control panel. From below came the building roar of Drive; the scout pushed up against them, and lifted off. Accel force made Bran heavy;

in the screen the sky went black much sooner than he'd expected. "Out of atmosphere," Quinlan reported, needlessly.

And then, conferring with Reggs, he set course, and eased the difference between accel and the counter-gee field down to Earth-normal. "Okay, Janith," he said. "Give 'em the spiel."

Janith Reggs was good with numbers, getting across what they meant. Accel, distance, time, Big Vee and how it *changed* time if you got it up there much, toward c. (*Vee. Arc. Sine. Cosine. one x. Correct as hell, ma'am!*) "We don't have the acceleration," she said, "of a full-sized ship. Even though this scout's power has been augmented by a considerable fraction." She paused, with her characteristic gesture of running a hand back through her dark brown hair. Always, Bran noticed, it fell back into the same pattern of short, crisp waves. Beat the hell out of stubble. . . . But she was saying "—will be in space for six weeks by Earth time, and upon our return you will all have two ages." She cleared her throat. "Let's assume that your chronological and biological ages then differ by exactly two days. And that we go out in a straight line, accelerating to a given velocity and then slowing to rest, and come back the same way." She smiled, and in that smile Bran saw something besides amiability. "Now who can tell me, from those data, what our top velocity will be?"

Getting out his calculator, Bran thought about it, and knew that his steady-vee assumptions lacked the answer. He'd have to work up an equation and integrate it, and *he had nothing to write on.* Well, neither did anybody else, so figure what he could first. Okay, five percent time-differential. (*one x. Arc. Cosine. Sine: BINGO—roughly 0.3c.*) But that was average, not peak Vee. He felt confused—was this aspect of the function linear, or should he skew his guess a little? Sure; enough to be in range either way.

He waved his hand and caught her attention. She nodded, and he said, "About half-c, maybe a little more."

Her brows raised. She said, "Let's see what our other students estimate, perhaps giving the question more severe analysis." But the others' results, coming slowly and stated haltingly, varied nearly from 0.1c to 0.9, and the explanations varied as much. Finally Reggs said, "Tregare? Explain *your* method. Because you're the closest to correct, and with the tools at hand, I'd like to know how you did it. If it wasn't a plain lucky guess." Scowl. "Well, speak up!"

So he told her, figuring that her question was honest, not a trick. At the end she nodded. "I see. You knew which facts you had and which you didn't, and then made an educated guess. Not bad, not bad at all—because someday in space, in a *real* emergency, any of you may have to make vital decisions on insufficient data. Well, one of you knows how, and I hope the rest paid attention."

Heading out from Earth, Bran had expected to get a tourist's view of the moon and maybe even a planet or two. Instead, the scoutship bent course north out of the ecliptic—not directly toward Polaris but only a few degrees off. So when increasing velocity began to Doppler-shift the colors of stars in the forward viewscreen and move their apparent positions nearer to center-front, there weren't all that many to color-shift or move, which made it easier to check the computer corrections that put real positions and colors on the aux screen. Probably, Bran guessed, this was the reason for heading on a star-scarce course.

Navigation turned out to be Bran's best skill—aside from dealing with communications gear, which he knew from childhood. Gunnery wasn't emphasized in scoutship training, because scouts carried only one turret that pointed straight ahead and had no traverse capability, so the pilot could either try to shoot or not, and the computer would either let the shot go or it wouldn't, depending on range conditions. Well, Bran wasn't planning on being a scoutship pilot, anyway.

One thing he couldn't help noticing was that Pell Quinlan was in command over Janith Reggs, who obviously knew more than Quinlan did. It wasn't that Quinlan was dumb, but that Reggs was smarter. The discrepancy puzzled Bran but he didn't know how to ask about it. Then one "day" it was his turn to be given his first space-walk training, and it was Janith Reggs who helped adjust the too-large suit to him as they waited in the air lock. She was making sure that their mutual life line was properly secured, both to them and to the stanchion by the entrance, when suddenly Bran realized that the air lock's bulkheads totally shielded their suit radios from any outside listener.

So he asked. "Ms. Reggs, you have seniority on Mr. Quinlan and you know more. Nothing against him, but how come he's in charge and not you?"

She had her gloved hand on the hatch control, but didn't operate it. Through his faceplate and her own, Bran couldn't be sure of the bitterness he thought he saw in her brief smile. She said, "How long have you been at the Academy? Not long, I imagine—or you'd know that UET *never* gives command to women. Not of anything at all . . . even a scoutship. We can be anything else, including second-in-command, but never first."

"But . . . that can't be true. Why, there are women on UET's Presiding Committee, that runs the whole *show*."

"I know," she said. "But that's *ownership*—the Committee is the majority shareholders, with some kind of arbitrary cutoff as to amount of holdings, that they don't tell us about. So not even Minos Pangreen, the Chairman, can keep women off his precious Committee." Bran heard her laugh but her face didn't show it. "The funny part is that Pangreen has no sons. His daughter will inherit." She shook her head. "Enough talk. We're taking too much time." The hatch opened, and Bran had his first experience of space itself.

For the first few steps he took walking the scout's hull, Bran thought he'd never get the hang of it—how to activate his bootsole magnets for solid footing, then release a foot to move, with any kind of continuity, let alone grace. But after an error that left him dangling at the end of his life line, so that Reggs had to pull him back in, the burst of panic-adrenalin seemed to give an edge to his coordination. And soon he was stepping along the hull, almost automatically handling the suit and its magnets, while he scanned the visible star field, distorted by the scout's fraction of light speed. He found himself forgetting to breathe.

Not thinking that others might hear, he said, "Oh, Ms. Reggs! *This*—it's worth all of it! The Slaughterhouse, all the crap. I—"

In a sharp tone she interrupted. "*All of us* know that the Academy can be rather grim sometimes." He caught the message—their talk here was not private. "But as you say, the goal is worth it." He looked to her, and nodded his thanks for her help, saying something trite and bland to cover his lapse.

All too soon it was time to go inside again. In the air lock they unsuited, and Bran learned that spacesuits make you sweat in a particularly stinking fashion. Reggs said, "Quinlan says we're crowding our water-recycling schedule. So I hope you don't mind sharing a shower."

He wasn't sure if he did or not, because he wasn't sure what the offer included. While he was trying to think what to answer, she said, "I like you, Tregare. I like your work and I like your thinking, though you'd be well-advised to keep some of it close to your vest." When he only nodded, she went on, now beginning to undress, "Six weeks is a long time, and there won't be all that many chances. Would you like to?"

"I—"

"Or do you only do it with the other boys? Or ever?"

He shook his head. "No boys. And just once, so far." Her clothes were off now, and without them, somehow the extra weight didn't show so much. She reached for him, and he nodded.

While she helped him strip, she said, "To the others, we'll have to pretend this didn't happen."

"Yes, I know, Ms. Reggs."

"Janith. Here, I mean. Ms. Reggs outside of here." She kissed him. The two of them crowded into the tiny booth, and had to move cautiously to get the spray everywhere that both needed it. Then, having sex standing up was fun but not easy—and a good thing, at climax, that there was no *room* for him to fall down. When his legs felt solid again, they washed a little more before indulging in a final hug. This time, in the kissing, he did a better share of it.

"Thank you, Janith."

"And you, Bran Tregare." They got dried and dressed. Just in time for dinner.

Later, Quinlan and Reggs did a wrap-up report on the cadets' spacewalk performances. Bran was pleased to place high in the evaluations, but he wasn't tops of the group. Where he truly excelled was in piloting maneuvers, nudging the scout through simulated combat situations. By instinct, before anyone had the chance to instruct him, in evasive action he was "cheating" on turns by throwing the scout semi-broadside and hitting max drive blast, firing his single turret on override all the way. After one practice session Pell Quinlan said, "If I ever rate command of a combat ship, Tregare, I'd like you to pilot for me."

Janith Reggs spoke in mild protest. "But can't everyone learn that?"

"Learn, sure," Quinlan answered. "But this kid did it *without* learning anything."

So maybe, Bran decided, Quinlan did know some things that Reggs didn't. He still liked her a lot, though.

After reaching a respectable but minor fraction of light speed, instead of going into straight-line decel, the scout turned. One day in classroom mode Reggs asked "At any velocity, how much energy does a right-angle turn require?" Bran fussed at the question, trying to rig equations and getting nowhere. Then the answer hit him: a right-angle means killing *all* your velocity and building a new vector from scratch.

So he had the answer: "Ms. Reggs? Same energy as to slow to zerch and then accel to the same vee."

"May we see your validating equations, Tregare?"

"I haven't worked them out. That's just how it is."

Reluctantly, she nodded. "True. But now try a thirty-degree turn." And it took him nearly an hour to realize that all he needed for *any* degree of turn was to plug in the sines and cosines.

The scout made its circuit and returned to Earth. Now Bran had, as the saying went, "two ages." His personal chronometer registered nearly forty-eight hours less than did its counterparts that had remained on Earth. Well, thought Bran, it's a start. . . . He exchanged leavetakings with his shipmates, paying special heed to Reggs and Quinlan. Was the slight twitch of the woman's eyelid meant as a wink? No matter. He kept his own face as straight as possible but tried to put extra warmth into their final handshake, and was rewarded with a barely noticeable nod.

Off the scout, then Bran toted his kit across the quadrangles to Cadre D. He found his squad room empty, but heard water running in its adjoining facilities. After he'd set his kit on his bunk and begun unpacking, the water noise stopped and he turned to see a new cadet, still drying himself, come out to the main area. A tall, skinny kid, sandy-haired and strong-jawed, with greenish eyes and a lopsided smile. Who said, "You'll be one who lives here, I'd think? As it happens, so am I, now. I'm Bernardez."

"Bran Tregare." They shook hands, after Bernardez took a moment to be sure that his was dry. "I'm just back from my first scoutship tour, as a new middie. Have you been here long?"

"As of yesterday, so such things go, I hadn't set eyes on the place. Nor am I entirely certain that I'd cared to . . . meaning no offense, you understand. But my father died, and my stepmama couldn't see me out the door soon enough, so here I am and now it's to make the best of it." The smile flickered. "I am, so it's told me, a snotty. Not a title I'd choose, but with the customs of the country we must all make do, and so shall I." With a grace of movement that belied his gawky appearance, Bernardez slipped into his jumpsuit and zipped it. "Tell me, Tregare, are you fond of Irish whiskies? For I've brought a trifle and I hear that this place has such things as inspections and confiscations. So . . . should we foil such malfeasance by drinking the lovely stuff?"

Bran felt his grin stretch his face. This Bernardez was *fun*—never mind how he'd last the course when the worst stuff hit, but maybe Bran and Jargy could give him some helpful advice.

For now, though: "I can't think of a better idea, and thanks." His try at imitating the Bernardez style, Bran thought, hadn't come off too well. But the friendly part worked all right.

Bran wasn't used to straight spirits, no water or even ice, but sipping slowly, he loved the taste of it. He sat back and listened while Bernardez talked a mix of personal history, opinions, and total sheer speculation. "While my father claimed the family to be vanguard of Spain into Ireland, I find this hard to reconcile with his claim of collateral relationship to the Pope." Bernardez paused. "What do *you* think, Tregare?"

Bran shook his head. "Damned if I know."

By the time Jargy Hoad and some other roommates came in, Bran was more drunk than not and had missed dinner. Jargy seemed to have a lot of news to relate, but said, "No, not tonight, Bran. Get some sleep and we'll talk tomorrow." Sleepy enough, Bran agreed.

The extra slumber eased the change from ship's to Earth time, and cleared his head. Although he'd hoped for more work on the *Caesar*, the morning began with calisthenics and the following gauntlet runs for losers, and then a free-for-all. Before his guts could knot into their worst agony, the announcement came that this one was for snotties, to disablement only.

The second name called for it was Cecil Bernardez.

* * *

Oh, damn! The newcomer had no chance to know any of the angles—how to protect himself or help his odds. And Bran *liked* the oddly talking, mouthy kid.

But all he could do was watch and hope. The eight victims were equipped with protection for eyes and balls, and herded into the central ring. "*Go to it!*"

The bout lasted quick. Bernardez charged in and decked an opponent with his first blow, and the other stayed down. The only trouble was that Bernardez dropped his man with a clenched fist to the head, and even before the decision was signaled, it was obvious that Bernardez was nursing a broken hand in the other. *Fist* fighting, of all things!

But events can't be argued with. Bran saw Bernardez taken off to the infirmary; he'd be back to the squad room tomorrow. Meanwhile Jargy was still bursting with news, but it wasn't until after dinner, he and Bran walking the twilit perimeter, that Bran got to hear any of it. Some, he wasn't awfully pleased about.

"Channery got himself Welfared!"

Well, that part didn't hurt Bran's feelings. "What happened?"

"After the graduation party he hauled a snotty into his quarters—guess for what!—and got caught in the act." Then Jargy shrugged. "They Welfared the kid, too—and the way I hear, anybody could see that Channery'd beaten him into doing it."

Bran felt the rage come, but didn't give over to it. He took a deep breath, and tried to keep his voice steady. "Nothing new, is there? When was there ever any fairness in this place?"

Jargy's speech, then, held an odd edge. "Could be worse. The old commandant, before Arbogast—the guys were saying . . . about five years ago, two kids got caught like that. And on the way to Welfare, stopped by the local Committee Police HQ and had what they call a minor operation." He paused. "The commandant circulated pictures."

Bran didn't have to ask. Not only that, but he couldn't. Unexpected shock had him close to fainting. He forced himself to smile, and finally said, "I guess it's lucky I like women."

Horror offstage, though—atrocities he hadn't really seen—couldn't drag Bran's spirits down for long. Next day Bernardez returned from medical custody. The new kid seemed to be popular with all the group, for he got a whooping great welcome. Jargy yelled, "You get a good heavy cast on that hand, did you? Fine for clubbing, next time you're picked."

Bernardez shook his head. "No. Soft cast. Which, I admit, does in truth restrict my options."

Bran asked, "If you get picked for it, what'll you do?"

Bernardez shrugged. "Combat, I must own, is not my specialty. But in some other sports I was never the most rule-bound of players." He grinned, and said nothing more.

Bran wasn't sure who'd sneaked the beer in, but there was a fair amount of it, which led to friendly wrestling and lots of off-key singing. Such as the Underground fight song's second verse:

> "In the Slaughterhouse, just to get along,
> Even if you're right, you admit you're wrong.
> How it works is, if you get off free,
> They change the rulings retroactively."

And everyone yelled: "So *that* is the reason, you can plainly see, why there's only one latrine in all of UET!"

And next morning when Bran woke up, feeling not too bad but not exactly tops, either, the refrain still rang in his head.

Whether out of spite or sheer chance, Cecil Bernardez did get chosen for the next snotties' free-for-all. Jargy said, "You could beg off for hurt, you know," but Bernardez shook his head. "Should they have such a want of me, I could hardly avoid the issue for long."

Bran watched as Bernardez with his crippled hand went out to the fighting area. The thing began. Bernardez dodged, feinted with his casted hand and avoided breaking the other by striking only light blows with it, still clench-fisted. Someone his height but heavier came charging. Bernardez slipped to one side and brought a foot sharply to the attacker's knee. The other went sprawling, and rolled over clutching his knee with both hands.

First disablement. End of bout. In barracks after dinner, Bernardez said, "I've lived a time in the eastern Canadian sector, and soccer was one of the sports in which I was sometimes less than totally sportsmanlike. He sighed. "But—" I much misdoubt that any one such trick will avail more than once. Twice, at the most."

* * *

Whoever controlled the draw seemed to have it in for Bernardez. Time and again, still with the cast on his broken hand, he was chosen for snotty fights and caught a number of bruising injuries. But his footwork kept him free of serious damage, and after a few bouts, even the instructors began rooting for him. "Kick'em, Bernardez!" And after one fight, when the boy dropped an opponent with a high, spinning kick but fell exhausted, Bran and his squad mates ran out onto the field and carried Bernardez off in triumph. "Come on, Kickem!" Bran shouted. "Let's go get chow!"

From then on, the young man was known as Kickem Bernardez.

If a minor triumph could elate cadets so much, it was because there were few bright spots in the Academy's grim brutality. Bran was so accustomed to living with fear that he hardly remembered what *not* being afraid was like. But still, as he said to Kickem once, "I don't think you *ever* get used to it, really." He said nothing, though, about his recurrent nightmares.

And recently, in fact, his dreams had begun taking new directions. He found himself dreaming of being with his family—either back with them, before coming to the Slaughterhouse, or else somehow miraculously reunited with them after escaping the Academy by some means he could never quite remember. Very pleasant dreams, these were. Bran hated them.

The first time he dreamed that way, he felt so wonderful! And then woke, and had to give it all up and accept his grim reality *again*. And again, and again—his dreaming mind couldn't seem to learn that it was being deceived, so every waking was a devastating shock. The result was that instead of merely missing his parents and sister, and feeling vaguely betrayed, he came to hate them. Because they had *promised* to get him out of here.

Until the new dreams, he'd almost forgotten any goals other than surviving the Slaughterhouse and getting into space. And in a way the loss of alternatives had made things easier for him. Now, though, the continual dream-reminders of a better life set his mind against itself, and the conflict was too much for him. His only way out was to *reject* Hawkman and Liesel and Sparline.

Sometimes, without wishing to do it, he found himself arguing both sides of a dialogue: They didn't *mean* to leave me here. Then why *did* they? Couldn't help it; something went wrong. Sure; people who break promises *always* have an excuse. They tried, though; I bet they tried. Not hard enough; I'm still here.

What it finally boiled down to, was that when he got to space and eventually Escaped, he would *never* have anything to do with his family again. That was the first time he realized that Escape was his second goal. Survival, of course, was his first.

The family dreams ceased. By contrast, the nightmares were welcome. Even when he *knew* he was going to be killed.

The Slaughterhouse never gave any reasons for what it did; one day early in Tregare's middie year, Kickem Bernardez was transferred to Cadre G, in the same quadrangle where Bran had once belt-whipped Channery. For the brief farewell party, Ellsworth sneaked some beer in. "Gonna miss you, Kickem," said Jargy Hoad.

"And be it known," said Kickem, "that Bernardez is of no mood to leave valued comrades." In spite of the boy's flair for big talk, Bran saw that he meant it. "Though I'm told that my new leadership can't be faulted: cadet-captain Ragir Parnell is, I understand, well-liked by his cadre."

Bran felt sadness; he reached to shake the other's hand. "Maybe we can visit back and forth, some."

"And highly welcome that would be, Bran Tregare."

For a time, Bran and Jargy and Kickem did arrange to meet. But the formalities of getting quadrangle-passes, the time-consuming delays, made the intervals longer and then indefinite. A few times Bran met and spoke with Kickem's cadre leader. Ragir Parnell had a quiet way about him, a bit somber but not unpleasant. The tall young man's long face, topped by sandy stubble, wasn't given much to smiling. But he seemed more amiable than not, and Kickem said he dealt a fair-minded grade of leadership. Since Tregare's own cadre had had three cadet-captains transferred in and then out again, in as many months—and not one of them could pour sand from a boot without cutting a hole in the toe, to hear Jargy tell it—the two friends felt that maybe Kickem had the best of it.

* * *

Not much later, the killing free-for-alls began, and with
them a recurrence of Bran's occasional nightmares. He'd seen
enough death by now that at spectator's distance he could
almost blank his mind and force himself not to react. Almost,
but not quite. Then, for the third death-fight, his own name
was drawn.

That night he went over the wall and came back drunk,
hoping to sleep without dreams. Mostly it worked, and he
woke feeling less debilitated than he deserved. Feeling a little
woozy but not much, he put away most of a fair-sized breakfast
and it stayed down. As soon as the meal "settled" he took
advantage of a free hour to run a few laps and do some
stretching exercises.

When time came for the combat formation, he felt as ready
as he could ever be for that sort of ordeal. He marched out
with his squad, heard Colonel Arbogast's insane announce-
ments, and walked to join the other seven cadets while they all
stripped and made the circle to face each other.

Then it began. The circle shrank into a knot of violence.

His legs weren't working right. They twitched and jerked,
instead of moving smoothly. Then a big youth lunged at him
and suddenly he could move the way he always had. Bran
made a leap, caught his attacker over the ear with one foot,
landed with a smooth roll, and came up to find nobody in
immediate threat to him.

He looked around. A lot of inconclusive grappling and
flailing was going on—as usual in the early stages. Well, he had
to look good for the records, so Bran decked one slow learner
with a chop block, bounced up to leap and a chest kick on the
biggest guy in the crowd, and found his target staggering from
someone else's hit—wide open for a flying head scissors. So he
did that, and there was a hit from the side, and a lot of rolling
across the ground while he still held his scissors clamp.

And when everybody untangled, the big guy's neck was
broken, and he caught Bran's breakfast all over his head, neck
and shoulders.

There was no point at all in eating lunch.

* * *

For the next two killing bouts he didn't get called, so he began to sleep better. But on a deeper level he knew his luck couldn't last, and sure enough, on a windy drizzly morning the drills were interrupted by Arbogast yelling on the loudhailer. An impromptu combat, a killing one. Of the eight names announced, Bran's was the sixth. His gut froze in him. To the center of the field, meeting the others, he walked like a half-paralyzed cripple.

Peace take it, they WON'T kill me! Forcing himself to deepen his fast, shallow breathing, to swing his arms and put snap into his steps, Bran thought of how to make his mind put its own force into every blow. Australia was behind him now, but there he had learned what he now needed to use.

But when the melee began, Bran's foot slipped on the wet grass; his thrust fingers scooped an attacker's eye loose to roll free. While everyone stood frozen, watching as the half-blinded youth pawed at his face and at the ground, also Bran swallowed the bitter acid that erupted into his throat. He made one step back, one forward, and kicked to the throat. The maimed boy fell, with no will left, even to clutch at the injury that killed him.

Looking through a haze that shifted, listening through sounds that made no sense, Bran Tregare saw Colonel Arbogast and heard words that complimented him on his victory.

But for violating the no-eyes-no-balls rule, he still had to run the gauntlet. Just belt-ends, though. No buckles.

Later he realized that for minutes he was in range to put Arbogast's head on backward. He thought about it, and shrugged, because he'd have been killed for it.

The thing was, Bran Tregare had more to pay back, to UET and its Slaughterhouse, than *any* one death could satisfy.

His work in the melees had earned Tregare a vicious kind of respect—seldom now did opponents attack him singly. Still thin, though he had added some height, his wiry strength and Hulzein training made him more dangerous than he probably looked. Well, after this year, only one more to go!

Except that no one had boots full of ice, the graduation ceremonies were much the same as before. Cadre D's relatively new cadet-commander hosted a niggardly going-away party; in less than an hour the beer was finished. Bran and Jargy managed a call to Cadre G and reached Bernardez. "Of a certainty," said Kickem, "you must join me here. I shall request of cadet-captain—outgoing—Parnell that he furnish you the necessary bona fides to bring you hither." Since the guards had also been treated to beer, there wasn't any great problem about it.

Kickem's squad room was nearly empty. One cadet was passed out on his bunk. The rest, said Bernardez, were over the wall. So for the three of them there was beer in plenty.

They sat, drinking slowly and talking in quiet tones. On their minds were their respective futures. One more year of Slaughterhouse for Bran Tregare, a bit less for Jargy Hoad who had entered at near mid-term. "And two more of these eternities," said Kickem, "for my not entirely wretched self." For in Cadre G, Bernardez had found better treatment, and better luck in the "draw."

Tregare began to answer, but the door opened and Ragir Parnell entered. The tall youth was weaving a little, but his eyes still tracked as he said, "Ah. Kickem's friends from his old squad. Am I right?" He waved a hand, spilling beer from the flask it held. "Be welcome, of course." He sat, a little heavily. "Well, lads, you may congratulate me. I'm posted to space. I'm not certain as to which ship yet, but one thing I do know. I was slated for the _MacArthur_, commanded by Arger Korbeith. But that ship isn't back yet; the murdering bastard is late."

Bran cleared his throat. "I don't understand."

Parnell shook his head. "Pray to peace that you never do."

Again the summer period was scoutship training time. Bran and Jargy drew assignment to the same vessel, QR-1610, somewhat older than the one Bran had ridden a year before. Jargy described its commander, Malloy, as wearing the map of Ireland on his face. Malloy had red hair and freckles, with an expression partly tough and partly pleasant. For the most part he talked seldom, but sometimes the dam broke— Not right away, though—not on the trip's outgoing leg.

As had been the case on SX-2517, the scout's _segundo_ was female. Unlike Janith Reggs, Dien Talmuth had a sour way to her. Youngish, slim, not bad-looking when now and then she forgot to wear her usual sneer, Talmuth rebuffed all attempts at friendly conversation. Bran thought he knew why. Reggs had told him that UET totally denied command to women. Janith could live with the restriction. Talmuth apparently could not.

So Bran tried to stay pretty much out of her way.

From a training standpoint, the scout's trip went well. In most aspects, Bran and Jargy ranked high in tested skills. Not first place usually, for either but second or third. The competition, out in space with no brutal penalties in store, was fun for both. And, as during the previous summer, Bran found he could outdo anyone on board when it came to *maneuvering* the scout. After one contest, Malloy put a hand on Bran's shoulder. "You've got the reflexes for it, same as I have. If they don't put you to an armed ship 'twould be an awful waste."

And hadn't Peralta written much the same? Bran felt good.

The trip ended, and Bran was sorry it had to. It was back to the Slaughterhouse, to the forced fighting, to the fear again. But when Malloy landed QR-1610 on the Academy grounds he held his crew aboard that night, ordered beer and booze brought in, and staged a party. "I'm entitled," he said, "and I damned well shall."

Good party, Bran thought. He was more used to drinking, now; he could pace his intake and avoid losing control. He made one pass at the young woman who had topped his and Jargy's efforts in several phases of training, and knew enough not to be disappointed when her answer was no. It was time for singing, anyway.

The third verse of the Underground fight song wasn't all that encouraging:

> "When you post to space, your odds are dim;
> Your life's at the mercy of the captain's whim.
> Ride with the Butcher and you'll get a shock;
> Just one error and you're out the lock!
> And *that* is the reason, you can plainly see,
> Why there's only one latrine in all of UET!"

Bemused, Bran sang through the repetition of the chorus.

Later, a bit more taken with drink, having been turned down by Dien Talmuth and not much surprised by that outcome, Bran found himself sitting alongside Malloy, who was talking.

". . . one of the first ships ever to vanish, and now it turns

up on Terranova," Malloy said. "Called *Ridgerunner* now—
went in and raided, and got away clean. That's how—" Malloy
fell silent.

"How what?" Bran asked. Malloy turned and looked at him,
owl-eyed, but said nothing. "*What?*" Bran repeated.

Squinting, one eye almost closed, Malloy nodded. "How *I'll*
do it someday, you hot pilot, you!" The man looked around,
saw nobody paying heed to him, and said, "*Pig In The Parlor.*"

Puzzled, Bran said, "I beg your pardon?"

"*Pig In The Parlor!* When I take my ship, that's its name."

Bran thought, then said, "You mean Escape?"

Then Malloy's hand was to Bran's throat, and the man said,
"You and I know what I said. Anyone else does, you're a dead
cadet."

Bran shook his head. He knew Malloy was too drunk for
thinking and he wasn't sure how to handle the mess. He said,
"I didn't hear you say anything." Then, seeing the light of
reason in Malloy's eyes, added, "But I won't forget the advice
either."

Malloy laughed. "Good for you, Tregare." And the crisis was
over. After a time everyone bunked down, and next day
debarked.

Beginning his third year, as an upper, Bran found himself
moved to a different squad room, becoming its leader. Jargy
also had a squad of his own—still in Cadre D though, so
visiting back and forth was no problem. But seldom could the
two of them get all the red tape coordinated to make a joint
visit to Kickem in Cadre G. Separately sometimes, but not
often together.

All seven of Bran's squad mates—four snotties, three
middies—were unfamiliar to him. And the way he was feeling
nowadays, he was content to leave it at that. He learned their
names and paid heed to their failings, and conscientiously
tried to help and advise them toward survival as best he could,
but all attempts at more personal acquaintance he dis-
couraged. Because he didn't *need* more friends who would
likely be hurt or even killed; he had enough grief of his own.

So all of them—Spencer, Delegans, Marshall, Tarenz, Bills,
Gannister, Kloche, and fat little Schweik—formed a tight loyal
clique of themselves, in which he had no part. Which suited
Bran Tregare just fine; he felt a relief from pressure.

But he sometimes thought, *is this place turning me into some kind of monster? Or just a machine?*

Riding on nerve's edge, Bran drove himself to excellence— or as close as he could manage—in all aspects of upper-year training: classwork, physical drills, even the dreaded death-fights. Plus, as an upper he now had access to training on ship-control computer simulations for as many hours as he chose, and after a time his reports began to carry an Outstanding rating.

The way he knew about the reports was that he courted the young woman who was Colonel Arbogast's most junior secretary. At first he didn't care that he was using her for his own purposes. Then he came to like her and felt guilty about his duplicity. And finally he liked her enough to confess, and by that time *she* didn't care, so he didn't have to either. Lindya Haines was a small person, thin and dark and intense, and with her Bran found that he had known as much about sex as a mole knows about agriculture. The learning was quite an experience.

Bran's proficiency ratings had him well into the running for cadet-officer honors. When the listings were posted, Jargy Hoad came over to Bran's squad room and they had a couple of beers. Jargy said, "We're neither of us likely to be up for cadet-colonel, like Peralta—but captain's a good bet, and *you* might make major."

Bran looked over his tipped-up beer, tipped it back down, and swallowed. "Don't bet any money on it. Not me, anyway. You, maybe."

Jargy protested, but when the promotions were announced, Bran's pessimism was justified. Jargy made cadet-captain; Bran remained a squad leader. *Colonels and elephants never forget*; Arbogast wouldn't have forgotten sentencing Bran to the special cell.

Bran had no right to be disappointed about the promotions and he knew as much. But when, a day later, he was picked for a free-for-all, inside him something froze. *Be DAMNED if I will!* But he knew he had to; there wasn't any way out of it. He'd heard of the group that sat down and refused to fight— some years back, that was. On a third refusal of the commandant's orders, they'd simply been gunned down where they sat. And then there was the group that had somehow communicated and agreed to gang up on one of their number and kill him fast. They were congratulated, then told to go ahead and fight to *another* death. Not that that case had any bearing on Bran's current problem; well, he hoped not.

No way out. But then—suddenly, Bran Tregare knew exactly what he was going to do, next day. Or try to do, anyway . . .

Standing naked, one of eight in the drill field arena, even with the heat Bran found himself shivering. Could he do it? Arbogast's hoarse voice brayed "Start." Without hesitation, Bran moved. No choosing of targets. Whoever was nearest, came first. Moving at top speed while others vacillated, he kicked an opponent's knee sidewise, gave a near-lethal neck chop, and broke an elbow.

Three down—four to go. He had to pause a moment to see where everyone else was. Then: jump, kick, drop the man. Stiff fingers to a throat; trip the next man for later. And then the remaining contender put out a defending hand. Bran took it, twisted, had the man in front of him and ran him full speed, head to head, into the one trying to get to his feet. *Seven down!*

Panting, he stood and faced Arbogast. Growling past the mouthed cigar, the colonel said, "Well, go ahead. Finish one of them."

Bran shook his head. "I don't have to. They're all disabled, out of action."

Arbogast stood. "You haven't *finished.*"

"I'm not under attack, colonel, sir. No need."

"Finish it. That's an order."

Too much. "Take your order and—"

Which is how Bran Tregare became the first cadet to survive a full ten days in the special cell, with the cold, the electric shocks, and the ice-water showers. He was tougher now, and the experience didn't even put him into the infirmary. Though for a few days after his release, he was glad that his reputation saved him from challenges he couldn't possibly have handled.

"Are you crazy?" said Jargy Hoad, visiting Bran's squad room.

"Probably. This whole place is; you know that."

"But to try such a trick . . ."

"I thought it might work. You disable all the rest, that should be enough. Only thing was, I wasn't all that sure of doing it."

"Well, you did it, all right. And got ten days in Special."

Bran shuddered. "I'll never get the chance to kill Arbogast. A cadet wouldn't have a prayer—and the way ships chew time up toward light speed, he'll be long buried by the time I'm back from my first real space cruise. If I—if they let me—if I ever get out there at all. . . . But—" Bran leaned forward. "He's just one of a *lot* of bastards. And Jargy—someday I'm going to get rid of some of those."

Before next visiting Lindya Haines, Bran waited a while. For one thing he wasn't sure how she felt about UET and Arbogast and the Slaughterhouse in general. And he wasn't certain that he could smooth out his own feelings and, if need be, use tact. Well, tact had never been one his greater talents! But one evening, sending a bottle of wine in advance as a peace offering, he went to see Lindya.

His fears were needless; her first words were, "Oh, Bran! *How* could that bastritch treat you so?" Arbogast she meant; sure. So they cuddled and kissed and drank some of the wine before they got laid, and the rest after, with the dinner she'd prepared. And later talked with the Tri-V running unnoticed, and hit the bed again. Twice, before Bran decided he'd better not risk staying the night and maybe being caught absent from his squad duties.

But before he dressed, they kissed goodnight while her tiny warm breasts nudged his chest and made him wish he could stay longer.

At the age of fifteen, Bran Tregare recognized few limitations. Except, of course, for the official and enforced ones.

Next evening, Bernardez came over for a visit. Not often could he manage it, for Cadre G was tight with passes.

They were talking—no drinks tonight, for the illicit pipeline was temporarily crimped—when Bran's squad came in. Looking embarrassed, they sat here and there, not saying much. Bran's conversation with Kickem also died. How could they talk in front of these strangers?

Then, clearing his throat, little Schweik spoke up. "Tregare . . . in these forced combats, how many kills do you have?"

Bewildered, Bran shook his head. "How should I know?"

Delegans drew a shocked breath. "You mean, so many you've lost count? Or just don't care?"

Rage came, but Bran sat on it. "It's not that. It's—I hate it, I hate to think of it, I try to put it out of my mind." He found himself close to going for Delegans, and held himself back. "Can you understand that?"

Looking pale, Delegans nodded. "Yes. I think so."

Kickem stood. "Gotta go, Bran. Long day tomorrow."

"Sure. See ya." After, the squad was quieter than usual.

Still no more than a squad leader, Bran graduated. The next day, the board showed him posted for space. Standing beside him, Jargy said, "Oh, Jesus, Bran!"

"What's the matter?"

"You see the ship you're on? It's the *MacArthur*. Bran, you're shipping under Butcher Korbeith."

5

The Butcher

The *MacArthur* was an older ship but very well maintained. Toting his gear upship from the main airlock, Bran noticed that the bulkheads were spotless and the "ladders"—stairs, really—had new nonskid plastic on the treads. As an officer-cadet he was quartered on the top level of the crew's space, one deck below the galley. The cubicle held two bunks, two chairs, and two small desks. It shared sanitary facilities with three other such rooms arranged in a cluster. Someone else's possessions lay on one of the bunks; Bran dumped his on the other and, as directed by the boarding officer, went up to the galley. Like the one on the *Caesar*, it seated about forty—a little more than one-third of the ship's complement. At the moment only a few off-duty crew members were having coffee and snacks, but off to one side sat about a dozen young people who were obviously cadets.

With them sat a uniformed woman with a tattoo on her cheek. She motioned to Bran. "Over here." "Soon as your whole group's here, the captain will be down to give you a talk."

"Sure. Thanks for letting me know." He was staring at the tattoo. In a pattern of red, green, and blue, it was the lower quadrant—right-angled point upward—of a circle, its radius about a centimeter and a half.

The woman cleared her throat. "Never saw an officer before?"

"I—of course. At the Slau—the Academy. Colonel Arbogast, and—" Other cadets were entering. He paused.

"A spacing officer, I meant. Arbogast only spaced as a rating. He got commissioned after he went groundside." She gave a quick laugh. "He used to be younger than me, if that tells you anything. Anyway, I noticed you gawking the tattoo—that shows I rank as Third Officer. Second adds the left quadrant." She pointed. "And First adds the right. Captain has the full circle. Admirals and such—" But looking past Bran, she sprang to her feet. "Ten-*hut!*"

Standing quickly, Bran turned to face Captain Arger Korbeith. The man was a hulking giant, with huge, knobby hands and the outsized, distorted features that told of a hyperactive pituitary gland. Acromegaly, Bran recalled. Korbeith's shaggy hair was a dirty blond color above his sallow face. His expression was that of someone confronting the latest error of an unhousebroken pet. "At ease." The term, gravel-voiced, might have been invented just for him. "Sit down before you fall down." Except for one who almost did fall down in the process, the cadets obeyed.

Korbeith looked them over. "Another snot-nosed batch. Take forever to make spacers out of the likes of you! A quicker way for some, though. Keep your tails clean or you'll find out." Slightly stooped, like an animal about to spring, he stood a moment. "Any questions? And state your name first."

Sooner than ask that man a question, Bran would have banged his head against a brick wall. He held his breath, hoping for silence, but a young woman said, "Megan Delange, sir. What did you mean?"

Korbeith's heavy brows rose, unhooding deepset yellowish eyes. "One more word, *slut*, and you'll be the first to learn." He paused, waiting. His questioner shook her head. Korbeith's laugh had the sound of gravel. "Hope for you yet, maybe. Not much, but some." Turning with speed and grace that belied his awkward stance, the captain left the galley.

Silence extended, then across the large room some crew members began talking together, one giving a high-pitched laugh. Bran turned to the third officer. "Is it all right to ask *you* questions? If it isn't, I withdraw the request." He looked, gauging her. Her broad-cheekboned face looked pleasant enough, with its wide mouth and firm chin below grey eyes and a totally inadequate childlike nose. She looked trustworthy.

As she said, "Ask away. But first, who's asking?" Bran gave his name. She nodded. "And I'm Eunice Parsons. To you cadet types, Officer Parsons. So now ask."

The answers were much as he'd expected. As her hand

worried the short, sand-colored curls below her uniform cap, Bran began to get the picture. At the Slaughterhouse, rumor repeated enough to gain fact-status had said that a graduated cadet's first space trip was an all-or-nothing final exam. If you screwed up, they spaced you out the air lock.

"On most ships," Parsons went on, "that doesn't happen much. Which is to say, maybe every second or third trip on the average there's a real muckup in the group and an example *has* to be made. But—" She paused, obviously hating what came next. "Four training runs this ship's made, with this captain. He never spaces less than three." Shuddering, "seven, once."

For a moment, Bran fugued back to the party on Malloy's scout.

> "*Ride with the Butcher and you'll get a shock;*
> *Just one error and you're out the lock!*"

Somehow he managed to take a deep breath without making noise about it. Others around him, who had also listened, weren't quite as successful. Bran said, "I thank you for the warning, Officer Parsons."

"I hope it helps you, Cadet Tregare."

Going down to his room, Tregare calculated. Two dozen cadets was max quota. The actual number might be two or three less, depending. The odds weren't all that bad, but they weren't too good either. In the Slaughterhouse at least you had a chance to *fight* for your life. Not here, though.

It took him a moment to remember the right number. Then he opened the door and got a surprise. Sitting on the bunk that wasn't his, a slim person looked up at him. His roommate was female.

The realization didn't come immediately, because the blouse showed no evidence of breasts, and the sidewise view concealed any spread of hips. The person had been an early graduate, because the black hair ran to nearly two centimeters, rather than Bran's five millimeter stubble. But, first subliminally and then consciously, Bran noticed the slimness of ankles, and of wrists that had no bony knobs to the outside. No Adam's apple. No sign of facial hair (and the sideburns ended in a curve, not a shaved straight line). Earrings, small, not immediately noticed. Then she turned to face him, and he was sure.

"Well!" he said. "We're roommates, are we?"

Her voice was husky, mid-pitched. "It seems so. Don't get any ideas, roomie. My contraceptive implant runs out this week or maybe last, and getting spaced for preggy isn't my idea of a great career."

Already she was ahead of him. He said, "You've heard about the Butcher? I didn't see you upside, in the galley."

"I wasn't there. Besides, I'd heard it all before. One of our instructors shipped with Korbeith once—and lived." She laughed. "Well, *obviously* . . . right?" She stood and reached out a hand. "Just because I have to be off-limits, I don't mean to be unfriendly. I'm Salome Harker. Sally for short."

Her handclasp was warm, firm. "Bran Tregare. From Australia originally, but that's a time ago."

"San Francisco. Well, a hundred miles east, nearly, but these days it's all the same." So then they talked for a while.

To start with, duty on the *MacArthur* wasn't too bad. Hard work, long hours, strict discipline. On watch duty (he caught the 1600-2400 stint, not—thank peace!—the 0800-1600 stretch when Korbeith usually sat in.), the cadets took turns on the comm board, weapons positions, first or second navigators' chairs, or one of the pilots' seats. They did not, ever, *do* anything unless given specific orders; their jobs were to make observations, calculations, estimates of what they would do if the tasks were truly theirs to perform. Their notes were handed over to the watch officer and, presumably, evaluated by someone. Stressful chores, but Bran enjoyed them more than not.

Then, following the after-watch meal, cadets put in six hours of scutwork. Mostly scrubbing—floors, doors, bulkheads, or anything else that held still for it. Then maybe a couple of hours at Drive-monitoring. Then sleep, which came easily.

But it beat hell out of worrying about free-for-all fights.

Ten days off Earth—exhausted, Bran had slept through liftoff and hadn't even noticed—the first scare came. Captain Arger Korbeith called a meeting of his twenty-two cadets. In the galley again, but this time he sat and they stood. In his rasping voice, the captain called each cadet by name and proceeded to read short excerpts from that person's Performance Report. As: "Megan Delange. Failed to note a rock on collision course." Headshake. "May not be with us much longer, Delange." His target was the young woman who had made the mistake of asking him a question; Tregare saw her go pale.

A few more, and then, "Bran Tregare." A nod. "Performance none so bad. Too bad your earlier record doesn't match up." The brows raised; the yellow eyes glinted. "Twice in Arbogast's special cell, I see. Too bad we don't have time for that onship."

Tregare felt his guts heave; "Too bad," he'd heard, was a term to fear. But he didn't throw up; he didn't dare to.

He was lying on his bunk, trying to get his breath to come evenly, when he heard the door open. "Hey! Are you all right?" And Sally Harker came to sit and hug him. He turned to look up at her, and knew his attempted smile wasn't making it. But she said, "He scared me, too. Come on, let's just hold each other."

But after awhile his natural impulse came to him, so he wiggled loose from her. "It's no good. You *can't*."

She grinned at him. "You've always done only the one thing? Let me show you." Her blouse came off, and Bran was surprised to find that breasts could at the same time be so small and so tempting.

Then she showed him some things he hadn't known, and after that they didn't bother to hide nudity from each other.

Bran was "on watch" when his comm instruments indicated an object approaching, on a converging course with slight skew. Parsons had the watch. Bran said, "A ship there, I think."

The woman's face went taut. "Get off the board, Tregare." Wondering, he stood and moved to another seat. Then after quickly talking into a hushphone, she said, "Only the captain speaks a ship met in space. Or his named speaker."

Bran nodded, and everyone waited until Korbeith entered, bringing with him a thin, slouching man who looked tired and perhaps defeated. Korbeith shoved him toward the comm chair. "Say it all just right, Meardon. No mistakes. You hear me?"

The man nodded, and his hands moved to open the offship circuits. "Open screens," said Korbeith, as he moved to be off to one side, out of the screen's view. "Now *talk*."

Meardon's voice sounded the way he looked: a whine. "Hello the ship," he said. "Can't make out your insigne from this distance. We're still keeping the *MacArthur* name on here for a while. Heading toward—" He spoke gibberish and at the same time overloaded his voice amplifiers to peak distortion, then eased the control back and said, "—but we'll be a time getting there. And what's your own course, and who have you seen lately?"

The offship viewscreen lit, but the picture wobbled. If Bran had ever seen the man shown there, he couldn't have recognized him. The voice came flat. "The *MacArthur*, eh? Or was. Tell me, how did Butcher Korbeith die?"

Meardon paused. "Now why should you ask that? And who asks?"

"Cade Moaker asks, and I don't mind telling you, since you're not armed and can't cut course to ram, that you're speaking *Cut Loose Charlie* now. Not the *Dictator*, these days. You got that?" Now, at the other end a pause, then: "Meardon, isn't it? You never could fool me and you can't now, either. The Butcher's still alive, isn't he? And you're still gobbling his leavings!"

"You're wrong, Moaker. I—"

"Eat crap, Meardon! And don't bother trying to peg my destination, because ahead in my course there's still a dogleg."

The circuit went dead. Meardon tried twice more, until Korbeith said, "Drop it, you fool!" and left the control room.

Then Bran dared to look up, and saw that nearly everyone else had been having the same problem. Lagging behind the captain by several paces, Meardon slunk out. Bran caught the gaze of Eunice Parsons; his raised brows and his gesture asked a question.

Parsons beckoned him closer, and he sat. She said, "Once Meardon—First Officer then—thought to mutiny and Escape. As you might guess, he lost. But Korbeith found it useful to have it leaked to the grapevine, on this and that world, that Meardon succeeded. So now he keeps the skinny rat as a slave decoy, to try to trap out passing ships and get leads to Hidden Worlds."

Bran shivered. "Why doesn't Meardon kill himself?"

"Same reason his mutiny failed. No guts."

Two "days" later the intercom alarm woke Bran in midsleep. A quick look told him he'd had less than four hours' rest. Then a voice rasped, "All cadets! Assemble for airlock drill! On the run!" The room lights came on; Sally had reached the switch first. "Thanks," Bran said. "What uniform, you suppose?"

"Regular duty, I expect. He said, a drill." So they dressed quickly and descended the stairs considerably faster than safety regs permitted, making themselves the fifth and sixth cadets to arrive at the airlock deck area.

It wasn't merely a quartet of their peers waiting, though. There Arger Korbeith stood, flanked by two armed guards to either side. Bran didn't dare speak, but he and Sally exchanged a quick glance, and he was pretty sure her thought was the same as his own: *Now the Butcher strikes!*

It seemed forever, but probably less than two minutes passed before the last cadet arrived, perhaps thirty seconds after the next-to-last. Korbeith looked at the laggard and cleared his throat. "Your name, *sir?*"

The young man's face reddened. "Pendleton, sir. Keith Pendleton. I—"

"If you were intending to make an excuse, I advise against it." He nodded to the guard who looked to be the oldest of them.

That man made a kindly-seeming smile. "Form one rank. Take normal interval. Dress it up, there; straighten that line!" When he was satisfied, he nodded. "Now strip. Clothes off, *now*. Fold them neatly and place them one pace behind your position, then form rank again." He broke hesitation with, "Move it!"

Shucking his uniform as fast as he could, Bran tried to think. Then he had the answer: not merely simple humiliation, but economy. If you're going to space somebody out the air lock, why waste perfectly good garments? Neither first nor last to do so, he rejoined the lineup. And waited, as Korbeith glared.

The captain strode to face the boy at the right end of the group, stared at him, said nothing, and moved to the next, paused, moved again. Tension built; Pendleton the late arrival was now under Korbeith's scrutiny. The big man started to turn away, swung back, jerked his thumb toward his target; the guards started forward, but then Korbeith shook his head. "No, not this time. Next drill, let's see if he can be *first* here."

Standing to Bran's right, Salome Harker was seventh to endure Korbeith's inspection. It ended quickly, and then it was Bran's turn. Resolutely he avoided the yellow-eyed gaze, staring straight ahead at the enlarged Adam's apple. Korbeith mumbled something, and only when he moved on did Bran realize the words had included, ". . . no good. Should space him. But later . . ."

The man stopped only briefly before the next few cadets, then paused a time at Megan Delange. Bran's sidewise glance showed him beads of sweat at the forehead edge of her blond stubble, and barely noticeable, she was swaying on her feet. Korbeith's smile had rocks in it. "You'll keep."

He went past the last two people without looking at them. The guards followed him, and they left the area. No one bothered to dismiss the cadets, or direct them to clothe themselves; for close to a minute they all stood there, unable to decide what to do. There were a number of relieved exhalations but no talk, until Bran said, "In two hours I'm due on watch." He put on his shirt, pants, and shoes, bundled the rest of his clothes into one hand, and walked away. Whether the others followed his lead, he didn't know or care. But Sally Harker entered their room while he was still putting the clothes away.

As she herself undressed, she said, "Peace take me, I've *never* been so afraid. But he didn't kill anybody, after all. Do you suppose, Tregare, that it's all a big hoax? A scare?"

Only one true answer. "No, I don't. This way the bastard can build up suspense more. That's all."

If Korbeith indeed enjoyed playing cat-and-mouse, he had little patience for it. On Tregare's second-next duty stint, about halfway through, came the "Airlock drill!" call. Rising from the comm board, Bran turned to the watch officer: "Relief, sir?" The man nodded, and Bran took off in sprint gear: Control was the topmost inhabited upship level, so of all the cadet group he had the farthest to go. He took stairs in three and four-step jumps, and when he came to a vacant flight, no one in his way, took a flying leap, a quick grab at the handrail, and swung to take a free bound to the next deck.

And still, by about two seconds, he was last to assemble. Well, *bluff, dammit!* Catching a deep breath he took a good cadet brace and threw Korbeith his best salute. "Cadet Tregare, sir, reporting directly from watch duty!" Explanation, not excuse—and grudgingly, the Butcher nodded.

"So fall in, cadet." And then the smiling guard gave the orders to strip, and again they all stood side by side while Korbeith stalked down the line. Bran struggled to get his pulse and breathing down to normal. There was nothing he could do about his fear, except try to conceal it. While they all waited . . .

So quiet. From well along the line, Bran could hear Korbeith's gravel-mumbled threats. "If you shape up, you might be *worth* spacing out the lock." "Can't imagine why Arbogast passed you." Long pause, and the chronic scowl intensified. "I'm saving you for later." To Bran's right stood Megan Delange. In his peripheral vision he could see that her knees were shaking as Korbeith moved to tower above her. "Any questions this time?" She shook her head. The captain took a step to face Bran, then jerked his thumb back to Delange. "That one."

Then it was horror. Korbeith stood back, and two guards, the older one still with his falsely-kind smile, came to grab the young woman by her arms. Her knees buckled and her head sagged back; she made a keening sound, a mewling whimper that hurt Bran's ears. All instinct said to *help* her, but he knew he couldn't. He could only watch—and that, he couldn't avoid.

While a third guard opened the main air lock's inner door, the other two dragged the woman toward it. Suddenly she stiffened, shaking almost loose from one captor—but the man grabbed her again, one hand on her arm and the other giving her left breast a vicious twist. Her eyes rolled up until only white was showing; her scream shrilled echoes in the place, but still the two guards pulled her along. Then all at once her body rejected whatever it could manage—urine, feces, and vomit splattered everything and everyone within range of her. Down along the line, Bran saw two other cadets throw up, and fought to hold his own gorge.

Ignoring their soiled uniforms, the guards heaved Megan Delange into the air lock chamber. The portal slammed shut.

Bran couldn't remember whether the thick plastic window fogged up with entrance of air or evacuation. In this case it didn't matter. The outer door opened, and Megan Delange went spinning, her balance not yet caught from the rough throw into the chamber, out into the vacuum.

Until that moment the captain's gravelly laugh had never paused. Now it did, and with the silence that came while no one else seemed to draw breath, Bran heard a harsh mumble. Maybe it was the chamber's acoustics that brought the words. But the voice was Arger Korbeith's. And as Megan Delange plunged dead into space, Bran heard, "*You* go out there, not *me*. *You* pay, not *me*. *Nobody* can pay enough, but you'll never stop paying. And *you* go out. . . ."

Then other people began breathing and talking, and Bran lost track of the Butcher's litany. If it were real. If *any* of this was.

At least it's done, Bran thought; but he was wrong; Arger Korbeith had more for them. Above the airlock door a viewscreen lit, and the harsh voice said, "You will now observe the results." A camera with a zoom lensing and a brilliant floodlight had followed Delange into her experience of explosive decompression, so now the surviving cadets were treated to a replay of young Megan's dying convulsions. The camera operator was no expert; the lighting showed only her decompressed body against blackness of sky, and the body grew and shrank as camera adjustments failed to match the dying woman's rate of receding from the ship.

The colors were off, but purple was probably about right for the face. Compared to what else happened to it, and especially the eyes, the rest didn't matter.

Shocked to calmness of a sort, Bran stood through several repeated showings, trying not to hear Korbeith's chuckles. All around Bran, people were tossing their cookies, but he held his down. Until Korbeith graveled out a particularly lewd comment that in other context Bran could have ignored; suddenly he spewed.

It wouldn't have made any difference; the entire cadet contingent spent the next hour swabbing up the whole mess.

When Bran and Sally finally got back to quarters and showered up, they held each other and that was all either wanted. Bran was shaking and couldn't stop for a while. When he did steady, he said, "Harkness, I'm swearing an oath."

Her hug tightened. "Yes, Tregare?"

Against her warm arms, his head thrashed. "I don't know how or when or where or how long—but one day I will kill Arger Korbeith.

"If he doesn't kill me first."

Again she hugged harder. "Or if I don't. Him, I mean." Then Bran wanted her, but even for surrogate sex, he was too pooped.

Tensed, unable to relax, Bran waited to see what Korbeith would do next. But for days there were nothing but normal duty assignments. Cat and mouse, yes. Mouse wasn't Bran's favorite role. But he didn't exactly have a choice.

He tried to learn more, about what the Butcher's *pattern* might be, but it was hard to figure who to ask. Ratings (and unrated) in the crew simply clammed up to cadets, and it was about the same with First Officer Orrin Peale and Second Officer Wendell Rheinhardt. The Engineering officers kept pretty much to themselves—not much chance there.

So it came down to Eunice Parsons, the Third. She'd talked with Bran before, but for a time the watch skeds kept him from meeting her in galley. But then he caught her having a midwatch snack, and sat beside her. After casual greetings he got his nerve up to ask.

She looked at him. "Well, why not? I've never seen that scared people work better, so—" The pattern was fairly simple. After the first cadet was spaced, Korbeith tended to call random drills, but usually staged an execution only at the end of a training program. The programs generally ran about two or three weeks. "Be careful who you tell this to," she added. "If it gets back to the captain that the cadets know anything, he'll change his system. It's happened." Bran thanked her, and told no one except Sally Harkness.

Training progressed, and in spite of himself Bran enjoyed it. At the Slaughterhouse there had been practically no drill with sidearms. On the *MacArthur*, the group regularly had target practice on a range set up in the ship's machine shop, just above the Drive room. The energy weapons, both the light ones and the big, heavy two-handers, had their outputs locked down to a level that would barely melt butter but which gave clear indications on the targets, both stationary and moving. The vicious little needle guns that fired a stream of tiny slugs at ear-wrenching velocity as air was riven were, for practice, loaded with fragile plastic pellets propelled at a much slower rate of speed. It wouldn't do to catch one in the eye, of course, but a cadet's jumpsuit would protect against anything more than an angry bruise. Since Korbeith himself frequently observed the practicing, Bran could see the point. Given real ammo, what cadet could resist using it on the Butcher?

As on the scoutships, navigation was stressed, and again Bran starred at it. The *MacArthur's* mission, aside from the training aspect, was to rendezvous with a series of patrol ships,

stationed at intervals along a line between Earth's solar system
and a planet known as Stronghold. The odd thing about
Stronghold, as Bran had noticed before on star charts, was that
it lay in the opposite direction from all of UET's other
explorations. Remembering his father's story of UET killing
the alien Shrakken and stealing their ship, Bran thought he
knew what Stronghold was all about. And the patrol ships too.
Again he told his guesses only to Salome Harkness.

But the *MacArthur* was going nowhere near Stronghold,
only a few percent of the distance to that world. Orrin Peale,
the First, handed the cadets the problem of figuring their max
distance. "It takes roughly a month for us to get up as near to c
as makes no calculable difference for scheduling purposes.
Using nearly twelve gees—and don't ask me how the Drive
field neutralizes all but one of those in the ship and its
immediate vicinity. My job's Control, not Engineering. Now
then, cadets . . . with that information, tell me roughly how
far we'll be from Earth after one month accel and the next one
in decel. For that's exactly what we'll be doing. Going to the
farthest ship first and catching the others on the way home."
He coughed. "And the ratio of subjective time to objective,
also."

Zerch to light? Bran already knew that one: t/t_o (elapsed) was
pi-over-four. He stood, said so, and got an approving nod.

The other part took him a minute, in his head, to set up.
Then with his hand-calc, it was easy. "Slightly under eight
hundred billion kilometers, sir. Between a seventh and an
eighth of a light-year." Which wasn't much of a bite toward *any*
extrasolar planet, but still one hell of a way from Earth.

Along with the nod, this time Officer Peale almost smiled.

Again the shout of "Airlock drill" woke Bran from sleep. He
thought of making speed by omitting socks and underwear, but
decided that Korbeith might take the omission as excuse for
having him killed, and spent the few extra seconds. Downship
as fast as he dared go, he was eighth to reach the air lock deck
and pleased to see Sally just ahead of him.

Quickly they all lined up. The guard with the plastic implant
for a smile (or so it now seemed, to Bran) checked off his list,
and Korbeith began his stalk along the rank.

Despite the assurances from Parsons, Bran felt sweat gather
at crotch and armpits, and begin to slither down his skin. *I*

never thought I could wish to be back at the Slaughterhouse!
In his mind a resolve formed. If Korbeith jabbed that great,
knobby thumb at *him*, he would immediately, without a
thought, take his best shot at killing the man. No matter, then,
what happened—if he could take the Butcher with him, that
would have to do. *You HAVE to become a monster!*

To Bran's right stood Keith Pendleton, the boy who had
arrived last at the initial drill but who had indeed been first
there for the second, when Megan Delange died. Squinting to
that side, Bran saw Korbeith make a dismissing motion toward
the guards—with the hand Pendleton couldn't see. Then the
captain stared Keith up and down, mumbled a threat Bran
couldn't quite make out, moved along to Bran and then jerked
his thumb back at Pendleton. "That one." Then Korbeith stood
still.

The condemned youth turned pale as death. But he didn't
sway or fall; his knees locked and he stood rigid. For about ten
seconds that seemed a hundred times longer, the tableau held.
Then came Korbeith's jarring laugh. "Not yet, Pendleton
. . . not yet. Have to keep you snotnoses alert . . . that's
all."

He moved to give Bran his glowering stare, but Tregare
hardly noticed; he stood, his mind in a confused whirl, as the
captain gave a snort and a few foul words, and moved to the
next person. *If he'd pulled that on me, I'd have jumped him;
I'd be dead now.*

So he changed his plan. Only when the guards came at him,
would he make his try to kill Butcher Korbeith.

But true to the Third Officer's estimate, that time no one
went out the air lock.

New training segments on the *MacArthur* tended to begin
abruptly and without notice. When Tregare next checked in
for watch duty he was told to report to the deck level just
above the improvised target range. Arriving there earlier than
most of the cadet group, he found Second Officer Rheinhardt
inspecting a mechanism, hanging from an overhead track, that
looked like a metal skeleton festooned with straps and
servomotor units. Bran found himself looking at something
that leaned in a corner of the room—an oversized spacesuit
that obviously carried a lot of mechanical paraphernalia.
Rheinhardt caught his gaze, and said, "That's a power suit.

This is the trainer for it." When all the cadets were present, Rheinhardt had two of them help him into the heavy suit. When he had himself fastened up properly, but leaving the helmet off, he said, "This thing gives you more than ten times normal strength, via the servo assists. It takes practice, because you have to learn not to overload the circuits or else you could wreck it. But I'll show you." He beckoned to Bran, and with one hand lifted him high and bounced him gently. Setting him down, Rheinhardt then picked up, again one-handed, a machine tool that had to mass at least three hundred kilos. He moved slowly, carefully, and put it back to rest. "I won't show you how this thing can jump, because I don't want to dent the deck. Here, help me out of this." Pendleton and another cadet obliged.

Salome Harkness asked, "Sir? What do we *use* it for?"

"Good question. Well, mostly for outside work, handling heavy components that would be hell to work with, no matter how many people you had, without the power assists."

Bran said, "Sir? Are we going to work in that suit?"

He wasn't surprised when Rheinhardt made a headshake. "No. You'll work with the trainer. Only officers use the suit."

Sure. Let me in that thing and I'd own this ship!

But the trainer, as Rheinhardt explained, simulated all the inertial aspects, the vast weight and the power-multiplication. Over the next three duty periods, taking turns, Bran got the feel of the surrogate mechanism—how to judge his timing and coordinate his moves. At the end, he felt he could operate the suit all right—if the trainer's parameters made an accurate facsimile. And Rheinhardt assured the group that in fact it did.

But when the cadets did their first practice at outside work, they wore ordinary, non-powered spacesuits. Orrin Peale took first position on the life line. Everyone seemed both nervous and eager, but then came a complaining voice: Keith Pendleton's. "This suit's marked redlined. Not safe."

"That's for extended use, son." In his own suit, waiting for his helmet to unfog, Bran couldn't see who spoke, but the voice sounded like that of the plastic-smiled guard. "Don't worry. I'll be right next to you, and keep an eye peeled to see you're all right. Which you will be. This time we're due out only half an hour. But I'll put us at the end, if it makes you feel better. So we could get back in fast."

It sounded like a lot more explanation than the question needed, but Bran was too excited to pay much heed. After a wait that probably wasn't as long as it seemed, the first half of the group entered the airlock. It cycled, evacuating its air back into the ship, and the outside hatch opened. Last in line, of his contingent, Bran crept out onto the ship's hull.

And gasped. Space seen directly from the scoutships had been spectacular, but *this*—the *MacArthur* was well past half of c, out where even at such speed the interstellar gas made no threat to a suited person—and the view was like nothing he'd ever imagined. Behind, except for the Drive's spreading aura, nothing but blackness—ahead, stars crowded into an unrealistically tight vista, and colors shifted out of all recognition.

The lock had closed, recycled, and opened out. Now the other half of the group emerged. Bran saw the two life lines being connected; then came Officer Peale's order to move off. "Just follow me. We're going all the way around the ship, a bit the long way with a lengthwise slant to our path. What you do is concentrate and get used to handling the suit outside."

So they began to walk, to clomp along with their magnetic boots on the ship's rind. Progress was jerky, as one or another cadet lost footgrip or held it too long. Life line segments tended to go too taut or too loose, disturbing someone's balance. But all in all it didn't go badly. Bran found that his earlier scoutship practice came back to him easily enough, and now and then he risked a look at that fantastic sky.

They were nearly all the way around, and he saw the airlock hatch ahead, when behind him he heard a commotion. Well, it had to be behind because the voices were Pendleton's and Plastic Smile's. "Help me!" "Watch it, boy. What—?"

Looking back, Bran saw the last suit in the line drifting away. Faster and faster, until it vanished in distance.

When they got inside both groups, Plastic Smile hurried the unsuiting and quickly sent the cadets to quarters. Bran wanted to look at something but didn't get any chance to do so.

When Salome joined him in their room, she grabbed to hug him. "Oh, Bran! I saw the lifeline. It was *cut*."

He nodded. "And on orders; sure. Well, if you're going to waste a suit, make sure it's worn out already."

Her eyes widened. "You think that?" She gave half a sob. "How much air do you think he had?"

Without meaning to, he snarled at her. "How should I

know? And what difference does it make? It all depends on how long the Butcher likes his victims to suffer first."

But now he knew. Air lock drills were only part of it. The Butcher had other ways.

6

Reunion

While the *MacArthur* still built toward c, the Butcher called two more drills. All the remaining cadets lived through the first one, but next time Plastic Smile and his sidekick took a young man to the air lock and he went naked into space. The victim seemed frozen by Korbeith's verdict; he said nothing, and his body held its contents until the vacuum hit. Two cadets vomited, but not Bran Tregare. Not before he was back to quarters, anyway.

The ship, Bran knew from briefings, was on sked to hit a Vee of $0.995c$—a t/t_o ratio, briefly at peak, of about ten. Or maybe one-tenth; Bran could never keep straight which was t and which was t_o, and who cared? Ships chewed time, was all.

Turnover date was no secret, though, and Bran looked forward to watching the maneuver. No such luck: Korbeith ordered all cadets to quarters, "—and strap in. Anyone injured during zero-gee time, I needn't tell you what happens."

Sure as hell you don't, you murdering bastard.

Bran would have settled for strapping in, but Salome came up with a more imaginative idea. So they rigged tie lines, and during turnover, floating free, they made love. One of their ways, that was safe for them, simply wouldn't work without gravity—so they made do with the other. And so much for the Butcher!

Now the *MacArthur* went into its month of decel. Training continued, and in three more airlock drills, only once was a cadet spaced. Always, every time, Tregare thought *he* would be the one to go. *But, peace willing, not alone!* The strain was costing him sleep, wrecking his appetite, winding him up to a tighter pitch all the time. If it hadn't been for Sally Harkness, he knew he'd have cracked, long since.

His closest call was the airlock drill two days before scheduled rendezvous with the patrol ship *Barbarossa*. Two places to Bran's left stood Sally, and at her turn Korbeith paused to mumble longer than usual. Then he jerked his thumb—"That one!"—and if Tregare hadn't seen the behind-hand signal, warding off the guards' move, he'd have charged and hoped to kill. As it was, he barely restrained himself. And back in their room fell shaking onto his bunk, needing love's comfort but physically incapable of taking it.

"That's all right," she said, holding him. "We're still alive and there's always tomorrow."

How Officer Rheinhardt came to his death, Tregare never knew. The ship was told only that Eunice Parsons had been promoted from Third to Second, that a rating was breveted to Third, temporarily, and (hardly made clear, but implied) that a new, permanent Third Officer was being transferred from the *Barbarossa*. This last news came after the two ships had met and docked, and the various Control and Engineering officers had exchanged guesting between vessels.

Rheinhardt had been a good, likable officer, clear in his instructions and fair in the ways he treated his cadet students. With some foreboding, Bran awaited meeting with the man's replacement. During ships' rendezvous the event didn't occur. After pullout, heading back for Earth by way of stoppage at other patrol-ship stations, he still hadn't met the new Third. So when he entered the galley, fresh off watch, the sight of a familiar face startled him. *Peralta!*

The man hadn't changed much: still slim, but more muscular. His face held firmer lines, and now the mustache was considerably more successful, though still trimmed to leanness. Bran saw that Peralta had recognized him, but showed no overt sign of the recognition. So maybe there were rules Bran didn't know yet. For damn sure he wasn't going to run up yelling buddy-buddy; for all Bran knew, that could mean a quick route to the air lock.

So, setting his tray aside because for one thing he really wasn't all that hungry, Bran got himself a cup of coffee and strolled over to the table where Jimar Peralta sat. If he got the invitation to sit down, fine. If not, he'd go eat.

Peralta *had* to see Tregare coming but he didn't look up.

Well, maybe this was how it was. Bran walked to the table, refrained from setting his cup down, and said, "Mr. Peralta?"

Now Peralta's gaze acknowledged Bran's existence. "Yes?"

"You'd be our new Third Officer, sir?"

A nod. "I would, yes."

"Congratulations, sir. From Cadet Bran Tregare."

He knew he'd said the right thing when Peralta grinned and offered a handshake. "Sit down, Tregare. Join me. It's irregular, but permitted." Bran sat. "Now what's been happening with you?"

Others were in earshot. Still he had to say what he felt. "I've been on this ship two months and I'm still alive. Sir."

With a slight frown, a twitch of head that wasn't quite a shake, Peralta answered, more loudly than seemed to be called for. "Very commendable, Cadet Tregare. Your attitude does you credit." Abruptly his voice dropped. "You talk too much. In public, don't." Voice raised again. "What news from our colleagues at the Academy?"

Chatter? All right; Bran gave some. "Jargy Hoad—you'll remember him—made cadet-captain our upper year. Kickem Bernardez—no, he was after your time—well, anyway . . ." Bran talked for the audience, assuming anyone was listening, and Peralta responded in kind. Then said, "You'd better go now, good as it is to see you." And, "Visiting must be at *my* instigation."

Bran nodded. "I understand."

"I hope so, Tregare." That was all of it, so Bran left.

In training work, Peralta treated Bran as if they hadn't known each other before—which, of course, was as it should be. The man was not unfair; if Bran or anyone else did especially well on any assignment, Peralta gave a compliment. On the other hand, any cadet who goofed caught the Third Officer's best grade of sarcasm. Bran didn't goof often, or badly.

Once he was able to answer a question without bothering to calculate—because, from curiosity, he'd already worked it out. "On your outward leg," Peralta said, "you hit very close to c before turnover. What did that run add to the difference between your two ages?"

"Not quite seventeen days," Bran answered, while others were just beginning to set up the problem on their hand-calcs. Peralta waited for an explanation, so Bran added, "It's the pi-over-four factor, for t/t_0 at steady accel from zerch to light, and back down. So sixty ship days roughly, equal nearly seventy-seven back on Earth."

"Did you do that in your head?"

"No, sir. I got to wondering last week, and figured it then."

Peralta made a faint smile. "Very good. Now we'll put a more complicated question. Our return to Earth is in two segments. Consider—" Bran's hand was up. "Yes, Tregare?"

"I thought we were to meet three more ships."

"And so did the captain. But the orders have been changed. Shall we continue?" Bran shut up, listened to the problem as given, and came in with the second-closest approximate answer.

Only the top performer got commended, though.

Back in quarters, Bran did some battery-assisted thinking. Before, he simply hadn't considered the matter. Now he realized that a four-segment return to Earth, each with accel and then with decel to rest (approximate), would have taken more than four times as long as the outward run. By ship's time, that was; on Korbeith's ship, Earth chronology meant doodly zilch.

So the change of orders was a break, and the nineteen surviving cadets could certainly use one. Still, they had four more months, anyway, under the Butcher's sway. *Scheist!*

So when Salome came in he was in no mood to talk. She tried to rally him but he wouldn't respond, until finally she jumped and grabbed him, laughing, knowing he was ticklish and would either snap out of it or get angry. Balanced on the edge of that choice, suddenly he laughed. "Watch it, lady! Tregare never forgives a tickle!" They had most of their clothes off when the intercom sounded.

"Third Officer Peralta here. Inspection tour in five minutes." Pouting, but grinning along with it, Sally Harkness got dressed. Except for mussed hair—now it was long enough to be mussed—she looked relatively sedate as she opened the door to Peralta.

Bran stood at attention. "Ready for inspection, sir."

Closing the door, Peralta waved a hand. "Inspection completed, cadets. Let's sit down. I have a few things to say."

Bran sat, with Sally beside him, Peralta taking the other bunk. Bran said, "Sorry, no beer to offer, sir. This ship doesn't seem to have much of a pipeline." Immediately, from Peralta's expression, he knew he was on the wrong track. "Sorry, sir. I'll shut up."

"You'd better." The Third Officer looked at Salome Harkness. "I see that in assignment of roommates, Bran Tregare has had better luck than he deserves." Her brows raised, and Peralta quickly added, "That's a compliment, cadet, not a proposition." Bran didn't know what to say, so he kept silent.

And so, for a time, did Peralta. Until he sighed and said, "This is a bad ship; we all know that. I'm relatively safe. Entirely so, I'd have said, until the circumstances of my posting here as Third Officer. If anyone knows what happened to Rheinhardt, no one's saying." He shrugged. "But I'll manage, I think; the captain seems to like my style and I shan't disabuse him of his opinion. You, though—" He shook his head. "I told you once, Tregare, I'd like to have you spacing with me. On my own ship, I meant, when I have one. *And I will*, peace allowing it. But how any of you cadets can guarantee to survive, I have no idea."

Harkness leaned forward. "You've heard something, sir?"

"Just grapevine. The captain seems to be working himself up to something."

"Is there anything—" As soon as he said it, Bran knew the answer.

"Anything *I* can do?" Peralta shook his head. "That's what I wanted you to know. I'm against this killing, the same as back at the Slaughterhouse, but there is not one damned thing I can do about it. I wouldn't even try." He leaned forward. "Because I want to command and I intend to have it. And nothing in this universe is going to get in my way. Nothing; not even friends."

And seeing the tautness of face and eyes, Bran knew that argument wouldn't help. Jargy had pegged Peralta right enough.

But on the next space walk around the *MacArthur*'s outside, when two cadets waffled at being placed at either end of the lifeline (well, look what had happened to Pendleton! But no one mentioned that), Peralta took one end himself and Orrin Peale took the other. Plastic Smile wasn't present, so Bran thought the fears might be unwarranted. But still he gave both officers a good mark in his mental book.

At the next airlock drill, two days short of rendezvous with the armed ship *T'chaka*, the cadets stood shivering, naked in a temperature hardly exceeding 12-Celsius, and saw Third

Officer Jimar Peralta standing at the captain's flank. After a
silent wait, Korbeith said, "Third Officer, you do the honors.
Inspect, and choose which of them to space."

Peralta nodded. "Yes, sir." He moved to confront the cadet
at the right of the line, looked her up and down, moved on.
Unlike Korbeith he said no word, taking shorter or longer
times to inspect each possible victim. As he faced Bran, one
eyelid dipped so slightly that Tregare thought he might have
imagined it. Then at the end, Peralta turned to face Arger
Korbeith.

"Sir?"

"Yes, Third. Have you chosen?"

Headshake. "No, sir."

"Why not?"

"Sir, I've had nearly eight weeks, working with these cadets.
And I must say, you've done an admirable job of culling, I—"

"You can't find *anyone*?"

"No one person. Captain, sir, in my opinion their performances are pretty much on a par. So in my judgment, if any
are to be spaced, all should be." Peralta didn't quite shrug, but
gave a faint suggestion of that move. "That would be up to you,
sir."

For a heart-stopping moment, seeing blood suffuse Korbeith's sallow complexion, Bran thought they were all dead.
But not alone! For he would take his last chance at Korbeith,
live or die.

Then the Butcher relaxed his stance; the gravel laugh came.
"If I dumped the lot, Peralta, you'd go with them." Then he
stalked away, and again Bran found himself able to breathe.

Later, alone with Sally and still winding down from tension,
he said, "He's a fox, Peralta is! If he's on your side, that's
wonderful."

"But if he isn't?"

"Yeah. That's the problem. How do you know?"

Rendezvous with the *T'chaka* came and was done with; Bran
didn't get onto that ship and saw no one from it. The
MacArthur went into accel mode: two months, roughly, short
of Earth return. Training stayed heavy but not intolerable;
scutwork details shrank to token chores. Despite what the late
Officer Rheinhardt had said, cadets did get actual training in
one of the ship's two power suits. But with the suit-powered

energy projector, much more massive and destructive than a regular two-hander, disconnected and removed. While a guard or officer, in the other suit, had the potent weapon ready for use. And the whole thing, the suit training, took place in a locked hold. No, Arger Korbeith was taking no chances of a cadet getting loose with a suit—not in *his* ship.

Never mind; Bran Tregare enjoyed the learning. At first the time-lags, the discrepancies between his body's moves and the servo responses, felt awkward. But then he caught the hang of it—a little, though not entirely, like swimming in Great Salt Lake (which he had done one summer, but had almost forgotten by now). In his third session he had the coordination down pat: the move, the pause, the suit's *action*. So when he thought he'd achieved mastery, what else but to *try* it?

Risky, it would be, for now Peralta inhabited the weaponed suit, and the man was cat-quick. But in a power suit, not quite so fast. All right, give it a go! So moving toward the other suited man, Bran said, "Let's see if I can do something, here," and heard his amplified voice boom echoes from the confining bulkheads. Peralta nodded; good enough. Bran feinted to the right, held the feint long enough for Peralta to react, then took advantage of the suits' delay-factor to come back the other way while Peralta had only begun to move.

The next instant, he had the other man's energy projector in his armored hands. But before Peralta, recovering his balance, could launch any attack, Bran was handing the weapon back to him. "No offense meant, sir. I just wanted to see if I could *do* it."

Halting his move, the Third Officer reached and took back the big gun. Inside the helmet, Tregare saw his nod. "Good action, cadet. You know, I trust, that if you'd failed to take the gun, you'd be dead now? Not by my will, but by my trained reflexes."

"Not quite that definite, no, sir. I did know I had to cut it pretty fine."

"Indeed." Peralta had punched the door control; it opened, and for the first time helpers came to get both men out of the suits. So Tregare knew something else now, or thought he did: a trainee's suit must have outside controls on it, so that someone else could turn it off. For otherwise the unprotected helpers could be made hostage, or simply slaughtered, by a really desperate cadet.

One more item to keep in mind . . .

* * *

When he told Sally about it all, she shook her head and then laughed. "You take such chances!"

He thought about it. "In this mess, is there any other way?"

"I guess not. But—" He was caressing her. "Careful, there. Mmm—that's safer. And now why don't you—?"

He did. Sometimes it bothered him, what they had to settle for. But as long as Sally agreed, it would have to do him.

Parsons had said the Butcher never spaced less than three cadets per trip; that much, he had done (if Keith Pendleton, cast adrift in a defective suit, also counted. And how many more deaths would Korbeith's urge need?). Patience wasn't Bran's best skill, and constant fear would never come to be a comfortable companion. He lost sleep, dreamed badly, and ran on raw adrenalin.

One day I'll kill him. If he doesn't kill me first. The saying helped Bran at first waking, and also in getting to sleep. No one, ever, had given him such fear; while Korbeith lived, Bran felt he could never be a whole person. Alive and functional, maybe, but incomplete. *So I have to. Someday, some way, I have to.*

He knew the goal was unrealistic, but still he was stuck with it. All his life, maybe, however long that might turn out to be. The main thing was outliving the Butcher; he thought on it.

When Peralta next paid Bran and Sally an "inspection" visit, he'd been wining. In fact he brought along a bottle, still nearly full. "Be my guests," he said. "I've had plenty. Not in the usual sense, but on this ship, more than enough." So, with thanks, the two sipped the tart, ruby red stuff.

"Very good," Bran said, and Salome nodded. Bran changed the subject. "What have you been doing since you left the— the Academy?" Thinking back, he frowned. "Someone said—I forget who—that you were trying for the next fleet to Stronghold."

"I was." Peralta's chuckle held no amusement. "But got bumped last minute into patrol duty on the *Barbarossa*. Been there ever since, 'til now. Not much action, and *no* promotions."

"But you're Third now. . . ."

"Your Mr. Rheinhardt's bad luck was my good. Oops . . . drink to his memory for me, will you? That's right. Anyway, I was senior to all-cadet status personnel on the *Barbarossa* and also here on the *MacArthur*, so I got the nod. Not my idea of a prize assignment, as you might guess, but Third Officer is Third Officer. And once back on Earth . . ."

"You have plans, sir?" Soft-voiced, Sally spoke.

Peralta laughed. "Always. But I never reveal them ahead of time." More soberly, he said, "This much I'll say. Some think promotions come faster at HQ, but percentagewise, they don't. You have to go out, to go places." Again he laughed. "Peace take it, I've made a joke!" He leaned forward. "Out in space, except for the piddle of patrol duty, your ship can—" He waved his arms wide. "—can find a new colony planet, nail an Escaped ship or its destination, maybe even locate a Hidden World. The bonuses for *that*, if it ever happens . . ."

"Nail an Escaped ship?" Bran thought. "Then you'd be trying for a berth on an armed one."

"If I could manage it. Of course." Maybe Peralta didn't think he was carrying much of a load, but Bran did. "And then there's the wild card situation. Which we need not discuss here."

But when the wine was gone, and Peralta also, Bran and Sally discussed it. "It stands to reason," he said, "that most ships make their Escapes by way of mutiny. Captains have the least incentive to bolt. Which, afterward, means promotions among the survivors, and one of these is to *command*. And that's what Peralta wants most. He can taste it."

On the *MacArthur* there was no question of mutiny or Escape. Off the grapevine, once crew members began talking to cadets, Bran had picked up several stories, and he passed them along to Salome Harkness. "It was tried once, on Korbeith's previous ship. I forget its name now. He got the ship back to Earth with only six other people alive."

"That's not possible. In these ships, for Control alone—and the Drive—"

"Korbeith proved different. He ran Control with two on duty in Control, rather than four, and two filling in for the usual three on Drive. Everybody standing double watches, sixteen hours out of twenty-four. And one in the galley, and no maintenance. He needed luck on that last, but he got it."

"Only seven alive?" She shook her head. "The others?" Then she said, "No, I guess I don't have to ask about that."

"Hardly." Inside him Bran grinned; he was starting to sound like Peralta. "Anyway, the word is that Korbeith has this ship loaded with special weapons systems, and carries the only keys to them. He can gas whole levels, if he wants to. And his guards—" (especially, Bran had heard, Plastic Smile) "—he has them addicted to some drug, and of course he has the only supply on board."

Sally frowned. "Are you *sure* about all this?"

"Course not. But it fits his patterns, and sure's hell I don't intend to find out."

At the next air lock drill, just short of turnover, the Butcher stood before Bran a long time. Mumbling, "No damn good. Past time—skinny, useless—waste of rations . . ." trailing off so that Bran, against his will, strained to hear. Then, with that quick way he turned, Korbeith twitched thumb at Bran.

"That one." Only the fact that momentarily he froze, before noticing that the guards hadn't moved, saved Bran then. Because he was primed to go, and his target was that jutting larynx. The hell with eyes and balls; their loss didn't kill.

But the tiny, involuntary pause, giving him time to realize that the guards' immobility meant Korbeith had waved them off, saved Tregare. He felt himself redden as the great rasp of the Butcher's laughter came. "Almost had you there, didn't I? Well, you're not home yet." But that time he killed no one.

Back in quarters Bran expected to be incapable with Sally. Instead he found himself ready, and again, and again—until finally she said, "I'm sorry, but it's starting to *hurt*."

So he apologized, and she said he needn't, that it was all right and she understood, and—somewhere in there, he fell asleep.

But that was why, at turnover next day, they played no games at all.

In some ways the last month was the worst. The closer they got to Earth, the more Bran felt they had to lose, should Korbeith choose one of them for spacing. Wound up tighter than ever, he had to forgo coffee entirely; combined with a constant adrenalin overload, it literally made him ill. Food was a chore. He needed the fuel value but had to force it down and fight to hold it there—not always successfully.

The next one Korbeith spaced was a quiet young woman whose work, Bran knew from the reports he'd seen, was exemplary. When the Butcher chose her, she simply fainted— or pretended the faint perhaps, since Plastic Smile was unable to force her to show wakefulness before he dumped her into the air lock.

As the lock's outer hatch opened, Bran saw the Butcher's lips move. Stationed at the far end of the line, this time he couldn't hear the words. But seeing the heavy mouth move, he knew what Korbeith was saying. "*You* go out there, not *me*. *You* pay . . . ." And pay for what? Tregare had no idea. Except that it might have to do with the ship Korbeith had brought home with only six other living persons aboard. At any rate, the Butcher left, and air lock drill was over.

After that one, Bran was not sane, knew he wasn't, and didn't really want to be.

In the galley, after watch-observation duty, Bran went to dump his tray and put it in the rack. As he set the tray down, alongside the stack he saw a thin, sharp-pointed tool, something like an old-fashioned ice pick. He had no idea of its use, but somehow he liked the looks of it. Under cover of pretending to adjust the stack of trays, he grasped the tool and put it up his sleeve. Then he left the galley.

Restless, he stalked through the ship—up a deck, prowl the corridors, up another, down three—he wasn't sure where he was going. But when he saw Plastic Smile ahead, turning a corner and going out of sight, he knew who he was looking for.

He followed the man, and the pursuit didn't take long, because Plastic Smile came to a door and rummaged to bring out a set of keys. As he put one to the door's lock, Tregare was close behind him and tapped his shoulder. The man turned. "What—" He got no farther. Between larynx and chin, the point entered slanting upward, rasped between vertebrae and hit the spinal cord. When the guard didn't drop immediately, Bran wiggled the haft to enlarge the wound. Then as Plastic Smile began to crumple, the cadet wiped his palm over the tool's handgrip. *No fingerprints.* And only then realized he hadn't even looked to see that the corridor was clear of witnesses.

It was, though.

* * *

Heading back toward quarters, feeling the cold sweat of reaction running down his body, briefly Tregare wondered if he should have kept the impromptu weapon. *There's always Korbeith.* But he decided if he had it, he could be caught with it. And if the galley stocked one of them, no doubt there were more. Now that he knew about them.

The sweat of fear stank on him; he showered clean before Sally got back. Then things weren't so good; sexually he was totally unresponsive. No matter what they tried, nothing worked.

Why? His total rage, his frustration when the Butcher baited him and laughed—he'd expected *that* to unman him, but the effect had been just the opposite. Now he'd taken revenge, and somehow the secret triumph left him drained.

There was no way to talk about it. He couldn't tell anyone, not even Salome Harkness, that he had killed Plastic Smile. So he hugged Sally and said, "Delayed reaction, I guess. Sorry."

"Don't worry about it, Tregare. I can wait for next time."

Bran dreaded what could happen when Korbeith got into retaliatory gear. For two days nothing. Then the Butcher called a selective assembly in the galley. Lower-rated and unrated crew members weren't invited, and the watch contingent was present by intercom-viewscreen only. Still the place was packed.

There weren't enough seats; some ratings doubled up and some sat on the deck, as Arger Korbeith stalked and glowered. "Won't put up with murder!" *Except by your own doing, you piece of dung.* "No shelter for killers, no mercy." *I'll drink to that.* "So—" Korbeith pointed to one of his other guards. "—get up here, and talk!" And to Bran Tregare's amazement, the guard who had been Plastic Smile's colleague in the spacing of cadets was dragged to a chair and tied to it. Whereat Arger Korbeith raged and swore and hit the bound man, and had other things done to him that Bran didn't like to see, until the man confessed to killing Plastic Smile—whose true name Bran never did register.

Korbeith turned to his two remaining guards. "Take him down to the airlock. Officers and cadets, follow. The rest of you, dismissed."

Bewildered, Tregare moved downship with the rest. Why had the guard confessed to what he hadn't done? The torture? Or a mind-softening effect of the drugs used by Korbeith's guard force? It made no difference; Bran was off the hook for Plastic Smile. And now he remembered: this guard, headed for the airlock, was the one who had given the vicious wrench to the naked breast of the woman Bran had first seen spaced, and then had helped to space her. *Go to hell, then!*

Airlock drill didn't seem the same with clothes on. Only the condemned guard was stripped. But this time the procedure was different; Korbeith ordered the man equipped with a breathing mask, oxygen tube, and life line. Then his two ex-cohorts horsed him into the air lock and secured the life line to a bulkhead bitt. When they were out and the inner door closed, Korbeith himself punched the opening of the hatch to space, to cold, to vacuum.

So that the man could breathe while his body's internal pressures bloated and ruptured him, while the chill of space froze him from the outside in. As the Butcher's lips moved. *You go out there, not me. . . .*

Bran didn't throw up. Korbeith had worn that reflex out. Among other things . . .

Slow, Bran was, going back upship. When he entered the bunkroom Sally was toweling and still part dripping from her shower. She looked at him, a question in her face. He shook his head, went to stand in hot spray longer than customs said he should, then came out to face her.

Frustration burst. "It's no damn *good!*"

She came to him. "I know. But it's not much longer. Back to Earth; then we get reassigned. They told us that."

He pushed her off; he had to. "You *don't* know." She waited. He said, "That bastard didn't kill the other one. I did." Then he told her all of it. "I didn't want to tell you."

"Oh, Bran! I'm so glad you did." And then, between them, everything was suddenly all right.

Why was it, he thought, that so many of the bright spots of his life had to do with women? Well, why argue?

In bed then, it was for him close to the best time ever. Afterward he told her so, then frowned. "Sally—is this ship turning me into a killing freak? I don't want it to. I don't want love tied into death. I *don't.*"

She held him. "No, Bran, that's not it. After you'd killed that smiling hyena, you *couldn't*—remember? But now that we

have it straight between us, you can. If you're a freak for
something, Bran Tregare, it just might be honesty."

Suddenly his tears flowed. He couldn't stop them, and after
a few moments he didn't try. When he was done, still in Sally's
tight hug, he felt a lot better.

And he slept without nightmares.

Approaching Earth, the *MacArthur* simulated invasion
maneuvers. Korbeith might be a sadistic murdering son of a
sow, but Bran had to admit that the Butcher knew his tactics.
Sitting up in Control on his watch-observer stints, he saw how
the *MacArthur* utilized its approach angle, coming from above
the ecliptic, then some deceptive changes in rate of decelera-
tion, and finally a twitch of course that hid the ship behind
Jupiter's radiation belts, to first appear on Earth's screens in
what would have been a highly effective attack stance. But of
course no such thing was intended; it was all for training
purposes, and the captain had given safe-conduct signals to all
outlying patrols. Still, it *was* damned good training.

Inside the moon's orbit, the ship neared Earth. Not long
now, Tregare thought, until they'd all be groundside. And *out*
of this insane mess. But that wasn't how it happened. A bit
lower than synchronous height, the *MacArthur* stopped
descent and went to circling the planet below. Cadets, having
strapped in according to orders, were then commanded to go
downship. Nude this time, leaving all clothes in quarters.

Airlock drill. What else?

With little earlier chance to learn weightless maneuvering,
Bran and Sally made awkard going of it. And so, it seemed,
did every cadet they met along the way. Nobody, though, after
three turnovers and two dockings, suffered from null-gee
nausea.

At the air lock deck, with his two remaining guards, Butcher
Korbeith *stood*. Sure; those three had boots with controlled
magnets. The cadets, of course, didn't.

There was a cable, though, strung across the area, and the
cadets were told to line up by grabbing onto it. When the
captain was satisfied with their spacing along the thing, he
said, with the laugh Bran had learned to despise, "Back to
Earth, we're all going. But maybe a head start for some of you;
beat the ship down there." And he stalked to scan the cable-
holding line-up.

There was no way to stand at attention so Bran didn't try; instead he twisted to watch the Butcher's progress and actions. Korbeith mumbled something to the first cadet, pushed the young man free of the cable and bellowed, "You have thirty seconds to get back into place." But then, as the cadet floundered, moved along and paid no heed.

Next in line was Sally Harkness. Gasping, as the Butcher put his great hands on her and *kneaded*, she turned pale. "And you'll reach Earth ahead of us, won't you? And make a fine bright light to guide us in, as you hit air. *Won't* you, slut?"

Sanity was lost. Tregare pulled on the cable, gathered his legs up to make thrust, and launched for Korbeith's throat. All without making a sound. His breath hissed through gaping jaws. But as the Butcher jerked Harkness free of her hold, the cable moved with his pull; Bran was sent spinning off the wrong way.

He met a bulkhead with one hand and one foot, tried to angle his carom back toward Korbeith, but missed again. The guards had the woman now, but somehow again she grasped the cable.

Then from the air lock—from outside it—came a muffled clang, and the other noises that happened when a small craft docked there. And the intercom sounded: "Attention! The vice-admiral's inspection lighter, approaching on the port bow, will be docking at the main air lock. The captain is requested to attend the vice-admiral there, as soon as possible." The voice was Peralta's.

Bran caught grip on the cable again, and turned to see Arger Korbeith's face twist into fury. "Two hours early, that bastard's here!" His knobby hand swept air. "All right, you cadets! Back to quarters and get dressed. Prepare for the vice-admiral's inspection." He glared. "Move it!"

But as Bran and the rest turned to shove off, to make their ways upship, the airlock warning sounded. Bran paused, and saw that the lock was opened to the other spacecraft, and five uniformed figures had entered. Then the outside hatch closed, the inner one opened, and the five boarded the *MacArthur*.

Since neither Korbeith nor either guard had worked the local operating levers, the lock had been handled from control.

Of the five, the leader was slim, and neither tall nor young. His greeting wave to Korbeith was not quite a salute, but thoroughly proper. "Captain! We've met, but not for some

years, even bio. I'm Vice-admiral Kaner. Was up to Luna, and
thought I'd stop by and—" Suddenly, Kaner seemed to notice
the covey of floating, naked cadets. He laughed. "Ah! Initia-
tions, at the end of their first trip? Not kosher by the regs,
strictly—but back on the old *Zhukov*, when I commanded
there, a little of such sport did add zest to the end of a long
trip. And no one was hurt—or hardly ever. I trust it's the same
here."

Korbeith's grey-sallow face held an ochre tinge. Before he
could answer, Kaner said, "Shoo these youngsters back to their
digs, will you, captain? Give 'em time to prep for my
inspection. And—" He tapped the folder he carried under one
arm. "For some of them, depending on proficiency ratings, I
have immediate space assignments. Ships waiting for personnel, so I may ferry a few down with me ahead of you." Bran
hoped he'd be one of those. Anything, to get off *this* death-
trap!

Neither he nor Sally were quite fully dressed when the
knock came. "Not the inspection *already*?" But, being closest,
she opened the door. Graceful, experienced in zero-gee,
Peralta glided in, caught a stanchion, and halted.

He motioned for Salome to close the door, then said, "I'm
passing the word. During inspection, or if you have the luck to
ride groundside with the vice-ad, make *no* accusations against
Korbeith." As both Bran and Sally tried to speak, the Third
Officer waved them silent. "His superiors know all about
him . . . have for years. He is, in a word, despised among
them. Don't ask how I know; I have my pipelines. But the
point is, the brass is an Old Boys' league. They cover for each
other, no matter what." One eyebrow raised. "Do you
understand?"

Reluctantly, Tregare nodded. "Yeah. I guess so." But then
he had to grin. "We sure lucked out back there. When the
Butcher couldn't kill Sally, because the admiral showed up."

Peralta shook his head. "Not all luck, cadet. The second
officer and I heard rumors. So somehow—and nobody can
prove it on us—Korbeith's invitation for Kaner to come
inspecting got updated by a couple of hours. Close timing, but
it worked."

Bran tried to thank him, but Peralta would have none of
that. "I hate waste. Here, as at the Slaughterhouse." Then the

man moved to the door, was out it, and pulled it closed behind him.

Inspection wasn't soon, but it was fast. Intercom orders were to leave room doors ajar, so Bran complied. Hearing the vice-admiral's group approach, Bran and Sally braced against bunks and held stanchions, to give a semblance of standing at attention. Kaner walked in magnetic boots as if moving in normal gravity. Entering, he looked around the cubicle, nodded, and gave a faint smile. "Quite satisfactory. Now then . . . Tregare and Harkness, isn't it?" Both affirmed. Kaner leafed through a notebook. "Yes, you're both posted for the hurry-up transfer. So get your gear together, and be at the air lock in thirty minutes. Or less."

He turned, and as though walking on Earth itself, strolled out. Just past the door, Bran saw Arger Korbeith standing, and before he also turned to follow the vice-admiral, the Butcher gave Tregare and Sally the most murderous gaze Bran had ever seen.

But now the Butcher was out of it. Or so Bran hoped.

Packing was no problem. Sally and Tregare were among the first to assemble near the air lock, beating Kaner's deadline by almost ten minutes. Then they waited, while Bran began to wonder if it might be all a cruel trick. Sally wanted to talk, but now he couldn't. Eventually, Kaner and his cortege arrived. The vice-admiral bade Korbeith goodbye—and after what Peralta had said, Bran could hear the sarcasm in the compliments—and all of them got into the tiny dispatch craft. Twelve, in all.

The vice-admiral himself took the pilot's console—and once the preliminaries were done and the lighter undocked, proved himself a pilot after Bran's own heart. As Bran and Sally, sitting side-by-side, gripped hands together, he laughed. "The man's taking her down like a real bat. Oh, peace! He knows how to *fly!*"

Sally released held breath. "I'm glad you think so."

Then they were groundside. Exactly where, on Earth, they weren't told, but it was a big spaceport and there weren't all that many of such size, so Bran had his guesses.

He and Sally were immediately hauled off to transient quarters and assigned a room. And, after dining at the mess

hall, mostly empty because they were between regular
mealtimes, they made the most of it. Because it was their last
chance for love or talk, either one.

Lying quietly for a time, drinking wine provided by a
friendly, bribable mess attendant, Bran felt both sad and
happy. "We lived through it, Sally. We got past the Butcher."

"Yes. I don't suppose we'll go to the same ship. Will we ever
see each other again?"

His free hand grasped hers. "I'd hope so. But with the Long
View, ships chewing time and all, might be our ages wouldn't
match."

Like a cat, she dipped to bite his knuckles. "I won't care. If
one of us is older, we'll simply not pay attention." She sat
straight now. "Bran? What are your plans? What do you want
to *do?*"

He knew he could trust her, and logic said that transient
barracks weren't worth bugging, so he spoke freely. "Escape.
What else?"

Salome Harkness frowned. "I thought it was Peralta, not
you, who wants command so bad he can taste it."

Bran shook his head. "Not just command—though I
wouldn't spurn it if it showed up under my pillow someday."
He leaned forward. "Bloody *freedom*, is what. Getting out
from under UET's heel. And then twisting UET's goddamn tail
'til it comes right off!"

Until he saw her shrinking back from him, he had no idea
how tightly his face was making some kind of predatory
grimace. Trying to relax, at least he softened his voice. "You've
been through most of it, same as I have. Don't you want to hit
back? Don't you burn to see those bastards *dead?*"

Eyes wide, she leaned to hug him, and hid her face against
his shoulder. "Oh, Bran! You mustn't let them *make* you like
this!"

Well, she was a fighter too; he'd put everything too strong,
was all. He soothed her until it came time for love again, and
afterward mentioned UET not once.

Next morning Bran was rousted out early and told to report,
gear and all, to his new ship. "You're Third Officer. Your papers
are aboard." So with little time to spare he got Salome
Harkness wide enough awake to know who she was kissing
goodbye, collected his belongings to go sit for his Third

Officer's cheek tattoo, and rode a shuttle-route groundcar out to the hardened area where the big ships sat. As the car approached one of those great towers, he stared at it. The insignia read *Tamurlaine*.

And even from some distance, he could see that it was an armed ship.

7

The *Tamurlaine*

Climbing the ship's ramp, Tregare realized he was still in cadet uniform. So before the air lock guard challenged him, he thought out what to say. "Bran Tregare: just completed my cadet trip with Captain Korbeith on the *MacArthur*." On the face of the guard, a thirtyish First rating, initial supercilious expression changed to something like respect. "My assignment here as Third Officer came as a hurry-up. In fact Vice-admiral Kaner brought several of us groundside in his inspection lighter, ahead of our ship's landing." What else? "My papers are aboard, they tell me. You can call up to Control and make sure. And I suppose I can draw proper uniform when there's time for that."

When the guard's tough-looking face made a half-smile, he didn't look like a bad sort at all. "No need to call; you're on my list, sir. Your instructions are to go to Third's quarters and wait for the captain's summons. My advice, though, is to stop by Supply on your way and draw the uniform first thing. You're reporting early, and the captain's a bit of a stickler for the formalities."

"I see. Thanks."

"Nothing like your recent captain, though; if I've heard right about *him*, my sincere congratulations for being here at all. At least three out the lock, it's said, every trip."

This could be a plant. "It is? That's interesting."

"As you say, sir. Well, welcome aboard."

Although the *Tamurlaine*'s internal arrangements differed slightly from the *MacArthur*'s, Bran found Supply easily enough. The man and woman on duty there found garments that fit him without need of alteration. He changed cap, jacket and trousers on the spot, the rest of the gear was interchange-able. Then he went up to Third Officer's quarters, on the deck between the galley and Control.

The room was slightly larger than the one he'd shared with Salome Harkness but it held more amenities, and had its own bathing and sanitary facilities adjoining. Before leaving his groundside billet he'd had no chance to shower. Banking on the guard's guess about the timing, he did so now, and shaved. He wasn't yet growing much in the way of whiskers, so it seemed as well to keep his face bare of the immature fuzz. Just in the interests of his Third Officer image, that was.

Then he waited until the intercom made its announcing sound, and a voice said, "Third Officer Tregare?"

"Tregare here." Was this the captain? "Sir." Just in case.

"Captain Rigueres speaking. Is it convenient for you to join me in my digs now, and meet your fellow officers?" From the assured tone of voice, Bran decided it had damn well *better* be convenient.

"Right away, sir. Tregare out."

Bran had never seen inside Korbeith's "digs" but Peralta had dropped hints that they were furnished in rather sybaritic style. Captain Rigueres, it turned out, didn't indulge himself in such ways. The ample space was more bare than not, with only a few very good pieces of space-adapted furniture, and on the bulkheads three differing but harmonious pieces of art work; he had a seascape, a half-lit Earth as viewed from low orbit, and a forest scene on a planet that obviously was not Earth. Rigueres apparently liked what he liked, and the hell with quantity.

Shorter than Bran but blocky-wide, not fat, the man gave a handshake that stopped short of crunching. Under crinkly iron-grey hair and heavy straggling brows, his squarish face seemed set in a scowl. "Tregare, eh? Welcome aboard." Without the intercom's distortion his voice was a rumbling growl, deeper even than Korbeith's, but with no rasp to it. "And wouldn't surprise me that you're glad to be here." Eyes don't really twinkle, but now Bran saw how the expression had come about. "Well, this isn't the *Mac*, but nonetheless I run a tight ship."

He stepped back, turned slightly sidewise, and gestured to the other two men in the room. "Your other two superior officers. Mr. Monteffial, my First—" An average-sized man,

olive-skinned and dark-haired, made a wary, quiet grin as he
moved to shake hands: firmly, no-nonsense, but no excess
pressure.

"Leon Monteffial. My pleasure."

"Bran Tregare. And mine."

As they stepped back again, the captain said, "—and Mr.
Farnsworth, my Second."

Tall Farnsworth's face went from blank indifference to almost
enthusiastic welcome. As his left hand pushed his bushy fair
hair back from a slightly sunburned forehead, his right hand
shook Bran's in a clasp neither limp nor aggressive. "Welcome,
I'm sure," he said. "Cleet Farnsworth."

Monteffial chuckled. "And that's two e's, Tregare," he said,
"not cleat as in track shoes."

"Thanks; I'll remember," and then Bran noticed that
Farnsworth didn't especially seem to care for the clarification.
"And I appreciate your welcome, Mr. Farnsworth."

The man nodded. "Well, we're all on the same team, aren't
we? Which reminds me—" He turned. "Captain, there's a
First rating holding down the watch for me. I realize it's only
groundside duty, but still—"

Rigueres nodded. "Of course, Mr. Farnsworth. Excused."
And as the tall man, his skin pale where the sun hadn't
pinkened him, left, the captain said, "Sorry to cut the
socializing so short, but Farnsworth's right. I have some cargo
manifests to check over. Mr. Monteffial, would you take over
the courtesies by showing Mr. Tregare around the ship?
Whatever he wishes to see?"

"Of course, sir." Monteffial gave a formal salute, so Bran did
also. Then they departed the captain's digs. "Where to?" said
Monteffial. "If you'd like, we could start with a drink, on me."

Tregare nodded. "Sounds good. Sorry I can't make the same
offer, but the *MacArthur* kept cadets in dry mode, and
groundside I had no time to stock up."

Monteffial paused at a door, opened it and ushered Bran
inside. His place was less than that of Rigueres but more than
Third's quarters. Which made sense. "Here we are. And not to
worry. As Third you can draw on ship's stores, within reason,
against pay. And you'll have your cadet pay on account, to start
with." Bran realized no one had told him about his cadet pay,
and he'd been too preoccupied to think about it. Mainly being
scared. He said something amiable and noncommittal, as
Monteffial asked him what he'd like to drink.

"Anything simple and not sweet. Beer, dry wine, bourbon . . ."

Nodding, the First said, "The latter, then. I had some old-fashioned sour mash once. This stuff imitates it almost perfectly." Whether or not, Bran found the flavor impressive.

"Cheers, definitely," he said. "And do I get the lecture now?"

"Lecture?" Monteffial smiled. "Orientation, yes. I knew you'd realize why we're here—one-on-one, as they say. All right. You want to know what this ship's like, and that's what the captain means me to tell you. You made it through and safely off the *Mac*; this one's nothing like that, praise peace!"

He stared under lowered brows. "As far as I know, the skipper's spaced only one person in his whole career. Off this ship, but before I joined it. What happened was, a senior rating talked on a monitored comm line and Rigueres heard the recording."

"*That's* all?"

"The rating, identified becase he initiated the call from his duty station, was trying to recruit cohorts for an attempt at mutiny and Escape. And on that subject, Captain Rigueres is death. Literally."

Tregare blinked. "Well, I can see—"

"Can you? Think on this. The Academy—and six years out of it I can say Academy without thinking Slaughterhouse first—it's an exercise in the harshest of conditioning, toward blind loyalty and obedience. But like all conditioning, the effects depend on what the conditionee brings to the process. On the captain it worked perfectly. On others, the opposite—they go into a trapped-rat syndrome and will chew their own leg off to try to get away." He shrugged. "Most of us—most fall short of complete acceptance but settle in, anyway. Do you understand?"

Bran wasn't at all sure he did, but he nodded. "Monteffial—"

"In private, make it Leon."

"Bran here. And how about Mr. Farnsworth?"

"Precisely. *Mister* Farnsworth. Until he tells you otherwise. Cleet's picky. He's only been out once, and new at Second. So—"

Bran waved a hand, just slightly. "Reminds me. What happened to your previous Third?"

"Our previous Second. That's what moved Cleet up. Well, nothing *happened* to her, except that she was overdue for a

First, and when we landed there was a ship here with that berth open, so she moved to it." He shook his head. "You missed a good farewell party."

Now Leon frowned. "Back to orientation. Tregare—you've been out on only a short haul. You must not have had time to see your family on this quick stopover, and your next visit might be twenty years from now, Earth time. How do you feel about it?"

Bran felt his face go wooden; he thought fast. The truth should do—or, rather, part of it. "I didn't have much family living. What was left went off Earth. The message that was supposed to tell me where, somebody lost. So—"

Monteffial grimaced. "No way for you to find them, then?"

"Just keep going out, I guess. And maybe get lucky." *But if I do find them, they'll never know it.*

"Maybe you're lucky already. Let me tell you something. . . ." And the way it went was that Leon Monteffial, fresh out of the Slaughterhouse except for his relatively brief cadet trip, had shipped out as Third on a ship that returned twenty Earth-years later, with him aging less than two. Family ties couldn't take the discrepancy; he was effectively orphaned and disowned. "Not because they wanted to, mind you. It's just—not everyone can deal with the Long View."

Bran signed agreement, to whatever the First meant. On the man's lean face a wry grin built.

"So I thought I'd take out some insurance, you see, against my next return. How, you ask?" But Bran didn't ask, so the other went on. "I looked for a very young nubile maiden to love and court, and I leveled with her that I'd be gone for years and come back younger than she, but meanwhile she'd have her allotment from my pay and I wasn't asking from her any such foolish thing as decades of chastity—but merely that she *be here* for me when I returned."

He sighed. "She thought it was all very romantic. We even married Oldstyle. I was in special training—my first trip out, I'd been only a rating at the start but moved up fast—so we had ourselves a great half a year before I went out again. But when I got back—"

Bran had to break the pause. "Yes?"

"I never found her. I didn't try. It was all clear in the records. I don't know how long it took her to decide to find somebody else, and I don't care. Or how long it took both of them to see their best course. But what they finally did was—

there's still a law that seven years' absence equals a spouse's desertion."

"So after seven years—"

"You're not thinking, Tregare. Seven years, hell! Not until my ship was announced coming in soon. *Then* she divorced me, and gave up her monthly share of my pay." His laugh grated. "At least I didn't pick me a stupid one." Draining his glass, the man stood. "Time, I guess, to give you the grand tour of the ship. Whatever you'd like to familiarize yourself with."

Bran's glass was dry long since. "Yes, sir. Ready when you are."

Ships were all pretty much the same. Where the *Tamurlaine* differed from the *Mac*—and now Bran could think of Korbeith's command by that nickname—it closely resembled the now-gutted but once-armed *Caesar*, where Tregare had trained as a snotty.

The *Tam's* (well, he wouldn't say that out loud) turrets were fully armed. As the First showed him the equipment in Turret Two, Bran saw that the projector was heavily insulated for as far forward as a gunner was likely to reach, even by accident. Farther ahead, the cooling fins were bare. But, as Monteffial said, "You'd have to reach hard to burn yourself. Unless you were a gorilla."

Dutifully, Bran chuckled. Then asked, "Are all the turrets set up with computer simulations? Practice runs . . . the way they did it back at the—oh, hell!—the *Academy?*"

Monteffial's laugh burst out. "Takes a while, doesn't it? Well, not all; just Two and Six. That's not policy; it's only that when we got the conversion, the shops were short on circuitry."

"I see. But anybody can schedule sim practice, on free time?"

Monteffial looked at him. "Not *anybody*. You can. I can. Anybody authorized. But not just anybody."

"Oh, sure," Bran said. "That's what I meant." But he hadn't.

When the First Officer told him it was coming on time for chow, Bran took the word gratefully. Trudging upship and down in Monteffial's wake, he'd seen enough of the *Tamurlaine* to last him a time. The Drive area was no different than any other he'd seen. Control was, for the operating consoles differed from those of unarmed ships and were of a newer design than the *Caesar*'s. But two or three watches at those controls, Bran thought, and he'd have it straight, where everything was.

So it was with relief that he followed the First into the galley. Ratings and crew stood in line with trays, but Monteffial nudged Bran away toward the table where Captain Rigueres sat. Now he thought about it, Tregare recalled that Korbeith and his officers were served in place. It had been a long day. . . . So he followed, and sat between his leader and a woman he hadn't met.

Well, he should say hello. He turned to her and she turned to him. "Bran Tregare, new Third. Pleased to—"

"Airda Kroll. Call me Airedale." The round-faced woman, sandy curls tumbling down to her eyebrows and around her face, came close to fitting her nickname and had a wrestler's grip to her handshake. "First Engineer." Meaning she was counterpart, among the Engineering officers, to Monteffial in Control.

Enduring the hand clench with only defensive resistance, Bran said, "Pleasure to meet colleagues. I—"

Headshake. Until her head tipped back a little, her eyes were hidden; then they showed grey. "You follow illusion. There is no pleasure, only duty. But enjoy illusion while you can."

Bran's dinner was served. Confused and silent, he ate it.

Afterward, leaving the galley with the First Officer, Bran asked, "What shakes with *her*?"

"I have no idea. It's some religious sect."

"New? I never heard of anything like it."

"No." Monteffial paused, looked to Tregare. "It's something that happened a long time ago. She's been out a lot, and I think her special religion came and went, died on the vine while she was away. Maybe sixty years back. You see?"

"Yeah, I think I do. The Long View, you mean."

"Right. Anyway, she causes no trouble, and does her job."

"Sure." But *the Long View*. At Bran's nape, a chill came.

Before Tregare's first watch duty he got some sleep and had only hazy, residual nightmares. He was off-duty when the ship lifted, but like any conscientious junior officer he sat in at Control—to observe and learn. The *Tamurlaine* went up not quite like a real bat, but not exactly coasting either; Tregare

watched his monitors and decided that Captain Rigueres knew
how to fly a ship. Especially when he skimmed past Luna and
set his course by making a sling turn that Bran himself would
not have dared try, without computer verification. And how
could Rigueres have had *time* to get that? Lifting off at a slant,
and—

Well, sooner or later, Bran decided, he'd figure it all out.

The ship's routine came easily to him. The feel of it took
longer. Rather soon it became clear that the captain's apparent
joviality was a surface thing. His reports entered in the log
were merciless on even the most minor errors. And although
not a killer like Korbeith, Rigueres had a mind for unusual
turns of punishment. As, the time a rating reported five
minutes late for watch duty. His next turn, the man stood
watch in full spacesuit, except for helmet and gloves. Besides
the discomfort of it, the order meant that to report on time,
the rating had to go to the equipment deck nearly an hour
before his watch began—to be fitted into the suit, and then to
plod upship wearing the heavy thing.

"And nearly as long afterward," Monteffial confided, "to get
back downship and check the damned thing in."

They were having a drink together—Bran's treat and in his
quarters. He answered, "So, two hours extra duty, and the
whole of it miserable. Seems a little strong."

Leon shrugged. "It's authorized in Regs. Well, hell—so are
the Butcher's killings. Not some of the finer touches he does,
though, if I've heard right."

Bran liked the First, but still he wasn't going to put anything
on record, just in case. "There's lots of rumors. I suppose some
may have a little truth to them."

Monteffial gave his quick smile. "Cagey, aren't you? Well,
that's good, Bran. I wouldn't feel safe drinking with someone
who spilled everything he knew. The dogs, you see."

"Dogs? There aren't any dogs on a ship."

The other man laughed. "You *are* new. Which is why I can
be sure *you're* not a Police dog. They don't come quite so
young."

Frowning, Bran asked, "Committee Police, you mean?
But—"

The First leaned forward. "Relax a minute. It's not a
traitorous act to hate the guts of the Committee Police, unless
they hear you do it. Because everybody does. My point is that

on every ship there's probably a dog or two, pretending to be an ordinary rating and bugging everything he can manage. Or a she; there's Police bitches, too. And one problem we have on here is that they scare hell out of the captain. He overreacts."

Bran was a point or two behind. "They bug the ship?"

"And Captain Rigueres keeps his comm-crew, which I expect you'll be heading before long, busy debugging it." Quick wave of hand. "Oh, it's all quite sublegal. The dogs aren't supposed to bug us. The captain isn't supposed to know they're doing it. But it's always legitimate to remove unauthorized electronics. Y'see?"

Tregare was catching up now. "He overreacts, you say?"

Nod. "He's tougher than need be because he's scared the dogs will catch him being not tough *enough*."

"Oh, shit." Bran looked at his wrist chrono. "Time for one more, Leon, before chow. Right?"

"Right."

In the galley, Bran found he'd drawn his turn at sitting honcho over at the cadets' table. Once before he'd had this duty, but then he knew none of the two dozen and simply ate first and asked questions over coffee. By this time he could put names to five or six of the two dozen faces, so he knew he'd have to talk more, want to or not. Under Korbeith on the *MacArthur*, certainly there'd been none of this fraternizing.

Being served at that table, waiting for it, would take longer than he wished, so Tregare simply formed up at the end of the cadets' line, picking up a tray, same as they did. He saw the captain at the officers' table, give him a stare that was less than approving and jerk a thumb toward the head of the line. In return, Bran made what he hoped was a placating wave of hand, and patted his stomach. Still grim of face, Rigueres nodded.

Finally seated, his tray loaded with food not so good as the other officers were getting, Bran ate. He sat at the table's head, saying brief greetings to the cadets at either side of him, since it happened he did know both by name. To his left was Waxy (Waxwell) Marston, a skinny blond beanpole who seemed to ask good questions—so far, at least. And at his right sat a stocky little woman with dark brown stubbled hair: Laina Polder. Whether from fear or shyness, she had trouble speaking up. Now, feeling tense from what Monteffial had said, Bran hoped none of them would ask too much.

He got through the meal without having to say a great deal, but over coffee the questions flowed. Most of them had no good answers: "Sir, if you were going to settle on a colony planet, which would you choose?" He'd never been to one and hadn't seen the brochures, so he had no idea. He said so.

"What's it like, sir, to return to Earth out of your time?" So he explained that as yet he had not had that experience.

"What about the Escaped Ships and the Hidden Worlds?"

He turned and looked at that questioner. Looked hard. A chubby, teddy-bear type, either all innocence or working at it. What was his name? Oh, yes—Cameron. Henry Lane (Hank) Cameron. According to Leon Monteffial, much too young to be a Police dog. But maybe not. So Tregare said, "You mean, what do I think about those rumors? I don't. I have no knowledge whatsoever."

The teddy-bear shut up.

"Are you glad you came to space, sir? If you had it to do over, would you?" The soft voice, with husky undertones, came from Laina Polder, to Bran's right. The very harmlessness of the question somehow set him scowling at her; he saw her lower lip begin to tremble, shook his head, and saw that the gesture only made things worse for her. Keeping his voice low, then, best he could, he said, "I think I made my best choice, and I stand by it." She nodded, and the next questions came.

But through those exchanges, Polder's question stuck to him. For he'd been given no choice at all. Had he?

Tregare's guess had been right; after only a couple of weeks at watch duties, he had the somewhat unfamiliar controls down almost pat. On the comm-board, which included viewscreen and other monitor controls, his work was excellent enough to draw a logged compliment from Rigueres himself. That came after the captain, sitting in to observe Tregare's watch, askedf for a four-way split picture on the main viewscreen: outside view of an approaching ship that would pass at rather near range, Control-to-Control voice-and-picture circuit for conversation while the proximity lasted, outside view of a group of cadets taking their first spacesuited hike around the *Tamurlaine*'s hull, and of course the normal "ahead" picture.

A lot of tricky coordination there, but Tregare brought it off nicely. At the time, Rigueres gave him not even a nod. But scanning the log, routine fashion, when he began his next watch, Bran found the commendation entered. Phrased in stuffy, understated language, to be sure—but better than a swift kick!

Not so good was that returning to his quarters after that watch, he found that someone had searched the place—and hadn't even bothered to try to hide the disarrangement of his things. The Police dogs? Probably. He had no idea what they could be looking for; certainly he had nothing to hide: no contraband, no incriminating letters or personal notes, no unauthorized weapons, nothing.

The incident's only result was in his own thinking: *UET is a shit trap and always will be. Whatever happens, don't forget that.*

Little, stocky Polder, Bran soon decided, had a crush on him. How he felt about it, he wasn't quite certain. She was a nice enough kid, and in the log her training reports weren't bad—she wasn't officer material but would probably wind up with a respectable rating. And Sally Harkness was a world ago, and Bran Tregare cared for celibacy hardly at all. But on this ship he wasn't too certain how these things were considered.

So, next chance he had, he invited Leon Monteffial to his quarters, for a couple of pre-dinner drinks. Well, dinner for the First; on Bran's watch-sked it was a late night snack.

After the pouring and the ritual "Cheers," Tregare tried to think of a way to ask his question, and said, "There's this young woman, seems to like me. And I wondered—"

Monteffial's smile went wide. "Advice to the lovelorn? I thought better of you."

"No, not that." Bran shook his head. "That part I'll handle all right, win or lose. It's—it's the ship's customs, that I don't know. What's allowed and what isn't? I mean, how would *you* conduct yourself in this kind of situation?"

The First laughed. "If you don't know, my own discretion is working better than I'd thought." His expression sobered. "Well, the captain's not quite prudish, but very traditional. Without some kind of contract—Freestyle marriage at the least—I'd advise you not to move a roomie in. I haven't; my own young woman and I maintain our official separate quarters and make do with visiting. What with the changing watch skeds that ratings have to put up with, the arrangement's

probably easier on both of us." He paused. "Does that answer
your question?"

"I think so. Thanks. Next time I have a chance to talk with
that cadet, I'll try to find out how serious she is about—"

Monteffial's hand gestured a stop. "Hold on there. Cadet?
No, Tregare." He shook his head. "If you were a rating, yes.
Or if she were. But officer and cadet? It's a—a sort of social
barrier, you could say."

"But that's silly. A cadet's only one step away from *being* an
officer." But then he realized that Polder wasn't.

As Leon answered, "You were. Some aren't."

And Bran nodded. "Yeah. I know. Well . . ."

"I'm not saying you couldn't play a little. Just keep it
damned quiet, is all."

"No, I don't think so. And thanks for telling me." But for
some reason he was depressed as *all* hell.

Monteffial was still talking. ". . . reasons aren't all bad. He
feels that with any great difference in rank, there's too much
likelihood of coercion entering in. Such as—"

"You mean clout, Leon?"

"Yes, I guess that's it."

"I can't argue with that," said Bran Tregare. *Channery.*

From then on, the way Polder tagged him at each chance,
big-eyed and hanging on his every word, seemed embarrass-
ingly obvious. To Bran, Monteffial's good-natured grin seemed
like a taunt. And Chilly Farnsworth, one day at mess after
Bran had—more or less gently—shooed Polder away, said,
"Tregare, if you don't want trouble, you'd best chase that
puppy bitch back to her kennel."

Because Bran had, after all, halfway encouraged Laina's
earlier attentions, he found it hard to answer the Second's
sneering comment. Finally he said, "Don't worry. There's no
involvement. She's new, and a little starstruck, and I guess I'm
the only officer who'd talk to her."

Giving a snort, Farnsworth said, "I should hope so! You
won't find *me* slumming with cadets." He stood, and left.
Looking after him, Bran wondered which would be doing the
slumming.

But still, Tregare had a problem. He didn't want to hurt the
kid's feelings, but he did want her off his back. So he waited his
chance for a private chat with Laina Polder.

That opportunity came when he drew spacewalk detail,

bringing up the end of the life line while once again the cadet group donned suits and marched a long slanting oval around the *Tamurlaine*'s hull. This time he knew there'd be pauses for inspection of hullside gear: outside camera modules, antenna arrays, and so forth. So, with any luck, time for talking.

He didn't have to arrange anything; Polder herself made sure she was next ahead of him in line. Leaning to help check her suit closures, he spoke quietly. "First substantial inspection stop, we turn off our suit radios and touch helmets. Private talk; okay?"

"Oh, yes!" Her eyes widened, and he knew she'd taken his meaning wrong. *Damn all!*

The lead group entered the lock; it cycled and they went out. Bran's group, he trailing, followed. The lines were connected. Just like on the *Mac*, Bran thought, except that he wasn't Plastic Smile, out to kill a cadet. The slow, clomping walk began.

Polder was probably goggling at the velocity-distorted view of space. By now, Bran was used to it; he waited for a stop that would last long enough for him to speak his piece. The first—to view a cluster of viewscreen inputs—was too brief, and so was a pause to inspect turret-ranging antennas. But then the group reached the smaller, topside air lock.

Too bad Polder would have to miss the lecture, but there'd be other exposures to that. Bran made a switchoff sign to her. As he turned his own communicator off, he saw her make a nod.

Gently, not to give noisy impact, he touched his helmet to hers. "Polder? I have to tell you something."

"Yes. I know." Very faint, her voice. "And I will. Any time you want me. Just ask."

"*No*, dammit! I mean, that's what I need to say. Cadets and officers can't fraternize that way; the captain won't stand for it. So forget the idea." He heard her gulp breath, and said, "Cadet, on this ship you're walking a tightrope. So am I. Don't let's get them crossed and raise our risks. You understand?"

"I—I guess so. May I still—?" But the life line jerked at her, and then as she moved with it, at Tregare. He turned his radio on and motioned for her to do the same. The tour went on.

Back inside, everyone unsuiting, he saw her looking at him. Where her look fell—between reproach and resentment—he couldn't know. But when she spoke to him after that, the circumstances were always public and her address almost stiffly formal.

He hated it—and at the same time, felt somewhat relieved.

Next time Tregare walked the ship hullside, it was in a power suit. Monteffial was in the other one, the two linked by a lifeline and further safeguarded by remote-control magnetic anchors at the line's ends. Purpose of the excursion was visual inspection of Drive nodes (through nine-nines-dark filters) at the ship's stern, and projector turret muzzles at the bow—with a perfunctory check, between antenna systems.

The drill was a bit cumbersome, but not hard to get used to. Carry your front anchor, slide it out ahead along the hull at bare minimum magnetic attraction, then sock it solid. Back anchor line being taut, ease that anchor almost loose and slide it in. A monotonous routine, but not difficult.

Neither Bran nor Leon were carrying the heavy energy guns that plugged into the suits' power sources. For one thing, no need on this chore. And for another—"Well," Leon had said, "there's no point in allowing capability for damage to the ship." That remark took Bran a time to digest, but he did manage it.

Back inside later, he didn't bother to ask Monteffial about the correctness of his guess.

Pale Farnsworth, the Second, was a real pain in all the wrong places. He was snide, upstage, and maddeningly likely to be correct in his gripes. Bran tried to be friendly, and was snubbed. He tried total formality, and as long as he could stick to it, the ploy worked fairly well—but formality wasn't really Tregare's long suit. At one drink break in the First's digs, he asked about the problem.

Slumped, relaxed as usual, Monteffial shrugged. "Cleet's a perfectionist, that's all. By now he's accepted that I'm not perfect and never will be. Unfortunately, he still has hopes for you."

To the downfall of such hopes, Bran raised his glass.

Rigueres hadn't disclosed the *Tamurlaine*'s destination, but he did condescend to announce, twenty-four hours ahead, the time of Turnover—when the ship would cut Drive, go zero-gee, turn end-for-end, and begin decel for target. Bran was on watch at the time. The captain didn't come to Control, but made his statement over the intercom, all-ship broadcast. Better than nothing . . .

Bran could see no particular reason why Turnover should be preceded by a quick eyeball inspection of the entire ship, but that's what the captain wanted, so that's what he got. Since Bran was at the bottom of the officers' totem pole, he figured to be stuck with inspecting the cargo areas. But Rigueres broke the job into more than three parts, delegating two Chief Ratings to assist. The cargo duty fell to a thin, blond man named Gonnelson, whose outstanding characteristic was that except to answer a question, he seldom spoke.

Bran drew the bow section, everything upship from Control—which meant the projector turret rooms and the staging deck below them (with its small aux air lock). He decided to start at the top and work down.

As he expected, the turrets were in top shape, except that someone had left Number Two switched to the Test Simulations position. Not serious, unless a gunner needed to *use* the weapon in a hurry and forgot to check. Undecided, Bran finally shrugged and logged the minor violation. He hated to get anyone in trouble, but maybe the minor black mark would cause the negligent party to pull his or her socks up. It couldn't hurt.

He still didn't like being a snitch, but sometimes you had to.

The staging deck looked good too. He noticed a couple of pieces of reserve gear secured rather sloppily, logged the matter, and corrected it. All right; nothing left but to check the air lock, to see that nothing had been left to rattle around loose in there.

The local operating panel—like the main lock, this could also be managed from a console in Control—showed outer door closed, chamber pressure normal. As it all should be. So he thumbed the switch to open the inner hatch—and nothing happened.

Either he had a malfunction, or the Close switch down in Control had been thrown. Or else the inside switch was holding the hatch secured. He looked through the heavy plastic window. No light inside, but in the dim shadows, did he see movement? Again he tried for Open, this time punching the Override button. And the door opened, and the inside lights came on.

What the hell? One man lay on top of another, just like

Channery and his victim. "*Get up!*" The first man came to his feet and began to arrange his clothes. He was small and compact, snub-nosed and dark-haired, a Second rating, a technician named Deverel.

The second man, tall and lanky, with thinning pale red hair above a high forehead, took longer about it. Quite calmly, he said, "So we're dead, Hain. Sooner or later, we knew it had to happen."

Not in negation but confusion, Tregare shook his head. "I thought—I couldn't see how such a small man could rape you. But—"

The bigger one made a one-sided smile. "No. It wasn't rape. We've been lovers for years. No point in hiding that now."

Before Tregare could think of what to say next, Deverel cut in. "Hadn't you better call up some troops, sir? After all, we're two to one here, and you're not armed." Tregare braced for combat, but the man said, "No. We won't try to space you. Want to know why?" Bewildered now, Bran nodded. "At the cost of an innocent man's life, ours wouldn't really be worth it." Deverel frowned. "You still don't see how it works, do you? Well, Anse and I knew our risk and chose to take it. You didn't. It's not your fault that you caught us—or that UET proscribed our natures as a capital offense. Besides, word is, you're a decent officer."

Tregare had to regain the initiative. "How about first things first? Names? Ratings? Assignments?"

"As opposed to assignations? Sorry, sir," Deverel said. "A little gallows humor, there. Yes—Hain Deverel, rating Second, electronics and servo gear."

"Anse Kenekke, rating Third, Drive technician. Dead man."

"Dammit!" Tregare said. "I can't—" He was going to say "—condone such behavior." But this wasn't like Channery's brutality. Was condoning or condemning any of his business? "I can't understand any of this is all. To me it makes no sense. Another thing I can't see is why you two didn't go for officer training. You both score high on the proficiency lists."

"We were in it," said Kenekke. "We dropped out, so we'd have a chance to ship together. And for five years, we've done so."

"And even now, with UET about to kill us, it's *worth* it." With that, Deverel's defiant air evaporated. He stood slumped.

Looking at the two men, Tregare wavered. The business of

their not threatening him hardly applied. Considering their repective grades of training, Bran was fairly sure he could have taken the both of them. But *they* didn't know that, and still . . .

Abruptly, he decided. But how to say it? He began, "I hope you're right that I'm a good officer on here. I intend to be. But what UET says and what I think, aren't always the same thing." Deverel tried to speak, but Tregare overrode him. "I may not understand you, but I don't see where you're harming the ship, or anyone in it. So I'm neither taking you in nor turning you in. I didn't see you. Got that straight? I didn't *see* you. So next time you get in a jam, if you do, don't make me out a liar." He paused. "And try to keep a little better track of what goes *on* in this ship. The captain announced this inspection hours ago."

He turned to leave, but Deverel said, "Sir? You say you don't always agree with UET. Do you mean—Escape, perhaps?"

Oh, no! A trap? "I mean no such thing. What I do mean— well, in your shoes I'd think seriously about jumping ship. The colonies, I hear, are more easygoing."

Then he did turn away and leave. What the two men said as he left might have been thanks, or maybe something else. He didn't care much.

Nor did he care what they did after he was gone.

8

Strains and Actions

Turnover came during Tregare's watch. Taking the seat he used when supervising, Captain Rigueres sat in to observe. When Bran, going by protocol, offered the job of turnover to the captain, Rigueres declined. *So the old devil trusts my skills.*

When the countdown clock was close to chiming, Tregare called down to Drive, to Chief Engineer Mallory. "Cut Drive, Chief. Ready to turn ship—*now!*" He didn't know Mallory at all well, had been in conversation with him maybe twenty minutes of the entire trip, so far. The man was older than most officers on active duty, and his record was very good indeed. Now Mallory acknowledged; the Drive hummed down to near-silence, and weight diminished to nothing.

Bran set to swinging ship. One-eighty degrees, no more, no less. The way he did this was to energize, carefully varying the thrusts, two of the three smaller aux-Drive nodes that at the ship's rear end formed a hexagon with the three mighty nodes of the main Drive. The way Rigueres had programmed turnover, the *Tamurlaine* wasn't going to pivot directly over one of the aux nodes, either singly active or silent with the other two sharing equal loads. It was going to be two nodes loading differently, and Bran's job to figure the balance and avoid skew in the turning. And then make the complementary thrusts, to stop the rotation.

Well, same as back at the . . . Academy. He plugged in the sines and cosines, and it worked.

Somehow, the decel end of the trip seemed to go more quickly than the accel leg. In truth it *was* slightly shorter, because of the resistance of the interstellar gas, which impeded accel but helped decel. But some of the difference, Bran realized, was subjective to him. For one thing, he'd done his learning, most of it; now he knew more of how he stood, on here. And for another, shortly after turnover—just off-watch, in the galley, in fact—he'd arranged himself a liaison.

Well, the officers' table was vacant so he'd sat with the ratings. Not quite according to Regs, maybe, but not prohibited. And as he ate, Chief Rating Nadine Ling sat down beside him. He'd seen her around a lot but they'd seldom shared the watch duty. Now he gave her a good look.

She was small, slight, and cute as all hell. Unusually, for a woman of Asian descent, she had her hair all in short tight curls, almost an Afro. The overall result, he liked.

If you don't ask, you'll never know. So he said to her, "You have a little free time now? Like for a drink, maybe?"

For a moment, eyes narrowed, she gave him a stare. And then nodded. "I think I can find the time."

So, once done eating, they went to his quarters. The drinks had to wait a while, because he didn't even have to ask; she came to him and that was that. First, because it had been so long for him, he blew it too fast. Then he got the drinks poured, but things started happening again, so the ice melted. That time worked better, a lot better. And there was plenty more ice.

Sitting up then, while she tickled his chest with her cold, condensation-moistened glass, he said, "Why, Nadine?"

She knew what he meant, because she said, "I watch the people I work with. I like the way you handle things."

"And here? We'll be back here?"

Grinning, she got him with an ice cube. When the writhing was done, and then the laughing, she gave him a sober-faced look. "Damned right we will."

On Tweedle, one of the Twin Worlds that present the same faces always to each other and make their own quicker dance together, along with their more leisurely path around the primary—on Tweedle, then, the *Tamurlaine* hit groundside.

In a way, Tregare hated to see the trip end. He knew there'd be personnel transfers; either he'd be one of them or he wouldn't, and the same for Nadine Ling. The way it went, she left the ship and he didn't. At least they had a mutual off-watch shift for the farewell, and made the most of it.

About half the cadets were offshipped, too. Among them was Laina Polder. Tregare would have liked to say something nice to her in the line of good-bye, but didn't get the chance to do so.

Two days passed before Bran got any time groundside. He'd hoped to be able to share leave with Leon Monteffial. No soap, though. Rigueres allowed only one officer offship at a time. He himself, though, Bran noted, took only his fair share of leave time, if that. "He's not all bad," said Tregare to Monteffial, at watch-change.

Leon grinned. "Probably afraid that if he gets too far from the ship, we'd take off without him!"

At any rate, one day at about noon, local time, Bran stepped groundside for the first time. Groundside was hot under a sky somewhat darker than he expected. Atmosphere was lighter, something like Earth at about twenty-five hundred meters. On this day no breeze blew, and the planet's sun shone whiter than Earth's but spanned a smaller apparent radius.

A group of ratings were climbing aboard a shuttle groundcar. The port was several kilometers from Capitol City, which mostly filled a river-mouth valley. Bran brought up the tail of the group, not pushing rank, and took the first vacant seat he came to, beside a red-haired First rating he didn't recognize. Not bad looking, he thought, even with the bright hair skinned back to a tight coil at the back of her head.

She wouldn't look at him, though; her face went blank and she sat as far from him as possible. What in the worlds—? He turned to her. "Seems strange, all this time on the ship, but I don't seem to know you."

First she blushed, then went pale. "Sir? I—I was just transferred onto the *Tamurlaine*. Off the *Bonaparte*, with nearly two months' wait groundside in between."

She went silent, so Bran said, "I'm Bran Tregare, Third Officer. It's my first trip as brass. Came aboard at Earth, straight from my cadet trip. On the *MacArthur*, that was." He waited, and finally had to ask, "And you are—?"

"Uh—Phyls Dolan, rating First, navigation. But, sir . . ."

"Yes, Dolan?"

"Officers and ratings don't socialize."

He had to laugh, regardless that the sound turned others to look. "Well, sure, we have to pay *some* heed to rank. For instance, the galley has an officers' table. But if I come in and find it empty, I can join the ratings, for company." She looked shocked. "I guess the *Tamurlaine* isn't as stiffbacked as the *Bonaparte* must be." She seemed to relax a little, so he expanded on the theme. "Mind you, we couldn't move your gear into my quarters. The captain wouldn't like that. But I can invite you up for a drink, any time you like, and—"

Really pale, she went then. And biting her knuckles as she said, "Oh, sir! Please don't. *Please!* I mean, if you say so, but—"

"Hey, wait a minute!" He wanted to ease her anxiety, but knew he mustn't touch her, not at all. "You're reading me wrong, Dolan. I don't know how your text reads, but mine says not a damn thing about command performances. When I said a drink, that's what I meant." He paused. "Tell you what . . . once into town, I'll buy you a drink in the first good bar we sight. Give you a look at my drinking manners, firsthand."

"Yes, sir." The rest of the way, she sat looking down at her clasped hands, while Bran wondered why he was bothering.

The bar was mostly red plastic and dim lights. It could have been any one of like thousands, on Earth. Bran found them an alcove out of the main line of blast. The drinks list carried bourbon. Dolan surprised Bran by seconding his order. She also consented to clink glasses with him—"Cheers"—and seemed a little less tense now.

Too bad to spoil it, but Bran had questions. "Dolan? I want some straight answers. On your last ship, you didn't have the right to say no?"

Her headshake was frantic. "I mustn't say anything. I—"

"Cool down. You're not talking to UET now. You're talking to Bran Tregare, who sometimes knows when to keep his mouth shut. And I don't care about names—probably wouldn't recognize them anyway, and what're the odds on our meeting that ship again?" She still wasn't saying anything. Bran leaned forward. "All I want to know is, are you scared here because you think rank can take you any time, like it or not?" A faint nod. "Well then, Dolan, drink up and cheer up. Because that's just plain not the case. With other personnel, it might be—but our sonsabitches don't happen to be *that* kind of sonofabitch."

With the second round of drinks, Bran ordered a tray of snacks. The cheeses were pleasant, the meat tidbits were unfamiliar but tasty. Except for a purple jellied mass that smelled like pickled overshoe, the treat was a success. And Dolan seemed more relaxed than not.

So Tregare said, "Now we'll try something. I am going to proposition you. 'You want to?' You've just been propositioned." He saw her stiffening, and said quickly, "If you say yes, you have to buy me a drink. If you say no—well, I'm afraid you still have to buy me a drink. Because it's just about your *turn.*"

It took maybe thirty seconds, but she laughed. So it was all right. Even though she never did answer the question.

Dolan's alcoholic capacity wasn't all that much. When Bran saw she probably shouldn't finish the drink she'd bought, he walked her outside and along the street to a shuttlecar stop. The walk helped. He decided it was safe to send her back to the ship by herself, and when the car came along, he did so.

"You'll be okay?" he said, as she prepared to get in.

"Sure thing," she said. "Sir. And thanks."

"My pleasure." She got to her seat all right, as he watched, the car pulled away. Even if she went to sleep along the way, and he thought, somebody would get her safely aboard the ship.

Restless now, he turned back along the street. He wanted no more drink just yet, but he was hungry. So he looked for a good medium-grade eating house. Nothing too specialized: he passed up a place that advertised "Highland Cuisine for the real Highlander." On the other hand, "The You Never Left Earth Restaurant And Boozerium" didn't take his fancy much, either; after all, what he'd tried of local stuff wasn't half bad.

The building he stopped to look at was a rambling shanty, much added-to. Its sign read "Ask For What You Want," and that seemed fair enough, so he went in. The high-beamed roof, with no ceiling below, made the interior cooler than outdoors had been. The decor was out of chaos by improvisation; Bran liked it.

Only about a third of the tables were occupied. Human instincts being what they are, those were the ones around the area's perimeter; the middle section sat empty. For no reason he could think of, Bran went to sit at the room's center.

Service was faster than he expected; a young woman, got up in an exotic fashion quite new to him, brought water and a menu. He was too busy looking at her to think of ordering a drink; as she walked away, he decided maybe that was just as well.

On the Tri-V, back on Earth, he'd seen some weird getups,

but nothing like this woman's. Her breasts seemed to be compressed flat to her chest, but through two transparent plastic bubbles, oversized nipples showed. Her hair stood straight out in all directions, in spikes about four centimeters long, each sprayed or coated with more transparent plastic. Between her thighs, just below her short skirt swung a metal bell, that chimed softly as she walked—in short, precise steps, because two ankle bracelets were joined by a slim, gold-colored chain not more than forty centimeters in length. Bran shook his head: *strange*.

The menu made little sense to him. When the woman returned he asked "What's your own favorite meal here?" and ordered according to her answer, including a small bottle of native wine. And when the food came, he found it surprisingly good. No pickled overshoes, not even one.

He was having coffee, and one glass short of emptying the wine bottle, when nearby movement caught his attention. He looked up and saw Deverel and Kenekke about to pass his table. For a moment he paused, then stood and said, "Join me? Though I'm nearly done here, now." The place had filled up quite a bit, so his offer made sense any way you looked at it.

Kenekke looked to Deverel. The latter hesitated, then said, "Yes. Thanks, sir. I guess we're hitting the crowded time."

They sat. The two new arrivals took Bran's recommendation on the wine. Each studied a menu, then ordered items Bran had never heard of. "You're more adventurous than I am," he said. Their expressions tightened. "The food here, I mean." Both men nodded, and the conversation went from sparse to nonexistent.

Hell with it. Gently, Bran swirled the remaining wine in his glass. "I'm curious. Would you be taking my advice?"

Kenekke said, "Which part, sir?" Before Bran could answer, the strangely got-up woman brought the two dinners. Looking and scenting, Bran was rather glad he had not ordered either of them. But the two ratings, digging in, seemed to enjoy them well enough.

"I meant, are you being sensible enough to jump ship?" His only question, really, so he drained his glass and stood, waiting. But Deverel's hand caught his wrist, and the glass was full again.

"I don't think so, sir," the small man said. "If it's all the same with you. We've dodged risk, Anse and I, since second year at the Slaughterhouse. I don't think we're done yet, and this world doesn't tempt us much." Deverel's eyes narrowed. "Unless, of course, sir, you're *telling* us to get off."

Again Tregare sat. He shook his head. "No such thing. Advice, was all; I think you might be best off the *Tamurlaine*, for your own sakes."

"And if we don't agree?" Kenekke said it.

"Then I wish you luck." Bran stood, drank his glass dry, and set it firmly on the table, upside down.

And said, before walking away, "Remember one thing. I *still* didn't see you."

He went to three different bars for one drink at each, found nothing much to interest him in any way, and caught the shuttle car back to port. Upship in the galley, two ratings were drunk.

So was Second Officer Farnsworth, Bran was told, but he'd been put to bed.

So who cared?

The next time Monteffial relieved Bran at watch-change, the First said, "Would you fill in for the ramp guard a few minutes? He asked me, but I didn't want to be logged in late." Tregare knew what the man meant: put a perfectly good *reason* into the log, and captains and promotion boards read an *excuse*. ". . . on leave yesterday, ate the wrong thing, I guess. He's been running a lot. So if—"

"Sure. And if there's much of his watch left, maybe I can find someone to handle the rest of it." Then, not forgetting the formal stuff—because any rating on watch might be a Police dog—he saluted. "Relief acknowledged, First Officer." Monteffial said his part of it, and Bran left Control.

Down at the main air lock, the ramp guard certainly looked miserable enough. "Here, give me your order sheet," Bran said. "I'll hold your post down for awhile. No hurry." The man started to leave. "Whoops, there—I'll need that gunbelt," so the man unbuckled it, handed it over, and hobbled away. Bran hoped the fellow would reach a latrine without mishap.

The guard station was quiet enough, with no one approaching either to leave the ship or from below, to climb ramp and enter. Tregare took time to scan the order sheet. Not much to keep track of. The leave roster wasn't included, so all he had to do about personnel leaving or entering was check their passes and log their passage.

He'd buckled on the gunbelt without paying much heed to

it. He noticed that it was too loose, so that the gun rode uncomfortably low on his hip. He adjusted the thing, then realized he hadn't checked the weapon itself, because it had been Monteffial who'd asked him to take this chore and he trusted the First. But what if the *illness* was faked, and the captain inspected him and he hadn't checked a faulty weapon? UET did love traps! So Tregare drew the gun—it was one of the smaller energy projectors, not a needler—and was relieved to find it fully charged. Still, being careful never hurt . . .

He looked back to the order sheet. Another group of cadets would be boarding today, but no exact time was given. Four this time, which would probably fill the ship's quota.

The ailing guard had been away for nearly a half hour, and Bran was beginning to wish he'd asked the man how much longer his trick would last, when he saw the group approaching the ramp below. He waited as they were led upramp to the lock, noting only that two cadets were male and two female.

It wasn't until he scanned the assignment sheet that he realized one of the cadets was Kickem Bernardez.

Remembering Peralta on the *MacArthur*, Tregare restrained his first impulse. He saw Kickem about to blurt a greeting, and gave a slight, headshaking frown. He decided to improvise a new formality: greeting each cadet by name and with a handshake. "Cadet Higgins. I'm Bran Tregare, Third Officer. Welcome aboard." And so on. Kickem was third in line. To him, Bran added, "Bernardez? I'd like you to report to my quarters at eighteen hundred hours, your other duties permitting."

Kickem's "Yes, sir" came in a voice as cold as his stare.

A few minutes later the guard returned. "Sorry, sir. I ran up to the medic station and got a pill. I think I'll be all right now—and I'll never eat *that* stuff again." He took the gunbelt, loosened it to fit him, and buckled it. "And thanks a whole great lot, sir. You saved my life!"

"Glad to help . . . Pritchard, isn't it? Well, maybe someday you can do *me* a favor. Or pass it along to somebody else." They exchanged salutes, and Bran went upship. A quick thought came to him. He detoured by way of the ship's Stores and drew a bottle of a liquor he didn't have on hand in quarters.

After a shower and his "evening" meal, he returned to his digs and waited. Almost on the dot of eighteen hundred, the knock came. He opened the door to admit Kickem Bernardez.

Ramrod straight, the cadet snapped a salute. "Cadet Bernardez reporting as ordered, sir. Since this is the way it seems to be, now that some of us have advanced above others."

For a moment, Tregare couldn't talk for spluttering. "Admirable, cadet. That's exactly the way it is in public. But right now, Kickem, we're not in public. For instance, I remember a business with some Irish whisky a long time ago."

"You'd be saying—"

"Well, I got a bottle of the stuff from Stores today. How'd you like to get down off your high horse, Kickem, and have some?"

And then they were whooping and pounding each other on the back.

"It was Peralta who showed me. He came on as Third, on the *Mac*. Anybody around except trusted friends, keep it formal. But—"

Kickem sampled his second drink. "Well, I *thought* that to be the case, Tregare, but was not wholly certain. And then to needle you a bit, in the bargain, was more than I could find it in me to resist."

So they traded stories. Hearing of Korbeith, Bernardez went sober-faced and shook his head. His first ship had been a strict one, sure enough, "—but nothing like the Butcher, was Captain Pemberton. A mercy you survived, Bran."

"Don't I know it! Now then . . . this is only your second run. . . . Am I right?" True enough; at the end of this one, Kickem hoped to be posted somewhere as a Third Officer.

"Except now it is that I'll be loath to move along, Bran. For wouldn't it be a marvel, were we to be shipping together when—" He paused. "But it may be I shouldn't ask of that."

Bran knew what he meant. *Escape!* He spoke carefully. "So far, I wouldn't have an answer for you. Nobody's said."

In no hurry, they finished the bottle. Flushed and cheerful but still in good control, Kickem left in time to get some sleep before his first watch period. Alone, Bran considered the question his friend had posed. Were Escape plans afoot on the *Tamurlaine?* Well, sure. The real question was who was in on

them, and how many, and how far along? Which meant
. . . what would the chances be?

Monteffial had *almost* dropped solid hints—that is, he'd
dropped some but they weren't very solid. Farnsworth
wouldn't tell you the time of day off your own chronometer.
The ratings always gossiped, but how much of substance their
talk held, Bran had no way of judging. He was still too new on
this ship.

But for now, the hell with it. He could use some sleep, too.

Two days later, as scheduled, the *Tamurlaine* lifted off.
Monteffial did the honors. When Farnsworth took the watch
an hour later, the First caught up with Tregare in the galley.
"Hey, there, Third!" He clapped a hand to Bran's shoulder.

Bran, seated, looked up. "Yes, sir?"

"Would you like to help celebate my lift-off? A small party,
but invite a guest or two if you like—people who can spare an
hour or two, maybe three, starting at fifteen hundred.
Compatible persons, you understand. Plus your own date, if
you have one."

Leon had already had a couple of drinks, maybe more. No
doubt of that. Bran thought, then said, "I don't know about a
date. Since Nadine was transferred off, I haven't—" He cleared
his throat. "Well, if I run into someone to ask. But one thing,
sir. There's a fella came aboard not long ago, we were friends at
the Slaughterhouse. He was a year my junor there. And—"

Monteffial frowned. "So what's the problem? Invite him."

"It's only that for this trip, he's still in cadet status."

Wave of hand. "Bring him along. What's his name, by the
way?"

"Bernardez. Kick—I mean, Cecil Bernardez."

Monteffial laughed. "Oh, that one. I've noticed him. Glib
tongue hiding a good brain is my guess. Yes, bring him."

So when Tregare went to quarters he got on the intercom to
Kickem. The cadet's roommate answered, and Tregare said, "Is
Bernardez here, and awake or due to be awake soon?" He was;
and came onto the circuit. Bran gave it the formal treatment:
cadet Bernardez, and please report suitably dressed, and so
forth.

So at the proper hour, after a couple of drinks in private,
Tregare and Bernardez arrived at Monteffial's party. Knowing
how these things went, Bran took along a couple of bottles to
contribute. Kickem, being a cadet, couldn't obtain any.

The two new arrivals made it seven men and four women attending. Nobody was drunk, nor totally sober either. Leon Monteffial was dancing with a tall brunette First rating. The others, sitting or standing, drank and ate and talked. After looking embarrassed for a few minutes, Kickem got into an amiable argument with the Second Engineer. With an arm around her, he looked well enough at ease.

Bran, though, felt edgy. He joined in conversations but didn't stay with them long. Finally he decided he didn't like being there solo, so he left and went down to the galley. Inside he saw no one he really wanted to escort to Monteffial's celebration, so he turned to leave. And met, coming in, rating-First Phyls Dolan. The redhead still had her hair skinned back tightly to a coil. She always seemed to do that.

As she moved to pass him, Bran took her arm. "Dolan? How'd you like to be my guest at a high-class party? It's the First Officer's, to celebrate his lift-off."

She began to shake her head. "Oh, no, sir. I—"

Softly but with emphasis, Tregare said, "Don't misunderstand, Dolan. This is a *nice* party. It may get a little loud, I wouldn't be surprised, but perfectly respectable, all the way."

"But I haven't eaten yet."

"The First has laid on a fine spread. Come on." For a moment she still pulled away; then she looked at him eye-to-eye and finally nodded.

In a group, Dolan was more fun. When other ratings whooped greetings to her, she smiled and waved back. She ate with enthusiasm, drank moderately, and danced with a lot more skill than Bran Tregare could muster. He tried, though.

As he had predicted to Dolan, the group did get steadily louder. Nothing raucous, no ill-feeling, just louder talk and the occasional burst of song. Yes, it was "getting a little drunk, out." Not Bran, though. Back at the Slaughterhouse he'd learned to pace his drinks, to get level and stay there, and now he did just that. Here and there he heard talk that sounded decidedly indiscreet; he hoped no dogs were present, or for that matter, bugs.

As he and Phyls Dolan finished a dance, her coiled hair beginning to sag loose and she trying to push it back into place, their host called to him. "Tregare? Over here."

Patting Dolan's hand, Bran said, "I'll be right back," and went to Monteffial. The First had a load, all right; he stood with one hand braced on a chair back. "Tregare? Gotta close down. Question first, though. In here." He moved, and Bran followed, to the side-cubby that held the bed. It wasn't closed off, exactly, but the alcove gave privacy for talk.

As Monteffial plunked down, heavily, to sit on the bed, Tregare asked, "Questions? At this time of the party?"

A nod. "Just one. Escape. How you feel about it?"

"That's not a good question to ask, out loud. Is it?"

"So don't answer now. Think about it, though. Because when it gets asked big, no *time* to think. Unnerstan'?"

"Maybe. And maybe thanks, too." Monteffial was leaning back, close to falling asleep. Bran said, "You need any help?"

Eyes half-closed, the First murmured, "Send her in here. Lady with me, you know. Close the party down first. Her, I mean. She'll do it. Just tell her, all right?"

"Sure. Right away. And thanks for the party, Leon."

He went back to the main group. Already it had thinned out some. The tall, dark-haired First rating—the one Bran figured to be with Monteffial—sat alone. He went over to her. "Leon asked you to close the party down. Then he'd like to see you."

She chuckled. "I hope he's still awake to do that."

"If you hurry it up, he will be." He gave her a wink for her smile and turned to find Phyls Dolan. The task wasn't hard; he heard a squeal and there she was, brushing liquid off her blouse. He went to her. "Everything all right?"

Someone else was brushing at her also, trying to apologize. Dolan said, "Never mind, Jennings. I bumped into you as much as you bumped into me and the other moved away, so Tregare guessed he knew what happened."

He said to her, "The First wants the party cleared now. I expect we ought to set a good example. All right?"

She shrugged; her hair sagged farther. "I suppose so. I did want one more drink, but Jennings and I collided, so—well, if the party's closing, I can do without."

"Maybe, maybe not." One hand gentle at her arm, he moved them through the latestayers toward the door. Out in the corridor, he said, "I offered you a drink once. The offer's still good."

For a moment she froze in place, then moved again, the two of them out of step now. "*Just* a drink, you said, though." He nodded, and she caught step with him. "All right."

Down the hall; then at the door he reached in to put the lights on and let her enter ahead of him. "Small place, isn't it?"

he said, and started over toward his minimal bar setup to mix her the drink. Her hand grasped his shoulder; he turned to face her. She was shaking her hair loose; the tumbled reddish mass fell to hang nearly at her waistline. Her face held no expression at all, as she moved, facing him but not quite touching.

Throat tight, he said, "Look; I told you. You can have the drink, Dolan. You don't have to do *anything*."

"I know." Now she smiled. "Maybe that's why I want to."

It was, for Tregare, a great trip, the short haul from Tweedle over to its twin Twaddle, to pick up cargo. And then another relatively brief jump to the Penfoyle Gate. As Tregare had told Phyls Dolan at their first meeting, they couldn't move in together on a ship commanded by Rigueres, but sure as hell they could enjoy time together, whenever neither was on watch duty.

It wasn't that Bran let the joys of friendly love get in the way of his shipside training—nor did Phyls Dolan. Merely, they made the most of what spare time the ship's schedules allowed them. And on the *Tamurlaine*, if you kept your official nose clean, you had some unofficial leeway. And certainly no Butcher Korbeith to give you nightmares.

As the grapevine linked her with Tregare, Dolan seemed to change a lot in a hurry. She dropped her anxious, defensive stance, obviously more at ease. She styled her hair in varied, less severe ways. When Bran complimented her, she said, "Maybe you're good for me, Tregare."

He knew what it was. He was Third Officer, and now Dolan was under his protection. No matter—he liked the result.

Among the cadets, Kickem Bernardez rated well, ranking usually in the top three. The exceptions came when Farnsworth did the scoring. As Kickem said to Bran once, "The Second—somehow I've got me on the wrong side of that cold man. Ah, well—not even the genius of Bernardez can charm everyone."

Bran was tempted to up his own scoring of his friend's skills in compensation, but decided against it. Once you start making allowances, where do you stop? So he kept his reports totally factual to the best of his judgment.

* * *

Any time he couldn't meet Dolan after a watch trick, Tregare spent some time training on sims. The second backup pilot position was hooked up to simulate various maneuvers, including takeoffs and landings. After one watch, Bran ran landings for nearly an hour. The computer threw him different situations; what he had to do was *adapt* to them. Such as gusting typhoon winds that shifted suddenly: that one, Tregare knew, was a real case, recorded at Hardnose. He hadn't run it before, and now he fought the simulated tiltings and drifts, and brought the imaged ship to ground—safe, but just barely so.

A voice behind him, not quite recognizable through his muffling headset, said, "Did that landing satisfy you?"

As he peeled the set off, Bran said, "Hell, no. Theoretically I made it, but I'm glad that was a sim, not real. Because I'm not sure I know enough, yet, to handle it."

"You think you're up to handling Penfoyle Gate?"

Before he answered, Tregare turned to see who was asking. It was Captain Rigueres, and the word for his grin, then, was mean.

Bran thought, then said, "Unless there's something tricky about it, sir, that isn't in the scoopsheets, I think I am."

"You are so assigned, Third Officer. Any necessary change of watch schedules, I'll arrange immediately." Tregare felt questions in him that he couldn't get into words; Rigueres answered them anyway. "Either you can or you can't; we have to find out. I'll be on the aux board, and if you're blowing it I'll cut you out and take over. And find me a new Third." Still shark-grinning, the captain turned and left.

For a while, Bran sat. Well, now it was on the line; for sure. Should he practice some more? No, dammit! He'd done that; now either he knew it or he didn't. Thoughts swirling, he went to his quarters. He could have used some company—Dolan, Kickem, maybe Leon—but one of those had the watch and the other two would be asleep now. Too tired to hit the galley, he had a snack from his goodies stash and lay much too long before he finally achieved sleep himself.

Three ship's days until the landing, and upshifting his watch trick by eight hours didn't help. Mainly, Bran stewed. Only once could he and Dolan get together to any purpose, and he was too jittery; he could perform but not complete it. He had no appetite. He forced himself to eat, but not much, after one full meal that didn't stay down. He wondered: would it have been easier if he hadn't known ahead of time, if Rigueres had simply called him to the job at the last minute? It didn't matter; he was stuck with what *was*.

So when the time came he went to Control with all his guts knotted into a lump just below his throat—or so it felt.

And the damned landing went off like clockwork. Not a glitch, not one. "Quite adequate, Third Officer," said Rigueres.

Penfoyle Gate. Discovered, naturally, by a Captain Penfoyle. The Gate part came from the planet's location, which made it a good refueling station on several runs between colony worlds.

The planet itself was only marginally habitable; located anywhere else, it would have been ignored. The temperature was chilly, sunlight red and dim. Air barely tolerable: thin and dry and impure. Take three steps and pant, take another and cough. Once Bran and Phyls Dolan reached the first group of buildings, covered by an airdome, they learned they could rent respirators. But new visitors to the Gate had to run the atmospheric gauntlet once, first. In a way, Tregare could see the point of it.

He and Dolan found a bar that served snacks, and were sipping drinks in wait of food when Bran said, "Sure, Phyls. They have to live with it all the time, here. So they want to make damn sure we know how bad it is, so's we respect them for it."

One copper-colored eyebrow she raised. "And do you?"

"I think so, yes." Pausing, he said, "Except, if I lived here, I imagine I'd be working on a way to get the hell out."

"Tregare," said Dolan, "somehow I'm not all that surprised."

Two days later, after the one brief visit groundside, Tregare's watch trick saw the windup of cargo offload and onload. Tired after a lot of cross-checking and correction of mistakes, Bran went to quarters and took a relaxing hot-water soak. As he came out, drying himself, at the door he heard a knock. He wrapped the towel around his waist and opened the door.

Kickem was there, bottle in one hand and sobriety a bit aft. "Tregare! News of Bernardez, and brought by none other than himself!"

What the—? "Get *in* here."

Laughing, Bernardez entered. "Oh, 'tis all right, Tregare.

You speak no longer to cadet Bernardez, but to the newly designated Third Officer of that illustrious name. I'm posted to the *J. E. Hoover*, Mister Tregare, sir and friend. Due to shove out in a few days, the exact number of which eludes me just now."

Tipping up his bottle, Kickem took a swallow, then handed it over. "Join me?" So although Bran didn't much care for tequila, he took a swig anyway. Bernardez said, "My shared room wouldn't hold so much as a bridge game. Tregare, would you host, here, my farewells?"

Bran hugged his friend. "Hell, yes, Kickem. Say who you want, and I'll get on the holler box for you."

The party was just the right size—almost too big but not quite. Leon Monteffial brought his tall brunette lady—by now, Tregare knew her name: Erdis Blaine. Kickem came with four other cadets: one male, three female. Bran got Phyls Dolan on the intercom and she managed to swap watch shifts with one of her counterparts; jumping shifts did beat the hell out of you, but that was no excuse for missing a good party. Farnsworth brought a woman from groundside; neither of them said much to anyone else, but at least he wasn't finding fault all the time. There were some other people that Bran knew fairly well, or somewhat, and some he knew hardly at all. Well, with over a hundred people on three shifts, that's the way it went. And the party, he thought, went better than not.

Even though it had to break up at a time when he and Dolan couldn't possibly enjoy each other before her next watch sked.

At main air lock next day, Bran saw Kickem Bernardez off the ship. "Best luck. And we'll be seeing each other."

Bernardez nodded. "I purely hope so. Good landings, Tregare." Seeing Kickem walk away, Bran knew how much he would miss him.

On Tregare's next watch trick in Control, toward the end of it he heard raised voices from one of the auxiliary positions, but couldn't make out any of the words of it. None of his business, likely, so when Farnsworth relieved him, Bran went down to the galley and had some soup and coffee. He was nearly done with all of it when Monteffial, carrying a cup of coffee, came and sat beside him. Scowling, and saying, "Oh, total rotten *shit!*"

Tregare looked at him. "Something *bad*, wrong now?"

The First looked back to Bran, then shook his head. "Max worst, I think." The coffee was good, but a sip didn't seem to help.

Bran hesitated; what *was* this? Then he said, "You want to tell it? Or not?" Because, don't push too hard. . . .

Leon Monteffial wrenched his shoulders through a tension-popping shrug that had to be painful. "Trouble just boarded, Bran. We have us a Major Bluten and two goons with him. Committee Police, the whole shit-eating lot!"

"But what can they do on a *ship?*"

Then Monteffial told Tregare what they could probably do. "They spy, they snoop; they get all the reports from their undercover Police dogs and bitches. They note down everything anyone says, that they could possibly consider incriminating. And at our next stop, which you can bet your ass will have a sizable Police garrison, their troops board us and arrest people."

Bran shook his head. "I hadn't heard of this before."

"I have. It happened on the *Leamington* a time ago. Two of my best friends were hauled off in cuffs and Welfared." Monteffial swallowed coffee and made a face.

To distract his friend—because Leon looked close to blowing wide open—Tregare said, "Bluten's an odd name. What origin, d'you suppose?"

Monteffial snorted. "It won't be his real one. 'Blut' means blood, in German. And that tells me something."

"Yeah? What?"

"The sonofabitch probably thinks he has a sense of humor."

It wasn't until his next meal that Tregare saw the Police group. Major Bluten was a slim, ruddy man of medium height. From the thighs up he didn't look all that slim, for he and both his followers, one male and one female, wore protective garb—bulky tunics that were armored against needle guns and insulated to withstand a certain amount of energy fire. The red-and-blue helmets, which looked like ordinary plastic but weren't, they carried slung at their belts, along with their weapons—Bluten wore the medium-heavy one-handed energy projector while the other two made do with needlers.

Just inside the galley entrance, the major stopped to speak with his troops. The man was short and bulky, the woman taller but equally large of frame. Both had heavy features under stubble haircuts. They might have been siblings, or cousins.

Nodding at Bluten's words, the two went to fill trays and then moved to sit at the senior-ratings' table, where no one greeted them or looked directly at them. The major himself came to the officers' table. It wasn't at all filled; Bran sat across from Chief Engineer Mallory and beside Second Officer Farnsworth. The Second Engineer was there, too—and as usual, not saying much.

Having seen how the ratings reacted to Police, Bran waited to see how his own colleagues would respond. As Bluten sat, Mallory gave him one quick look, said, "Major," nodded, and looked down to his food again. So Bran did the same, and the other two followed suit. A mess attendant brought Bluten's dinner, did not make the usual queries about beverages or dessert, and left. Everyone kept eating. Nobody spoke.

After a time, Major Bluten set his fork down loudly enough that it had to be on purpose. Side-glances showed Bran that no one was admitting having noticed, so he didn't either.

Bluten cleared his throat. "I want your attention and I will have it. Look at me." All right. Bran did so, keeping his face as expressionless as he could manage. "That's better. Now let's understand each other, right from the start. I am on a routine surveillance mission, not a witch hunt. If our HQ thought this ship had any special problems I'd have brought at least a full squad aboard with me, not a mere two aides. We allow for a certain bias by your branch of the service, against mine, but I sincerely advise you not to push it too hard."

He'd been leaning forward, tensed. Now he eased back. "Any questions?" Silence. "All right. You had your chance."

Appetite somehow gone, Bran finished his meal anyway. He'd be damned if he'd let the bastard know he'd scored, any!

When Tregare got to his quarters, having taken an hour of sim training in Control, he found all his gear out in the corridor. *Now* what? *Damn!* He keyed the door open and swung it wide, to see a naked Cleet Farnsworth in the act of disengaging from an equally nude woman—the one Farnsworth had brought in earlier from groundside.

"I'm sorry," Bran said. "Didn't know you were in here." But— "Come to that, Second Officer, why the hell *are* you?"

Showing no embarrassment, Farnsworth headed for the bathroom cubicle. "Tell you in a minute." The woman followed him and shut that door; Bran was left standing, looking at his room filled with Farnsworth's belongings. *What the hell?*

After a time Farnsworth emerged, took the woman's clothes into the other room, came back out, and dressed without hurry. "The major's equivalent rank is just behind the captain," he said. "So he bumped the First. Who bumped me. And I've bumped *you.*"

Sure. RHIP. "Yeah. I see it. But who do *I* bump?"

Farnsworth, shirt half on, shrugged. "You don't have to. Down on the next deck there's at least two Chief Rating rooms empty. Pick the one you like." He sniggered. "Just be glad, you and your redhead, you won't be stuck with a roommate."

Why did Farnsworth make himself so impossible to like? Never mind; Bran made a lukewarm reprise of his apology for intruding, and went out to haul his stuff one deck downship. Of the two vacant Chiefs' rooms he picked the smaller, because it had been cleaned more recently.

When Tregare went to Control to observe lift-off, he looked for a seat near enough to follow the pilot's moves on monitor instruments. Before he found one, Captain Rigueres called to him. "Sit over here, Third. Beside me. Let's see if you can take the ship up."

All Bran's nerves flashed fire. He stood frozen. Well, he'd wondered if no notice would be better than prolonged anxiety. Now he decided there wasn't all that much difference. Numbly he moved and sat beside Rigueres. "Thank you, sir." Without thought he began his pre-lift checkoff list, feeling nothing more than if the occasion had been merely another sim.

When the count hit sixty, he turned and asked, "Sir? How fast a lift would you prefer? Gentle, or more vigorous?"

Squinting, Rigueres gave his shark grin. "I had in mind to leave you the choice. Now that you ask, though—let's make a real exercise out of it. Consider that our survival depends on getting us upstairs at max—except, Tregare stay one notch below *real* redline, for your max. And—" A moment's pause. "I want some evasive action, soon as you have a bit of speed up; two dodging moves, and then back on course. Understand?" Not waiting for answer, the captain shouted, "Get *on* it, man! Your count is three."

Two, one—*lift*. Evasive action, the man wanted? Bran tilted the ship at first movement, let it skitter sidewise across the empty side of the port as the *Tamurlaine* built thrust, blowing gouts of dust and melt as the Drive nodes beat at soil and paving. Then the Drive took full hold; the gees hit, and the ship accelerated faster than Bran would have imagined.

His funny stuff at lift wouldn't count. Tregare threw a side-vector, angled off course and took two seperate corrections to bring the *Tamurlaine* back to its programmed route. He checked his figures against the computer's expectations for an average lift, and said, "Lift-off complete, sir. On course, forty seconds uptime from sked. Continue as ordered?"

Until Tregare looked over to him, Rigueres said nothing. Then he said, "Not bad, Third. But I don't recall asking you to sweep the field on your way out."

"Sorry, sir. Just wanted to see if I could do it."

The captain nodded. "I see. Well, you did. You get a commendation—and two days' house arrest, for not asking first."

Well, you can't win 'em all. . . .

Rigueres hadn't specified solitary confinement, so during Bran's two days of restriction, Phyls Dolan took the chance of bringing him his meals and staying to visit. Tregare enjoyed the visiting, but not the news Dolan brought. "That Bluten, the Policebastard—he and his two enforcers are scheduling everyone for interviews. It scares me."

"You haven't been called in yet? Who has?"

She told him, and there didn't seem to be much pattern to it. Monteffial hadn't been tagged, but Farnsworth had. Mallory had been in, but none of his junior Engineering officers. Of the ratings, and unrated crew, Bluten's selections appeared random.

"Any leakback?" Bran asked. "Anybody have an idea what they're after?"

She shook her head. "Not a peep, Bran."

He pulled her to him. "Then the hell with it, for now. Tomorrow I'm back on duty. Time enough to worry, then."

But after Dolan had left, and six hours before Bran's house arrest was supposed to end, Bluten called him by intercom.

"Tregare? We have an appointment. In First's quarters, as I assume you know. In one hour."

Watch this vulture! "I'm afraid there's a mistake, major. Any appointment I keep at that time will have to be here. I'm still under house arrest—as I assume *you* know."

"Don't hand me that space cadet stuff. This is a direct order, not an invitation to tea. Are you going to be here?"

"Not without the captain's permission, I'm not. Or rather—" overriding Bluten's angry voice, "I'll report to you when the captain okays it to me directly, or in six hours. Whichever comes first. Will that be satisfactory?"

Without answering, Bluten cut the circuit. Bran thought fast. If the major griped to Rigueres, the odds against a straight story ran to a lot of zeroes. He checked the time; the captain would likely be in Control now. He punched for the comm officer and asked to speak with Rigueres. For a moment he heard the captain saying, "Just a moment, major. I'll get right back to you." Then, to Tregare, "Yes?"

Bran told it fast and kept it factual, putting in no personal opinion until the end: ". . . seemed to irritate the major. So I thought I'd ask your permission, sir, to meet his schedule. I would add the out-of-quarters time to my period of house arrest, of course."

He was almost sure he heard Rigueres suppress a chuckle. "You needn't do that, Third. Permission granted. I'll tell Major Bluten to expect you, right on time."

"Thank you, sir." *So now I can stick my neck in the noose.*

The Policebitch opened the door to him. Of the two goons, Tregare decided, she looked to be the meaner. Not that there was much choice between them. Bluten sat behind a desk. Looking up only briefly, he pawed for a folder and opened it, then again looked at Bran. "A right smart ass, aren't we, Third? Got to the Old Man first, with a slanted story, eh? Well, well . . ."

"I told the captain our problem and asked his permission to keep this appointment. He granted it. That's all." Bluten hadn't offered him a seat, but he sat anyway in the chair facing across the desk. *Take charge a little. Not too much* . . . The man glared, but made no comment.

Leafing through the papers, Bluten stopped at one. "Bran Tregare." He read off the biographical data as fabricated by Hawkman for the Academy, and the gist of the records from then on. "Substantially correct?"

"No errors, major, that I can detect."

"Punishment twice . . . in the special cell. That's odd. Once does it, for most. Explain?"

"No excuses, major. I made mistakes. That's the size of it."

"Error-prone cadets seldom finish a trip with Arger Korbeith."

"Maybe by that time, major, the lesson stuck."

"Maybe." Bluten shoved the folder aside. Elbows on the desk, hands clasped, he leaned forward. "All right—who else is in on the Escape plot? If you give me a full list, I can save you."

If anything saved Tregare then, it was the total idiocy of the whole thing. Without intent or control he burst into helpless laughter. He saw Major Bluten's face turn red, but it only made him howl the louder. He tried to stop, but couldn't. Bluten shouted; it didn't help. Finally the major sat back, scowling up a storm, and waited for the paroxysm to run down. Then, still fighting the occasional fit of giggles—and inwardly appalled at himself, for peace knew *what* this maniac would do now—Bran said, "I—major, I'm sorry. It's just that—" Giggle fit. "—that I'm on my third hop with this ship, and I've yet to hear a *hint* of conspiracy." He wiped his eyes; his laughter had them streaming tears. "Peace be witness, major; that's truth."

And it very nearly was, too. At least, the vague bits he *had* heard were so far from the major's ideas that—well, that the pompous accusation had kicked him offbase. Giggle.

Stern-faced, the major tried a new tack. "What drugs do you happen to be on, just now? Oh, I can tell; you spacers can't fool me. Don't be afraid to admit it; we have treatment programs, and—"

Tregare suppressed a resurgence of the laughing. This part wasn't as dumb as it might sound; there *were* some exotic offworld drugs making the rounds of UET's ships, and Bran had heard of several though he hadn't yet been offered any. But what to say, now?

He shook his head. "No. Nothing, unless you count a drink now and then." Bluten looked skeptical; Bran said, "A blood test would verify what I say. If you like, I'll volunteer for one."

The major stared, glowered, and finally shook his head. "No. You're not smart enough to try a bluff, so you're clean." *Just keep thinking that! It might come in handy.*

There were a few more trick questions, but they were all so far off any personal mark of Tregare's that they gave him no trouble. Apparently Bluten had a fixed routine that he pulled on everybody whether it fit or not. This time it hadn't, much.

At the end of it, Bluten stood when Tregare did, and came around the desk with his hand outstretched. "I'm glad we got our earlier problems straightened out, Third. The grade of cooperation on this ship is hardly outstanding, but a few people like yourself help the average a lot." *Me, he's talking about?* And the bastard wanted to shake hands! Deliberately, Bran thought of the time he'd cleared away some chicken manure with his bare hands; that way, when he shook Bluten's hand he could smile about it.

The female goon showed him to the door and a bit outside it, holding his arm as she edged the door back to block the view from inside. Then she turned Bran to face her, her sullen face in a frown, and dug a vicious finger into the nerve at the back of his elbow. The arm screamed pain as its lower part went numb. Bran's feet shifted in reflex moves: *one hand now, and she has twenty kilos on me! But—* But she let go of him, made a sour smile as she stepped back, and said, "Just to show you, buster, you're not all *that* smart. You didn't fool the major none. So watch it."

The cheap trick wasn't worth retaliation just now, and any threat would be stupid, so he let her back away and close the door to him. Rubbing his elbow, as sensation painfully returned, Tregare went downship, to soak under a hot shower.

He got some sleep then, until time for his first watch at the end of house arrest. He didn't know which Chief Rating had filled in for him, and frankly didn't care. The watch shift ran smoothly. From the log he learned that the *Tamurlaine's* destination was Terranova's spaceport at Summit Bay. So Monteffial was probably right; at that well-established colony, UET would have a sizable Police garrison. The idea worried him, but he didn't know what he could possibly do about it.

His next two days, things seemed to be easing off; in the galley or up in Control, people weren't so tense. During one break he and Dolan managed a visit in his room. After his next watch, Leon Monteffial invited Bran up for drinks.

And then, while they were talking, relaxed and amiable, it all hit.

Farnsworth on the intercom from Control: "First! Up here right away!"

"Sure, Cleet. But what is it?"

"Not for open lines. Get here, will you?"

"Right." Monteffial shut the squawkbox down. Turning to Bran he said, "If I need you, Tregare, I could best reach you in your temporary quarters." He paused. "Where all your equipment is." And Monteffial tucked an energy weapon inside his belt, under his jacket. Bran felt his eyes widen, as he nodded.

"On my way," he said, and then was.

Down in quarters, Bran wasn't sure what he wanted to carry. Because what *was* this hassle? Monteffial seemed to think it could need weapons—well, Tregare had a lightweight energy projector and a needle gun. He didn't like the charge indication on the blaster, and the needler was smaller and easier to hide, so he tucked that one in his waistband. At the back, the way Hawkman Moray had shown him long ago. "They don't expect that. . . ."

He was armed, but nothing was happening. Nervous, Bran thought to add a concealed knife to his armament. *If nothing's blowing, I'll look silly as hell.* He waited.

Then the intercom blared, and it sounded as if all hell was breaking loose.

9

The Mechanics of Mutiny

Monteffial's voice. "—Police major raped her and maybe worse, so Dolan killed him. I don't know how, yet. The other two Police are running loose and shooting on sight. Captain took Dolan downship; he intends to space her, to clear the ship's record with the Police."

Farnsworth: "Monteffial, we *have* to go along with that!"

Bran opened intercom to Control: "Like hell we do! Leon—this is Escape! Are you with me?"

"But you can't—" That was Farnsworth.

Monteffial, then: "I think we have to, Cleet. Tregare's right."

"Hell, he's not even briefed, Leon. And there's no schedule."

"Are you with us, Cleet, or are you dead?" A pause. "That's better. Now then—" Monteffial's voice changed, as he loaded the intercom with more circuit outlets. "All hands—"

Not waiting to hear more, Bran left quarters, plunging downship as if the Butcher himself had summoned.

Still he wasn't first to the air lock. Captain Rigueres, disheveled and wild-eyed, held the half-clothed Phyls Dolan by a choke collar. Her head flailed; she didn't seem to know where she was, as Rigueres shoved her into the lock and closed the inner hatch. He put his hand to the lever that would space the woman. "Everybody hold it . . . right there!"

Everybody? From one side Monteffial entered. From the other came the Police goons, their handguns out. And Bran found he'd pulled his needle gun and was aiming it.

Following Monteffial, Farnsworth waved his arms, shouting, "Be calm! Don't dispute the captain's authority. . . . but sir, maybe you should delay your decision and—"

Everybody was in the way; stepping from side to side, Bran still couldn't get a clear shot. He moved closer, as Monteffial said, "Don't do it, captain! You won't have to—this is Escape, now."

Rigueres made a snarl. "Oh, no! You'll never make *me* a traitor." Tregare saw the man's arm start to move. The Police male was in the way, so Bran fired through him. As the man fell, Tregare took better aim, but then Monteffial's charge took *him* into the line of fire. Cursing, Bran moved to try for a better shot, and the Police female blindsided him and knocked him flat.

He rolled and came up, in time to see Rigueres pull the air lock handle as Monteffial reached him, and to see Phyls Dolan blown out into vacuum. In less than a second she disappeared from view.

Slowly, it seemed to Tregare, he got up. His gun was gone. But then, until slugged down from behind, he killed some people.

He woke up strapped to a cot, with a head he wished he could give away to someone else. For a time he didn't make sense and knew it, but couldn't help it. Then, a few hours later, he had to face Leon. The man had a bruised face and a bandaged hand.

He said, "A right mess *you* made. Are you all right?"

"No more than you, maybe less. What happened?" Before Monteffial could answer, Bran said, "He spaced her. The bastard spaced her. That's the last I remember." He tried to sit up, and Monteffial loosened the straps, so he could. "If he's still alive, he's mine!"

"He's not. I cut his throat. A second too late, dammit." The man shook his head. "I hadn't wanted Rigueres dead; hadn't planned things that way. But the way it went—too much killing, but that one I can't truly regret."

"Killing. And you say *I* made a mess. Tell me?"

Leon's hand on Bran's shoulder found unexpected soreness. "Rigueres had the intercom open; that's why the pack of loyalists came in and rushed us." The First squinted. "You really don't remember? Well, you cut the Police goon nearly in half with your needler, trying for the skipper, and hit *him*, too—but penetration slowed the needles down: no stopping power left."

Tregare nodded; the other went on. "I'm told it was the

other goon who decked you from a little behind your view. Anyway, when—when Dolan was blown out, you made a yell I never want to hear again. And you took a jump at the Police one, and spun in midair, and she went down with her head on backwards. Then you had your knife out, and spread four sets of guts on the deck, and—well, I think you lost track of who was who. When Deverel rabbit-punched you down, it was *me* you were headed for."

"Deverel?" *Peace take me—six, I killed?*

"He saved your life, Tregare. The way you were, then, I'd've had to shoot you to save myself."

"Berserk, eh? Never happened to me before. Not too unusual in the family stories, though." But that was Hawkman Moray's family, and here Bran's Moray ancestry was unknown. He said, "I'll thank Deverel, then. Assuming I'm allowed. Leon, you haven't said, yet, whether I'm under charges for any of this."

Monteffial laughed. "Charges? Hell, Tregare, you're Second Hat now, behind me as captain and Cleet as First. And by the Agowa formula—you've heard of it?—that Escaped ships use to allot shares, you *own* ten percent of the ship. We had to hold the divvy meeting without you; that kind of thing mustn't wait."

The rumor-mill info came back to him now. Agowa, sure: Control officers split a fifty percent share, 20-15-10-5; the Engineering officers did the same with twenty percent, 8-6-4-2. The other thirty percent went to the crew, with ratings getting double shares. And now he also remembered that on Escaped ships you'd be "Second Hat," not Second Officer. Any buildup of tradition, he supposed, was good for morale.

Now he said, "That's good to know. You have any idea when I can get up and go to work?" Because he didn't want to lie here, trying not to remember Phyls Dolan.

"Soon as the medics check you clear." The new captain looked at his chrono. "You get your next look in about an hour, I think." He stood. "I have to go now. We're shorthanded, you understand. Sixteen dead in the fighting, and something like twenty diehard loyalists locked in Hold, Starboard Lower for safekeeping."

"You're not—" He couldn't say it.

"Spacing them? Not unless we have to. If we make it to a Hidden World, maybe the place can use some cheap labor."

Alone again, Bran tried to wall himself away from grief for

the dead woman who, frozen now and far behind the ship, swept through the interstellar gas. Slowing gradually, from the friction of that tenuous medium, to coast forever—or maybe to make a small spark someday, against a star's glare.

But when someone standing by the bed coughed to get his attention, tears blurred his vision.

Quickly, he wiped his eyes. "Who—?"

"Hain Deverel, sir. I wanted to say—hitting you and all—"

"Deverel!" Bran reached out a hand, and the man took it. "The First—I mean, the new captain—told me. Said if you hadn't put me down, he'd've had to shoot me. I owe you, man."

"No you don't, sir. But maybe now we're even."

It took Tregare moments to think what the rating meant. Then he said, "All right. That's fine. And now you're safe, aren't you? You and—" The other name escaped him.

"Anse. Anse Kenekke. Yes, we're safe now. And that I *do* owe you, because they tell me it was you who pulled the trigger to force Escape."

Headshake. "Not me. A dead woman did that—or maybe the Police bastard who drove her to killing him. All I did was—" Well, hell, he *had* forced the issue at that. Change the subject. "Kenekke's all right too, I take it?"

Deverel grinned. "Anse? He's the one that secured the Drive for us." Now he talked fast. "When the new skipper made his all-ship call, announcing Escape, the Drive room had its problems."

"Mallory?" Sure, the older man could be a strong loyalist.

"Not him. But it was watch-change; the First and Second were both there. Chief Mallory just stood back and said he was out of it; whoever won, he'd tune the Drive for. The Second had a gun; he said we'd stand by UET or he'd blow the Nielson cube and all of it. The First, the one they call Airedale, she yelled something about duty and pleasure and illusion—Anse says she never did make much sense, except doing her work right—and tackled the Second. He killed her, and Anse killed him, by hand, before the man could get his gun free to use again. Stronger than he might look, Anse is. And then he had Drive secured, and no more problems. The Third, when he got there, he's solid with us—and up to First now, come to think of it." He paused. "There's several Drive techs in line for the Second and Third openings. If you could put in a good word for Anse?"

"I'd like to. Two problems, though. I don't know anything about his training scores, and I don't have all that much clout, anyway. But if Captain Monteffial asks for my opinion, I'll try."

"That's fair. Thank you, sir." And Deverel left.

A little later, the Chief Medic came in. Not a full-fledged doctor, but trained well enough. Bran knew her only slightly, from a physical exam during which she jabbed like hell at all the tenderer spots she was supposed to check. Must have trained at the Slaughterhouse, where cadets got used to cringing during physicals. Eda Ghormley was thin, middle-aged, with iron-grey hair and a slight stoop. Aside from the jabbing fingers she was easygoing enough, and spoke pleasantly despite her chronic frown.

Right away she took the conversational lead. "Tregare . . . haven't seen you much, in the line of business. Can't hurt an officer by hitting him on the head, but let's check a few things anyway." So—some questions, while she measured pulse, temperature, peered at his pupils, tested reflexes and coordination. And then said, "About an hour from now, after you eat, you get a sleepy pill and one shift's snooze right here. Then, unless you find something bothering you besides bruises and such, you're cleared for duty. All right?"

"Right. Thanks, Chief."

"Yes. Well, thanks for *your* part, in getting us free of those shitbags. I've waited a long time, for Escape."

Getting up after after sleeping and dressing, Bran found stiffness and soreness he hadn't noticed. Nothing serious, though; he went up to Control to check the watch sked, and found he had several hours free yet before relieving Farnsworth. He also found that there'd been some fighting here. Needle projectiles and energy bolts had clobbered some instruments. Well, that was his line of work—but first he needed something to eat. He went down to the galley.

Alone at the officers' table, Monteffial was finishing his meal. Tregare filled a tray and joined him. The new captain said, "Feeling better?"

"I'll live." He explained about the repair he planned to start, then asked, "Have you picked a new Third yet? And the new Engineering officers?"

"Leaving that part up to Mallory. He knows his people

better than I do. But for Third Hat—Tregare, I have a problem."

"Nobody's qualified? Or too many?"

"Neither. I could pick any one of three Chief ratings and justify the choice. Or rather, *we* could, because you and Cleet get a vote each, too. But the best qualified person isn't a Chief yet, just a First."

"So promote him, Leon. I'll vote your selection."

One sided, Monteffial grinned. "Afraid not. The trouble is, you see, the First I mentioned is Erdis Blaine. Now wouldn't the new captain make everybody happy by naming his woman Third Hat, over the heads of three who have seniority on her?"

Bran nodded. "Yeah, I see it. Well, make her a Chief anyway, for future reference."

"I plan to. There's more than one vacancy at that rank now."

Impatient with the subject, Tregare said, "Okay . . . but who *do* you peg for Third?"

The captain paused. "It's a tossup, mostly, but I lean toward Gonnelson."

"The man who never uses one word if he can get by with none. At least he won't be nagging the watch to death. Well, if you think he can handle the job, I'm for it."

"He looks to be turning into a fine pilot—good marks, fast reflexes, solid judgment. Gets along well with the Drive room—just tells them the bare bones of what he wants and lets them do it, without fussing over details."

"Yeah." Bran knew what he meant. Farnsworth, for instance, practically told Mallory which knob to turn, and how far.

Monteffial stood. "Gotta go. Oh, yes . . . one more thing. Not right away, but when you find time for it, I'd like you to replace the antenna cluster just aft of the topside air lock. Groden, down in Stores, will have the parts assembly ready for you, and the tools."

"Sure. It'll have to be after my upcoming watch, though." Then he thought. "Just a minute. Who do you want me to take along on the job? I mean, that stuff's more than a one-man load."

"Gotcha!" Leon grinned. "Not in the power suit, it isn't. Use the two-anchor system, though; no showboating."

"Right. I'm not much for hitchhiking."

* * *

Before his watch began, Tregare had more than half of the damaged instruments replaced. He sent the removed items down to the Shops level by one of the cadet observers. Then after relieving Farnsworth he let his Comm board technician take the pilot's chair, telling her to notify him of *any* change on the monitors. So, during the first half of his watch, he restored the consoles to full function—except for one aux board, where he put a cable splicer to work on a burned-through trunk line.

At the half-watch break he patched the main forward screen, and the intercom, down to the galley. And was starting to leave for that oasis when the intercom came on. "Captain here. Tregare, would you mind taking your break in my quarters? Little meeting going on. Shouldn't take long."

So he changed the patching to put view and squawkbox to the captain's digs. Bran hadn't had time yet to move into Second's quarters, but Monteffial and Farnsworth, he knew, had made their own moves already. Gonnelson, whether he'd relocated into Tregare's previous room, Bran didn't know about.

Entering the skipper's suite, Bran found the lanky, blond Gonnelson there as well as the two senior officers. Walking over to the stand that held the coffee urn, Bran made a head move at Gonnelson and said, "You tell him yet, Leon?" Monteffial nodded, so shifting his coffee cup to his left hand, Tregare went over and offered a handshake; Gonnelson took it. "Congratulations, Third Hat. I expect we'll all work together just fine."

"Yes. Thanks." Two low-voiced words, then nothing more.

Well, there were worse habits than not being gabby. Bran turned back to the other two. "A meeting, you said?"

"Yes," the captain said. "Let's sit down." That done, he went on. "Question of where we go next. Cleet thinks we should go on in to Terranova, per sked, bluff it out and get refueled on the strength of our original mission documents. Fake the log from about two jumps back, to leave Rigueres off and promote everybody. What do you think?"

It took no thinking. "We don't have a chance in hell, getting away with that. And the Uties we have, locked up—we'd need to space the lot. I—"

"No such thing," Farnsworth put in. "Stick 'em in freeze, listed as high-priority passengers for our next stop."

Freeze. Tregare knew, when he stopped to think, that the ship had freeze chambers. The *MacArthur* had none, because

Korbeith in his independent way had had them removed. But
Bran had seen the *Tamurlaine*'s during his first hurried tour of
the ship; he'd forgotten about them, was all. But how many
were there? He frowned. "Twelve of those, we have; right?
And twenty prisoners."

"Which is too many," Farnsworth said. "I keep telling
you—" He spoke now to Monteffial. "—nearly half of those,
now they've had time to think, are safe to let loose and put to
work. Then we wouldn't be so bloody shorthanded, and—"

"And on Terranova," Bran cut in, "they'd all go on groundside leave and keep their little mouths shut. *Sure* they would."
He shook his head. "I can't go with any of that. Captain, what's
your idea?"

Monteffial cleared his throat. "Well, it also has its risks. But
different ones. I haven't told anyone before, but I have what
purports to be a coded set of coordinates for five Hidden
Worlds. To reach one of these would require only a thirty-
degree course change, which I believe is within the limits of
our fuel reserves. So—"

Thirty degrees. Let's see: pi-over-six radians. Plug in the
sines and cosines; yes. A right-angle change took as much
energy as slowing to zerch and coming back up to speed, like a
planetary stopover. But a lesser turn—decel would be one-
minus-the-cosine of the angle, and accel factor would be the
sine. Pi-over-six; okay: decel, dot-one-three-four. Accel a flat
point-five. A little over five-eights then, total, of stopover fuel
need. Discounting gravity, because the Drive field fed it back,
mostly. Tregare blanked his hand-calc.

He said the numbers. "Leon—do we *have* that much extra?"

"And enough more to let us sleep easy."

"Then do we vote on this, or what?"

Monteffial said, "I suppose so. I vote for the Hidden World."

"Terranova," said Cleet Farnsworth.

Bran laughed. "I'll take thirty degrees and out!"

Gonnelson, as they all looked at him, kept them waiting.
Having been granted a vote, he could lock it all up now, if he
chose, in stalemate. Finally the serious face tilted to face the
others. "Not Terranova," he said.

Monteffial whooped, then said, "A drink on that. Bran, you
have time for a short one, not enough to muddle you for
watch!" He poured neat spirits; the four clinked glasses and
drank.

Farnsworth, though, looked as though his drink was sour.

* * *

What with one thing and another, including Monteffial's change of course to the Hidden World, it was two more ship's days before Tregare found himself with enough free time to do the outside work, replacing the antenna array. First, of course, he tried fiddling with the gear from Control, hoping that the glitch was merely an adjustment problem. *Always try the easy answers first.* No luck, though; the problem was definitely outside. So he called down to rating-First Groden and made sure the parts and tools were ready to go. Then he gave a little thought to the logistics of outside work, and went looking for Hain Deverel.

He found him just leaving the galley. "Deverel? You got a minute?"

"Yes, sir. Can I help you?"

At Tregare's gesture, the shorter man accompanied him along the corridor. ". . . outside, see, in the power suit. And I need somebody dependable to cover for me at the main air lock. Maybe an hour, not more, is my guess. Would it be convenient for you, now?"

"No problems at all, sir. And I'm glad it's me you asked."

Gently, Bran tapped the man's shoulder. "So am I."

With less whinging and creebing than Tregare expected, "Gripin' Groden" issued the necessary equipment. Carrying the stuff out of Stores and along a passage to the stairway landing, Tregare and Deverel found it a full load. They left it, to go up a deck, where Bran was able to instruct the other man how to help with the power suit. He checked the thing out; all systems seemed to be working well, except for one gyro that was a little slow at engaging and disengaging. Well, he didn't plan to have to bend over or straighten up in any big hurry.

They went back for the parts and tools. In the suit, Bran carried the lot like an armful of kindling. They went to the air lock staging area. There wasn't any reason for personnel to be there, and no one was.

The lock's inner hatch was open. As Bran prepared to close and seal the suit's helmet, he said, "Okay, Hain. All you need to do is stay here and see that the lock's kept open for me to come back in, and that nothing interferes with coming in *all* the way."

"Yes, sir. But what would interfere?"

Tregare shook his head. "Maybe cross-up from Control. Somebody doing an inspection and putting the outhatch closed. *I* don't know what's antsing me. . . . just plain jitters, maybe. Anyway, I'll feel lots better with you standing in, here."

"Come to think of it, sir, so will I."

"Okay . . . here goes." Tregare sealed up, entered the air lock, and attached his lifeline with the two anchors. When the lock cycled to vacuum, the outer hatch opened. He climbed outside.

Working both magnetic anchors by himself was a nuisance, but Bran kept patience and used care all the way. When he reached the antenna clump he saw why it wasn't working; some chunk of cosmic debris had wiped half of it off and twisted the rest.

The wreckage wasn't worth taking inside; the shops wouldn't be able to salvage any of it. When Bran got it free of the connections, he heaved it off into space. He'd used four different tools; now they all floated on the short lines that fastened them to his suit belt. Carefully he untied the replacement bundle, fitted it to the heavy connector, and pulled in the wrench he needed to fasten the assembly in place. Once it was secured, he did the unfolding and attached the accessories, taking loose only one at a time and cinching it down firmly before reaching for the next part. In the back of his mind he thought that for a first outside job, he wasn't doing half bad!

Then he was done with it. He had no idea how long he'd taken, but hoped he was within the limit he'd told Deverel. He started back, and restrained the impatience that made him want to shortcut the twin anchor routine. So it took him longer than he liked, to get back to the main air lock. At one point he thought he felt the ship jerk under him. But he got there without mishap, climbed in, and secured his life line and anchors in their usual places.

Through the heavy plastic window of the inner hatch he could see Deverel, and gave him the high sign. The outer hatch closed, pressure swirled in, and eventually the inner door opened. Bran went through it; it closed behind him.

Deverel was talking, but until the helmet got unsealed, Bran couldn't hear him. Then he did. "The ship, Tregare!

Farnsworth's retaken it—him and the Utie loyalists. It's been announced—Captain Monteffial's dead, and we're back on course to Terranova!"

At first he couldn't make sense out of any of it, so he kept asking. Coming inside from outside was always disorienting—but *this?* "Say again, Deverel—*how* did they do it?"

Farnsworth. A sleeper. Well, he'd always dragged his feet on Escape. Now with only officers and a few selected people carrying arms, Farnsworth and one or two of his flunkeys had opened the arms room and put weapons in the hands of all the UET loyalist prisoners—and turned them loose to conquer.

Deverel shook his head. "I don't know who killed Captain Monteffial. It wasn't Farnsworth, because he was up in Control, announcing himself captain, when somebody reported having killed Monteffial in his quarters." Deverel's face tightened. "Tregare, sir, what can we *do?*"

Sometimes things took no thinking at all. "Seal the helmet on my suit, Deverel. I'm going upship. You stay here; you should be safe enough."

"I want to help!"

"You already have. But from now, you hardly can't."

There wasn't time to sidetrack and get the suit's energy projector—even if he could have hooked it up by himself, from inside the suit. No—best to go straight upship and take what came. So Bran Tregare headed for the nearest landing and began climbing.

At first he didn't see anyone else. Then he came up to a group of unarmed people who seemed to be screaming as they ran away. They were probably on his side, but there wasn't a way he could spare the time to tell them that.

A few decks before the level of his own quarters, he was intercepted by four gunholders. A quick glance told him they were among the Utie ex-prisoners—now, according to Deverel, part of Farnsworth's troops. No time to quibble about it—both needle pellets and energy beams raked his suit's armor. Well, *hell!* One man was within reach, so Tregare reached. He swung the man against the other three; it took two swipes but he decked them. Then he found he wasn't holding the man any longer—just the man's arm. He used it to club down one Utie who was still trying to get up, then threw it away. That move was a mistake; the faulty gyro, when he went to straighten up too fast, began to process and almost turned him sideways.

All right—easy now! He paused to look. One man wasn't quite dead, but close to it, so Bran stomped on his head. No point in leaving loose ends. Weapons might be a good idea; he looked around and picked up one medium energy weapon and one light one. There was a needler lying handy, but he had only two hands and no place to tuck anything away. So— upship again.

Somebody must have ducked away and made an intercom call, because three decks up he ran into an ambush—maybe a dozen armed people blasting at him when he came up into view at the landing. *Peace on it!* Spraying energy bolts with the heavier gun in his left hand, he ran at the two closest attackers. They were standing against a bulkhead. The suit's impact made mush of them.

Well, nobody said it was going to be neat and tidy. Three were still alive. They ran, and he didn't bother to shoot.

Farther upship. He was shot at, and he shot back. He left several dead and let some flee unscathed. The suit's right knee mechanism was heating up; the gyros for bending down and straightening chattered and paused at the wrong times. He had to keep his moves simple now, or the damn suit could collapse on him.

Coming to the galley level he heard a lot of shouting. Whose, he had no idea, and by now he couldn't afford to care. He thought of something Hawkman had told him once. When he climbed far enough to look across at floor level, he flipped on the suit's outside speakers and *yelled*, then dropped out of sight for a few seconds. And then raised his heavier gun up and sprayed the level without even looking. When the noise stopped he raised himself up and scanned the area. There were three corpses and no one alive. Whether the three kills were his or someone else's, he'd probably never know.

Not far now, to Control. And to Farnsworth, who'd had Monteffial killed, who had tried to give this ship back to UET. Farnsworth, that pigass—oh, forget about cussing, *get* him. So Bran started up the last climb.

He expected a grenade, but maybe Farnsworth had forgotten to stock up on those. He expected a flood of armed troops, but maybe good ol' Cleet had run a little short. He didn't know *what* the hell he expected. So he just climbed on up.

Farnsworth didn't have much ready for him, special. A few

troops, and one of the projectors that would have fit onto the power suit. Not much, but enough. "Hold it right there," said Farnsworth. "I don't know who you are, in there, but I'm captain now and I offer you amnesty if you'll surrender. Is it a deal?"

"Tell me a little more, captain," said Tregare. He was inching the suit forward, trying to look as if he weren't. "I'm not sure I understand all what's happened."

"Well, it's simple enough," Farnsworth said. "There was a traitorous mutiny, and now that's rectified. Except that you and I have to reach an understanding."

"That's no problem. I understand fine. A deal, then?" He strode toward Farnsworth. Everything would have worked if the heavy-projector man hadn't caught on; the blast caught the suit's control pack and jammed the lower limbs. Bran grabbed for Farnsworth; the thrown missile that smashed into the gunner's face and knocked him unconscious, was Farnsworth's head. Then, the explosion came.

"I'm getting tired," said Bran Tregare, "of waking up in hospital."

"Then try taking better care of yourself." Eda Ghormley's voice still belied her sour expression. "Captains shouldn't take so many chances. Can you tolerate visitors? There's one here."

Bran took a quick self-check. Head thudding, ears ringing, stomach vacillating between hunger and nausea, but—"Visitors. Yes." Because if he was captain, he had to know more about it, and fast.

The visitor was Erdis Blaine; she looked a little red-eyed puffy but mostly in control. Bran asked first. "Who's got the watch? What's the drill? Tell me fast." Then, realizing she had her own problems, "I wish to hell they hadn't got Leon."

She sniffed once and almost managed a smile. "Me, too. Nicest guy I—well, Gonnelson's standing in for you, Tregare, and just temporarily, Max Druffel and I are filling in on the other watches. The other Chief rating in line, he was on the wrong side. Somebody killed him. Probably you."

What a mess. Tregare said, "Tell Gonnelson I confirm his choices. You and Druffel, which of you is senior?"

"He is; he's a Chief."

"Then I guess he's Second Hat and you're Third. All right?"

Now she did smile. "Anything that works." She paused. "Tregare—did anybody ever tell you you're a real pisser?"

He looked at her. "I wouldn't know what that means."

"You don't have to; you just do it." Then she left.

Not feeling up to it, Tregare after one sleep cut loose from medical custody and called council in Control, since he also wasn't up to moving into captain's quarters. On hand he had Gonnelson, Druffel, Blaine, and old Mallory representing the Drive room. To avoid distracting the ratings who were holding down the watch positions, Tregare's group took seats well away from them.

"I missed the other meeting," he began, "so if I pass up anything we should do, somebody clue me in. First, who's got a roster of surviving personnel?" Gonnelson handed him a flimsy. He made a quick count. "Sixty-seven of us. Jeez, we *are* shorthanded."

"Five of those," said Al Druffel, "were Farnsworth's."

"How come they're still alive?" Tregare raised one eyebrow.

"Because you haven't ordered them killed," said Erdis Blaine. "And three of them are cadets. . . ."

He thought. Hell, he wasn't Korbeith! "Then let's leave it at that. Any holding ratings are unrated as of now, though. And no two of those five are to work together or live together. So I don't think they'll give us any trouble." Blaine pointed out the names, and Bran checkmarked them. "If they keep their noses clean, they can earn promotion like anybody else."

Again he looked down the list. "We need to make some promotions. Well, for starters, let's make it official that I'm captain, Gonnelson First Hat, Druffel Second, Blaine Third. Any questions?" Most of them nodded. "How about your people, Mallory? Your Third Engineer—what's his name?— he'll be First now, I imagine."

"That's right. Junior Lee Beauregard. Georgia boy." Mallory cleared his throat. "My Chief Tech moves up to Second Engineer: Ingrid Nakamura. Now for Third I've jumped a fella several grades, just because he's a damn good Tech. Man named Anse Kenekke."

"I've met him." At the corner of vision Tregare saw movement. The man in the pilot's seat had looked around; it was Deverel. "Good choice."

"And I've made other promotions, to fill in the supervisory spots, which I'll log in after this meeting. If you approve."

"I said it before, Mallory. You're the one, knows your Drive people. You call 'em, I'll okay your choices." He paused.

"Upship here we need some promoting, too. I have some ideas for about half the top rating slots and can use suggestions for the rest. Here's who I favor for the vacancies at Chief level." He named the people; one of them was Hain Deverel.

The only question came from Druffel, about upgrading Groden, down in Stores. "That man would bitch at his own funeral."

"Does his job," said Gonnelson, surprising Bran.

Tregare thought of something. "How long's he been a First?"

"Five years, maybe," Druffel said. "Rubs people the wrong way."

Chuckling, Bran said, "Let's see if a raise might help his disposition some." Druffel nodded, and Groden got his Chief's rating. Then suggestions were offered for the lesser promotions; without any real arguments, most of them were passed.

That much done, Tregare said, "Gonnelson, I noticed by the log that you corrected Farnsworth's change of course almost as soon as somebody got me out of that suit, cold as a clam, and cleared you some space to work. So—" The man looked alarmed, about to apologize; Bran waved a hand. "I checked it; you're solidly on the route Monteffial punched in. All I want to do, here, is give you a public commendation for initiative. *And* accurate work. By not waiting, you saved us some fuel, too."

What else? Oh, sure; the new divvy. The figures were no news to anyone, but his reciting them made it all official. "We'll need to refigure crew's shares, rated and unrated, but that won't take long."

"How about Farnsworth's Uties?" Blaine asked it. "Are you giving them shares?"

"As unrateds, sure," Tregare answered. "Way I see it, since we're not killing them they have jobs. Jobs determine shares. Anything else wouldn't be fair, all around."

After a couple of minor questions, Bran called the meeting closed and went to log the results into the ship's computer. He grinned at the young woman in the seat beside the terminal he used. "Better be careful when I feed this stuff in. Wouldn't want to give Tinhead a headache."

As he started to leave, Erdis Blaine intercepted him. "Captain, you'll be moving into your new quarters, I imagine, as soon as possible."

He hadn't thought that far ahead, but . . . he nodded. "Yeah. I suppose so. Why?"

"It's just—well, I've tried to get Leon's things packed for

storage, figuring what should be sent to his family if he still had one, and if there's any way to do so. What to simply throw out—" He saw tears forming but she blinked them away. "But I just haven't had *time* to get it all done. And my own stuff. I'd moved in with him, you know. Or maybe you didn't. So there's all *that* to move, too. And—"

He touched her shoulder. "Hold it, Blaine. There's no rush, except that I do need to do my sleeping where the remote command facilities are. But my own personal junk—there's not enough of it to crowd anything. Just clear a corner maybe, and part of a closet. I'll wedge in okay. And you don't have to move right away either, if it's inconvenient."

She backed away from his touch. He hadn't meant more than comfort, so he felt foolish. She said, "Look, captain. I like you, and I think we all owe you a lot. But I *loved* Leon, and I can't switch men that fast."

Angered for no real reason, Bran Tregare kept his tone calm. "All right, I see why you'd take the offer that way. But believe it or not, all I meant was—" Grief came. He fought it, and couldn't quite hide his feelings. "Blaine, I'm still hurting over Phyls Dolan. You might think a fast tumble would help, but that's not how it feels. What I meant was, just that you could *stay* if you wanted, long as you wanted." Now he could smile a little. "Hell, wouldn't be the first time I had a lady roommate in a 'mustn't touch' setup. So *now* how about it?"

"Tregare . . . I mean, captain—"

"We're off duty. Tregare's okay. So's Bran."

"They'll all think we are."

"Do you care? I don't."

"I snore. Or so Leon claims."

"People snore. I nudge 'til they quit."

"Then it's a deal."

Bran hauled his gear—three loads, but he didn't bother asking anyone to help—up to captain's digs. Erdis Blaine had cleared him more than enough space; when she got everything out, the place was going to look rather bare. Oh, well, things always tended to accumulate faster than a person expected.

He moved some clothing—Leon's—that Blaine had piled on the chair facing the remote-command facilities module, and set to checking that equipment. Druffel had the watch; Bran coached him through some of the operating functions and found that skipper's quarters could monitor not only the main viewscreen, with whatever he ordered combined on that versatile instrument, but could also obtain miniature insets of the two aux screens that flanked the big one. And he could separate or combine various facets of the intercom net, and—well, when he'd checked out nearly all the console, he decided he could damn near fly the ship from here! Well, he didn't have access to direct control of gunnery or of the Drive, or the air locks. But to everything else, or nearly so.

Somehow, Bran had in mind that Leon Monteffial had taken all necessary action with regard to the *Tamurlaine*'s new course and destination. When he checked the log and it told him differently, he was too depressed to bother with cursing. Or to blame anyone else for not noticing. All he said was, "Druffel. Ask Malloy how soon he can be ready for Turnover."

"Turnover?"

"I believe you know the term." Then, ashamed of taking his irritation out on the man, Tregare added, "I should have checked earlier. Just found out, here, Turnover was due about the time I was flatbacked after Farnsworth's caper." So that, of course, was why Monteffial hadn't done it; the man was dead then.

Mallory needed only an hour or so to prepare; Bran spent the time in useless stewing. What the delay meant, was that to bring the ship to the Hidden World known as New Hope, he was going to have to run decel near to max, or else go past, too fast to land or even orbit, and loop back. Either way a waste of fuel, the same as pushing a groundcar or aircar at full throttle. Well, either the fuel reserves would be enough, or they wouldn't.

Turnover went smoothly; Bran tipped the *Tamurlaine* over, directly in line with the idle thruster and balancing with the other two, then used the third to dead-stop rotation at as near a solid one-eighty as the instruments would measure. The calcs were more complicated than that, of course, because the ship was still in change of course. But the vectors could be considered separately and still add up right, so Tregare didn't worry about the overall equation.

When he told Mallory to set decel at point-nine-two max, the old Chief Engineer said, "Nine-two? Confirm, please?"

Tregare sighed. "Confirmed, I'm afraid. We turned late. Call it my fault. There's nobody else alive to blame."

Clearing his throat, Mallory said, "I see. Don't fret, lad . . . Captain, I mean. The Drive's tuned quite finely, as I always try to keep it—but I'll just see if from now on we can't tune it a little finer."

"Thanks, Chief. I'm sure you will." Well, if Mallory couldn't do it, Tregare knew no one who could.

Blaine had exaggerated about her snoring. Once in a while a soft burring vibration, but never loud nor for long at a time. The way the watch sked was running, they didn't usually share the big bed for the full sleeping period of either. Sometimes Tregare came to bed while she was sleeping and found her gone when he woke, sometimes the other way around.

When their skeds did synch, for once, he found himself embarrassed. He entered quarters, and there she was, undressing for bed just as he intended to do. The thing was, it was only about the second time they'd both been around for disrobing together, and the first had been when he was bedding down and she arising. Which was, somehow, different.

Bran nodded to her. "Hi, Blaine." And went into the bathroom for a while. When he was done there, he picked up his clothes and went out to the main room, and hung them over a chair. She'd left the light dim for him, so he supposed she was trying to go to sleep. But when he went to the bed, he saw her lying there looking at him. He got in, staying on his own side as usual. "Good night, Blaine."

"Are you sure, Tregare? I've been wondering."

He came close to snapping out a curt reply; dammit, was he supposed to be able to respond to this kind of turnaround in thirty seconds or less? So he said, "Can we talk some?"

Her words came fast. What were they *doing*, living like monks and nuns when maybe the ship couldn't even hit groundside and they'd just drift and die? And—but tired as he was, he could see what drove her. And it wasn't sex, as such.

"Come here, Blaine. What you need is a good cuddle. And me too, maybe. But that's all, for right now."

So they did.

Mallory nursed the Drive; Tregare refined his navigation figures and finally saw his way clear, when the *Tamurlaine* hit half-c going downhill, to cut decel to point-eight-seven of max.

When they came in hailing distance of New Hope, they had close to three days' fuel in solid reserve.

10

New Hope

What Tregare expected of a Hidden World, he wasn't sure. But this one didn't make things easy. The voice from ground-side came from a loop tape, and repeated, ". . . colony world New Hope, to the approaching ship. Identify yourself, please. Name, last port of call, roster of officers to check against our own records, and other ships of recent contact with you. We welcome all news and will reciprocate in kind." Pause. Silence with slurred undernoise. "This is the colony world New Hope—"

Bran cut the sound to a murmur. *Colony* world? That meant UET, but Monteffial vouched for this one as Hidden. He looked over to Gonnelson, who nominally had the watch, and decided not to ask questions.

But he couldn't help muttering out loud a little. All right, he had an *armed* ship. But little use would those turrets do him, sitting groundside and pointing straight up. So if New Hope turned out phony, how would he handle it?

"Scoutship." The voice jarred him; then he realized it was Gonnelson answering his unheeding mumbles.

He turned to look at his First Hat. "Thanks, Gonnelson. You're right." For he'd forgotten the scouts. Rigueres had ignored them in training, and unarmed ships (like the *Mac*) didn't carry the little spacecraft. Tregare first began berating himself for losing track of things, then thought: *well, it got a little hectic on here.* So he shrugged, and thought some more.

"Gonnelson? Those scouts checked out for use?" The man nodded. "Who by? You do it yourself?" Another nod. "Good enough; I think you just now gave me some answers." He reached for his offship transmit switch. "So maybe it's time to talk to groundside."

Tregare didn't bother with the loop-tape approach; he spoke live on circuit. "The ship *Tamurlaine*, calling New Hope spaceport. Captain Bran Tregare speaking. We last lifted from Penfoyle Gate; before that, the Twin Worlds. Our officers' roster? Your news might list Rigueres, Monteffial, and Farnsworth; unfortunately, none of those gentlemen have survived to greet you. Tregare over."

He turned to Gonnelson. "If this is a UET plant—if they send up missiles—I'll walk this ship across their town and wipe it off!"

"Fuel," said Gonnelson, and Tregare sagged in his chair. "Fuel, yeh. All right. You can land this thing?" The man nodded, and Bran knew that Gonnelson never overstated. So he said, "Then you do it. And just outside atmosphere, I'll take one of the scouts out and ride you shotgun, going down and until we know things are right, groundside."

Gonnelson shook his head. "Talking."

Bran knew what he meant. "Druffel and Blaine'll be with you, to handle that part. I'll brief 'em first. All right?"

Groundside, after a pause, was answering now. "*Tamurlaine?* That's an armed ship. None of those ever Escaped before. *If* you did. Which is to say, if you're Escaped, what's the ship's new name? And why aren't you using it? Answer immediately!"

Bran shook his head. No time to think up excuses. Level first and maybe regret it later. He said, "Peace take you, I came on this ship as Third Officer, after one cadet tour with Butcher Korbeith. Whom one day, if ever we meet again, I will kill. Escape happened on here before I had any chance to learn the rules of it, or the niceties and protocols. We are coming in to land, New Hope; we intend to give fair treatment and expect the same in return. Are my intentions satisfactory to you?"

The pause was too long; groundside was having fast confab. Finally the voice came. "Set your computer for fast feed and we'll give you a landing trajectory. New Hope out."

Tregare said to Gonnelson, "Put this input in storage first; before it goes into Tinhead, we inspect." But when they checked the data, it came out solid enough. So Tregare called Al Druffel and Erdis Blaine, explained what he wanted them to do during and after landing, and signed off. He told

Gonnelson, "I'll grab my kit and go snooze in the portside scoutship. Call me about a half hour before you hit gas, and then keep a channel open between us." He grinned. "If you want, you can put Blaine on it."

The snooze part had been a touch of bravado on Tregare's part, but once aboard the scoutship and leaning back in its pilot's seat, he actually did doze off.

Druffel's voice woke him. "Skipper? Captain Tregare?" Bran acknowledged. "Roughly thirty minutes to hitting atmo, sir. Instructions? And do you want the landing site coordinates, and the trajectory, in your computer, sir?"

All that stuff? Hell, he had no map recorded, and—"No need, Druffel," he said. "In about twenty minutes we talk again and you spit this scout out. Once through the no-comm ionization layer, we talk again. But no point in bothering the computer with it."

"Yes, sir." Druffel paused, talking to someone, not loud enough for Bran to make it out. "One thing, Captain. Will you want to dock with us groundside, under gravity?"

Oh, hell. Bran thought fast. "No. I haven't done that. Don't know if I could. No . . . we get things settled, I hope, and I'll land alongside. Then either these people have a big hoist we can use, or we dock this scout after we get upstairs again."

Another pause. More talk Bran couldn't quite hear. Then, "Yes, sir. That will work. One way or the other."

"Good." Another thought. "Flash me the map once, though, I can spot the port. I might just want to be there first." On the screen the image flickered, then steadied; Tregare put in into the records. "Okay, thanks. Call me in twenty minutes."

He cut the circuit, ate a quick snack, and hit the john. His nerves could have used a quick drink but maybe his reflexes couldn't, so perhaps just as well he had no booze aboard. He sat again, fingering the controls, and waited. When the voice came again—Blaine's, this time—he was more than ready for it.

"Docking chamber pumping to vacuum, sir. Count ninety, to opening. Further instructions, sir?"

He couldn't think of any, except—"Anybody takes offensive action against the ship, walk the Drive across them. And then sit down near as you can to the fuel dump, if you can spot it. I'll try to give you backup."

"And if our landing is peaceful, sir?"

Tregare laughed. "Hell, you don't need any orders for *that*."

The time came, the hatch opened, and the scout made its exit to clear space. The *Tamurlaine*'s inward path was crossing the terminator into a hemisphere of daylight on the world below; Tregare checked his map on the screen and—off toward the horizon—he spotted the port. Already the edge of atmo dragged and jerked at the scout, making it look as if the larger ship, to one side, bucked and pitched. But Tregare knew the *Tam* was holding course; it was his own scoutship being bounced around as it entered the top of atmosphere.

He watched his hull-temp readings; they looked fine. The ship, though, was lagging him, drifting off the back edge of his portside screen. Well, should he hang back and stay with it, or go groundside like a bat?

A moment, Tregare thought. Then he grinned. The *Tamurlaine* had to do a conservative, least-fuel grounding. The scout's fuel needs, by comparison, were hardly noticeable. Tregare pointed his small aux craft straight down. *Like a bat!*

Surprising, how long the scout took, getting down to aircraft altitudes—and then how little time he had to level off, and not churn dirt. He didn't actually plow a furrow, Tregare didn't, but he decided not to tell anybody what his altimeter read when he pulled out of his dive. For one thing, they probably wouldn't believe him, and accuse him of bragging. Hell with it. Next time, if ever, he'd know to take it a little easier.

Slowing now to speed that wouldn't break windows groundside, if they *had* windows, Bran spotted the approach route to the mapped spaceport. He opened channel to the *Tamurlaine*; in a little while the ionization roar cleared. "Tregare here. Downside and close to the port. Going to make a pass there. Keep in touch."

Static partially obscured the answer, but Druffel was agreeing. Tregare saw the spaceport just ahead; he went across it at just below sonic speed, looped around and eased past the place again, slower. Nobody shot at him so he pulled up and circled, waiting for the *Tam* to descend. And finally he watched the ship land, on the one of four landing circles nearest a building. Port Control, probably. When the dust settled, he saw a group of people leave the building and approach the ship. If any were armed, it was with nothing more than handguns. So, keeping the *Tamurlaine* between the groundside people and his scout—to protect them from his own, lesser landing blast—Tregare set down.

He did the shutdown checkoff in a hurry, lowered his ramp, and went down it three steps at a time. By walking quickly, he intercepted the groundside people as they reached the place where the *Tamurlaine*'s ramp was descending and would soon touch.

Leading the party were a man in late middle age and a somewhat younger woman. Bran couldn't figure who was in charge, so "ladies first." Extending a hand, he said, "Bran Tregare, captain of the *Tamurlaine*, which we haven't got around to rename yet." He saw them looking past him, between the big ship's landing legs, at the scout. "I came down by the scenic route, you might say."

Squinting against bright sky, the woman pushed back short, tousled hair, more sandy-colored than anything else. At close range Bran saw that maybe she was younger than she looked. Her skin was weathered and darkened. Outdoors too much? She said, "I'm Corlys Haines, Port Commander, and I'd like you to meet"—Gesturing to the man beside her—"Council President Edd Crilly. With two d's." Crilly's gaunt, lined face creased into a smile as he in turn shook hands. He mumbled something that sounded polite, before Haines introduced Bran to a stocky, freckled man, roundfaced under greying, reddish hair. "Ezra Drake, our security chief. He's the one who'll want to know all your spacing histories, to put together a picture of who's been on which ships and where they've been."

Another handshake, and Bran nodded. "The Long View, eh? I hope the information flow goes both ways."

"Once we've checked you out," Drake said, "it does."

Down the ship's ramp, now, came Druffel and Blaine, followed by a squadsized group of senior ratings. So Gonnelson, to avoid a talking situation, had stayed in Control. Tregare introduced his two Hats to the three persons he'd met, mentioned that his First had stayed aboard to hold down the watch, and wondered how to get down to business. Well, just *start*: "We'll have to go over our cargo manifest together, I expect, to see about trading for fuel and supplies. I suppose you do some long-term trading with other Hidden Worlds, so maybe we can work up a dicker to handle some cargo for you. And—"

Palm out, Drake's hand came up. "Hold it. You're not

cleared yet. You can get on with your preliminary negotiations if you like, but no fuel or data goes on that ship until I okay it. Understood?"

Bran scowled, then thought about it. Drake didn't sound unfriendly, nor like being arrogant for the fun of it; he was doing his job. "Understood," Tregare said. "But if the checking's holding us up, let's get on with it."

"Fine. Your group here first; all right?" Drake waved a hand toward the nearby building. "Over there."

"Sure," Bran said. Then, "Just a minute." He hadn't taken a talkset aboard the scout, so he borrowed Druffel's and called Gonnelson. "Post somebody to the scout, will you? Can't leave it vacant and open." Gonnelson acknowledged. "Right, then. Thanks, First." Tregare waited until a rating came down from the ship, entered the scout, and drew the ramp up. Then he turned back to Drake. "Sorry to hold things up. Let's go."

And during the short walk to the amber-colored concrete building, which looked like any box of offices on any world, Bran finally had time to notice and enjoy the clear air—plenty of oh-two here—and the springiness of step that came with a lighter-than-Earth gravity. Sky glare was a little more than he liked; next time he'd bring sunglasses. He had no close look at local vegetation; the port area was bare, and the brush around the edges too far distant to show any detail, except that it seemed to be mostly a pale grey-green, and wafted no scents across the landing area.

And then they all went inside.

Drake himself questioned Tregare. There was nothing tricky about the man's approach, no traps in the Major Bluten fashion. Drake simply wanted all the info Bran could remember about ships and rosters and destinations. Also anything he could recall from the Slaughterhouse. "If somebody graduated in the year Z," Drake put it, "then when he shows up in another report, at Z-plus-ten, we have that much more tie-in on him."

Bran had just about run out of data, which was why they were into chatter. "Do all Hidden Worlds have data banks like yours?"

"I hope so. I try to send the word along, and copies of our stuff, with any ship that cooperates." He paused. "Actually, I didn't originate the idea. I got it from Cade Moaker on *Cut*

Loose Charlie. He brought a packet from Number One, a sort of starting kit."

Moaker. Bran had forgotten the *Mac*'s fly-by with that ship. Now he told it. Drake nodded. "He wouldn't have been from here, on that one. The coordinates and vectors don't fit."

Relaxed now, sitting back, Tregare said, "Any more you want?"

"From you, no. Unless you think of something else for me. And far as I'm concerned, your ship's cleared. You can go ahead with the dealings." Drake stood. "But I'll appreciate it if you'll send your people over in groups of twelve, to fill in anything else they may have for us. Will you set up a circuit to me from your Control room, so we can cut out the delays with the walking back and forth?"

"Sure." Ready to leave, Bran shook hands. "See you." He found his other people had finished too. They walked back to the ship.

Drake's systematic checking went fast. On his advice, Tregare dumped the five survivors of Farnsworth's team offship, bag and baggage. "We'll relocate them to a settlement a few hundred kilometers north," the man said. "They won't be the first of their kind, by any means. It's an ongoing problem, and our solution usually works out."

Another order of business was recruiting to fill the ship's vacancies. There were plenty of young people with an eye to space for the unskilled slots, but a shortage of trained spacers. Bran wound up with a full roster plus a few supernumeraries, but realized he was going to have to set up an intensive training program. So, not to waste time, put his officers on it immediately.

On the financial end of things, Tregare lucked out. Quite a lot of his cargo was electronic components, stuff that carried high value in small bulk. His fuel and supplies put a smaller dent in his assets than he might have expected. And rather than commission to carry New Hope's cargo, he bought it outright and would sell it the same way. The Long View . . .

When the Council threw a banquet for the *Tam*'s officers and top ratings—about twenty in all—Tregare turned up with a couple of good ideas. He was seated between Corlys Haines and a Professor Landis. First, Haines asked him if he intended to visit only Hidden Worlds in future, or bluff it out at UET colonies also. "Raiding can be profitable, I'm told."

"Yeah, I've heard that. Matter of face, I've been working on a faked log to use for bona fides if we hit UET territory."

She touched his left cheek. "Then you and your new officers had better do something about your symbols of rank."

Right. His cheek proclaimed him Third Officer, while Gonnelson and Druffel and Blaine had no markings at all. Now why hadn't he thought of *that* objection when Farnsworth wanted the ship to go on in to Terranova? He said, "You have anybody here who can do it for us?"

"Yes." It was agreed; Haines left to make a brief call, and returned to say that the needle artist would visit the ship the next day.

Meanwhile, Bran had been talking with the professor, and he found the talk interesting. Landis headed a technical group stranded here by Escape of the ship they'd been riding. "And I have a prize gang of lab jockeys, captain, and a rather good lab"—he spread his hands—"we could hire out to design all sorts of gear and arrange the building of it, but all this place wants is better farm machinery!" He laughed. "Well, not quite that bad, but nearly."

The man started to change subjects, but Tregare raised a finger. "Let me think a minute." Actually he didn't have to think about anything except how to say it.

The equation was this: he wanted to do UET in the eye, and peace take it, he would! But one ship wasn't enough; he needed allies. The trouble was, far as he knew, no other armed ship had Escaped, ever.

But that didn't mean that maybe an Escaped ship couldn't be armed later. So Tregare asked Landis about that. "Say I give you a spare turret projector out of ship's Stores, along with the specs for it, and for the circuitry. And the other stuff—missiles and counter-missiles, which I haven't studied all that much. Hull plate adapters, all that." He stared at the prof. "How'd you like to build me some weapons, and arm other Escaped ships I send here?" Because there *was* a Hidden Worlds grapevine, and ships left messages for each other; *it could work.*

Landis squinted. "It won't come cheap. You will pay how?"

"Plain old Weltmarks." The *Tam*, Bran had found, carried UET's money in good supply. Well, a ship would have to. And New Hope, at least, operated on that same currency. So?

"We can deal, captain. And I know a way to improve on UET's turrets. You'll come, yourself, for the weapons?"

"Or send somebody, with my personal password. Say, my name, plus my ship's new name."

"Which is what?"

"Unknown at present." Call it *Unknown*, maybe? No, but the French word for it. Yes. "*Inconnu.*"

So with one word Tregare made a deal and renamed the *Tam*.

The tattoo artist wasn't all that expert. The Hats' emblems looked well enough, but when the scabs came off, Tregare found that on his own cheek the colors, new parts and old, didn't quite match. Which would have been okay if he'd realized ahead, and asked for each succeeding segment to differ a little. But this way it was obvious that he'd gone from Third to Captain in one jump. And the faked log was already getting too complex to tamper with, to try to make plausible three promotions all marked on him at the same place. Tregare shrugged. *Hell with it.*

The ship, its scout docked by Gonnelson following liftoff, was in space again. Or rather, *Inconnu* was there for the first time. Still wearing the *Tamurlaine's* insignia, though, because nobody had designed one for *Inconnu*, and the ship was headed for UET's colony on Hardnose, an icebound world.

The need for heavy training schedules made the trip seem to go faster. And while Hardnose was a small colony and not apt to hold much in the way of high brass or Committee Police, still it seemed a good idea that officers and ratings get the faked log down pretty well. Thinking in terms of the Long View and of spatial geometry, Tregare decided there wasn't much chance of any vessel from Earth leaving data this soon, that would contradict his effort at computerized fiction. Or so he hoped.

At icy, high-albedo Hardnose, the approach and hailing and landing all went easily. Now the question was, could *Inconnu* get away with pretending to be UET's *Tamurlaine*?

How easy it was, Tregare could hardly believe. But all officialdom was in a dither, trying to hunt down a group of deserters from the only other ship in port, the *Attila*. That ship's First Officer had headed a leave party of nearly a dozen, including the officer's lady, and the group hadn't returned. Two were caught, but seemed to know nothing of the others' whereabouts. Since Committee Police had done the interrogating, Tregare tended to believe that the two, before they died, had been telling the truth. So even in this relatively small place there had to be a local Underground hiding the fugitives.

On Hardnose, ships' business went slowly. Before Tregare was done with his, the *Attila* lifted away, maybe with replacements and maybe not. Bran didn't care and didn't ask.

What he did care about was how to find the deserters. Still shorthanded when it came to skills, he could use some experienced people, and obviously the ones hiding out would like a way to escape UET.

But how to go about it? Tregare was too easily recognized to try scouting the local underworld on his own. His officers, each sporting the appropriate cheek tattoo, were no better qualified. So who in hell *could* he send on such a mission?

Then, walking along a corridor, he met Deverel and Kenekke. *These guys know how to keep cover. They have to.* So he said, "Talk with you two for a minute? My digs. And drinks go with the offer." After a quick look to each other, both nodded, and followed Tregare's brisk gait. In his quarters, Deverel accepted the drink. Kenekke settled for water.

Bran explained the problem. "I don't know how you can make contact but I'd appreciate your giving it a try. If you do locate these people, especially that First Officer, port security here is so lax that we can sneak people to the ship in the courtesy groundcar."

He waited, then Deverel nodded, and Kenekke said, "I guess we can give it a try, sir. But why us?"

Bran tried to think how to put it. "Because, to stay alive in UET, you *had* to be pretty good at keeping the bastards guessing." Both men laughed; then, with handshakes, the deal was on.

For three days, no luck; Tregare had to start thinking in terms of how long he could stall his scheduled lift-off. Then, late one night, Deverel brought two Tech ratings around to be hoisted in by the cargo hatch—no air lock, that point of entry, and only Tregare's own alerted guard watching. Bran interviewed the two, a young couple. The male did most of the talking but looked to the woman for corroboration and was sometimes corrected in his details. "True; the First didn't *tell* us to jump ship. He just talked slow, around a table in this big bar, and said if anyone was going back to the *Attila*, don't say anything about some of us maybe not going back." It sounded reasonable.

The next night, Tregare met that prodigal First and his freemate. The officer, now wearing crewman's fatigues, gave a bad first impression. Hulking and swarthy, a bit stooped, the man wore gargoyle's scars on his face. Blinking as he came from dim corridor into Tregare's better-lighted quarters, he faced Bran and offered a handshake. As Bran took it, the man said, "I'm Derek Limmer, off the *Attila* and done with it, I hope. With me is Vanessa Largane." The scarred face grimaced. "I am not to blame for my looks, captain. At the Slaughterhouse, when I was fourteen, it was a matter of too many belt buckles and not enough dodging."

As the low, resonant voice stopped, Tregare didn't know what to say. Finally, "Those bastards do have a lot to answer for."

Now the woman stepped forward. "And I'm Largane." As Tregare accepted her handshake, his breath caught—she was so damned beautiful! Tall, slim, with delicate features and tilted grey eyes, a mass of honey-tinted hair falling well past her shoulders. Strength to the slightlywide mouth, though, as she smiled. "Derek and I are a team. For some time now."

"Yes." Bran nodded. "Welcome aboard, both of you. Drinks, maybe?" They agreed, and he accommodated them. "Now— two of your people are here already. Any more, that you know of, looking for a way off this icecube?"

"All the remaining five, I'd judge," said Limmer, "if they and your people can make connections."

"We'll try," Bran said. "Now let's exchange news."

Two more refugees from the *Attila* were aboard when Tregare lifted from Hardnose. Of the other three no trace could be found, and time was running out; sooner or later UET was going to get suspicious of the delays.

Bran felt lucky to have Limmer on the ship; the man was obviously capable, and from the start, after those first moments, Tregare felt full trust in him. And a good thing, too, because *Inconnu* was short one Control officer. Not in body but in function: Druffel, groundside, had tried a local competitive variation of downhill ski racing, and now had one leg in a cast from waist to ankle. Maybe a couple of drinks too many and maybe not; only the result mattered, so Bran didn't ask.

What he did was call a meeting of officers, in hospital which

was really more of an infirmary, and invited Limmer also.
Deverel was on watch along with Erdis Blaine and could hold
the job down alone long enough for the necessary talk, Bran
felt. Arriving while Eda Ghormley was still fussing over
Druffel's complaints about the way the cast itched, Bran waited
for the others to get there.

When everyone was on hand—and Druffel wasn't in such
bad shape that people couldn't find seating on the edge of his
bed—Tregare opened the proceedings. "While Second Hat Al
Druffel is out of commission I want to appoint Derek Limmer,
here, as Acting Second." He paused. "Any comments?"

Gonnelson said, "He held First." No more; he'd said it all.

Tregare nodded. "True. But I'm not demoting my own
people."

Erdis Blaine frowned. "Why Acting? I mean, I know it's
temporary, until Al's back fit for duty, but—"

Low-voiced as always, Limmer spoke. "Because permanent
ranks carry shares with them; I know that much. And I
brought nothing with me, from the *Attila*, that would enable
me to buy in."

Waiting until he saw that no one else had anything to say,
Tregare wrapped it up. "Then it's settled. And Derek—your
time as Acting Second will earn you work-credit shares in
Inconnu at that rank's rate. All right?" Some nods, no
objections. "Adjourned."

The UET trip-sked handed to Tregare on Hardnose had the
Tamurlaine going next to Johnson's Walk. But the hell with
that; scanning Monteffial's list of Hidden Worlds' descriptions
and coordinates, Bran changed course—out of detection range
from Hardnose but still at such low-vee that the change cost
little in terms of fuel—and headed for a planet called
Freedom's Ring. According to the list it had a lot of Escaped
traffic, and Tregare wanted all the information he could get.

So *Inconnu* built vee. And Bran looked at the circuit
modification diagrams he'd got from Landis on New Hope. It
was about time he did that, for Landis had a good thing here.
The trouble with ships' projectors, as Bran already knew, was
that the heterodyne was off-peak at the start, drifted through
peak for five or six shots and then went off the other way,
weakening again. Landis had circuitry that gave the gunner
control over the heterodyne frequency—peace take it, that
gunner could *stay* at peak energy. If the thing worked.

Tregare put Deverel on the modification job, handing him the specs, and letting him pick his own work crew. And a couple of days after turnover, listened while the small man explained the modified turret controls, and tried them out. They worked!

Took a little getting used to, though. Tregare sat in at Turret Six on some sims Deverel had improvised. You still had your range lights, for convergence, to keep unlit, and the hand lever for that function. And still the override pedal for desperation shots. But now, between the range lights, Tregare faced a small screen that lit up with a glowing ellipse. When heterodyne frequency was perfect, you had a circle. Off either way, the circle tilted, became an ellipse, and what you had to do was push your other handlever against that tilt, ease it back. Took a bit of doing, to learn the coordination, double observation and both hands, but after a while Bran thought he had the idea. At the end of the sim run he pushed up out of the gunner's seat, and turned to face Deverel.

"Hain," he said, "between you and Landis, I think we can shoot UET's ass off. If ever we get the chance."

Sooner than he expected, that chance came. Off-duty, coming out of the shower, he heard his intercom chime and went to answer it. "Captain?" Some rating talking; Tregare didn't recognize the voice. "Come up here? There's a ship overhauling us."

Half-wet, half-dry, he pulled on pants and shoes, and ran upship to Control. Gonnelson had the watch, but Erdis Blaine was there too, and it was she who explained, pointing to the main screen that pretty much told its own story. ". . . still on accel, captain, but the speeds are close; it'll be a relatively slow pass. Slight skew in our courses but not enough to shorten the contact period. And as you can see—"

"Yeah." Tregare nodded. "I see it's armed. So one gets you twenty, it's UET."

Blaine moved over to give him the aux pilot seat. Gonnelson had started to vacate the main one but Bran wasn't going to take over from his First Hat. Not that blatantly, anyway. He turned to the comm board. "Any calls coming yet?"

"Signals, yes, sir. But not strong enough to read yet."

"Stay on it." The woman nodded, fiddling with her tuning knobs. As voice tones grew toward intelligibility, Bran waited. ". . . the *Tamurlaine*. For the *Hannibal*, Commodore

Sherman calling the *Tamurlaine*. Come in, Rigueres, you old war horse! If you're still a captain, you owe me a bottle!"

A *commodore*? This one would know too much to be fooled by the ship's usual cover story. So fake it! But how much? Well, for starters: "First Officer Tregare speaking for Captain Farnsworth, who will be up to greet you if there's time. Sir, I'm sure Commodore Rigueres would congratulate you on equalling his rank, but you'll have to compare promotion dates to see who won your bet, and I'm afraid I have no exact data for you, sir."

"You don't, eh?" Now, inset on the screen along with the picture of the accelerating *Hannibal* facing *Inconnu* on decel, the commodore appeared: a lean-faced man with a mustache waxed into toothpick-length spears. The man scowled. "Answer me two questions, First Officer! Name your last two ports of call, and your next destination. And fast!"

Without even a star map, Bran couldn't begin to invent a plausible set of routes. He shook his head. "Begging your pardon, sir, but without the captain's authorization . . ." He let it trail off, hoping to stall a little. This pass couldn't last forever.

Not much luck. The commodore's voice raised to a shout. "To the *Tamurlaine*—I order you, a *direct order*, damn it!—to cut your Drive. *Now!* The *Hannibal* will match velocities and dock air lock extensions with you. Then we'll see what's going on."

Tregare panicked. "Sir . . . I can't . . . the captain's authority . . ." He knew he was dithering but couldn't think what to do.

"You will do it," the commodore yelled, "or I'll blow you out of space!"

Bran's thoughts came together. He looked to Gonnelson. "How long until they're into effective range?"

"A minute. Less."

Tregare was out of the seat and moving. "Swing us to *point* straight at them. No time to mess with traverse, but hook all six turrets to slave on Six. I'm going up there."

Protests came but he overrode them. "Gonnelson, you drive this ship! Blaine, feed me a running report up to Turret Six. And right now, everybody *shut up!*"

Then he ran.

In Turret Six he found the function switch on Simulation, thanked something or other for the time he'd had to correct that mistake once before, strapped into his seat, and activated his gunnery position. No bother with Tinhead-the-computer fiddling with traverses; Gonnelson had *Inconnu* headed dead-on, and heterodyne was warming up as Tregare batted the other control back and forth, while he got the feel of his range lights.

He felt a jar; the *Hannibal* was firing. He got a circle on the middle screen, held it, and wiggled the controls until both range lights went dead. The odd part was that only a tiny indicator light told him he was firing. Then Blaine's voice came. "Oh my God, Tregare! You got them. You blew that ship apart!"

Stiff-legged with soreness incurred somehow when he wasn't noticing, Tregare went downship to Control. "All right," he said. Tell me what happened. No screens up there, y'know."

"Better," said Gonnelson. "Show you. Tape." He switched the forward view to an aux screen; on the main one Tregare saw the *Hannibal* approach, swinging to screen-center as Gonnelson had turned *Inconnu* for dead-on aim.

Incredibly fast, the *Hannibal's* image grew. Then, between the two ships came flashing bursts, as UET's gunner strove for accurate beam convergence; Bran couldn't see the twin UV beams, and the lights vanished as heterodyne went into the peak-heat infra-red range. Suddenly the picture jerked and jiggled; almost, Tregare could feel again *Inconnu's* shudder at the impact. Sheer radiation pressure, that was! "—much more time," Erdis Blaine was saying, "and they'd have got us."

Flashes going the other way now. "That's where *you* started shooting," the woman said, unnecessarily, as a little behind the *Hannibal's* turreted nose, blinding bursts of plasma erupted. "Dead on into Control," she said. "The Drive didn't blow, but—"

He wasn't listening now; he saw the other ship go into a slow pinwheeling motion toward the screen's edge. Cargo holds, under his fire, exploded. Just before the *Hannibal* went off-screen, two specks, showing Drive radiation, left it and also vanished. "Scouts," said Gonnelson. "Got away."

"Which direction?" Tregare asked. As Blaine figured the defining angles, Bran shook his head. "That was in real time, wasn't it? Up in the turret, seemed to take a lot longer."

Blaine quoted her figures now. "A UET colony off that way, I think," said Derek Limmer. "I've seen the listing but don't remember the name or coordinates."

"Close enough, they might make it?" Tregare asked.

Limmer peered at him. "I wonder how you mean that."

Bran shrugged. "I mean, I hope they do. But sure as hell we can't go picking up after UET's mistakes."

"The *Hannibal*," said Gonnelson.

"You can't worry about that one, Tregare," Blaine protested. "It went spinning off our screens before you got back down here."

Well, sure, it *would*. Up at these speeds, a very little bit of Drive change could make a lot of distance in a big hurry. Bran shrugged. "Sherman was the one, wouldn't let it go."

Derek Limmer blinked. His scarred face made the sneering grimace that Bran knew he meant for a smile. "One thing's certain, captain. If any from the *Hannibal* get back to UET, you'll have a new nickname. . . . Tregare, the Pirate."

Limmer was there to relieve Blaine from watch; she'd stayed over, was all, but finally left. Tregare remained longer, talking and winding down, then stopped for a galley snack before he headed for quarters and sleep. He found the captain's digs lighted only enough so that a man wouldn't trip over the furniture. In the big bed, slight sounds of fuzzy breathing came from Erdis Blaine, who hadn't moved out yet.

Tregare hit the bathroom and then came out to go to bed.

Maybe he should find out about Blaine—and about himself. He climbed in, turned and put a hand to Erdis Blaine's shoulder. "You awake?" In case the guess was wrong, he said it softly.

"Yes. And I sort of expected you tonight, Tregare."

"How's that?" The idea was going sour already.

"You're the kingbird now. Don't you need to celebrate?"

Celebrate making death? Not hardly. But he pulled her to him. "No, Blaine. It's like the time, a while back; I told you, you needed a cuddle. Now *I* do. So get you over here."

But one of these days . . . It's been too damn long.

11

". . . Like Hogan's Goat"

When he and Blaine did become lovers, about three days
short of Freedom's Ring, it happened almost by accident. He
came half-awake to find himself somewhat entangled with the
woman, and more than somewhat aroused. Her hands had
something to do with it, and his own, moving more or less by
instinct or habit, weren't quite idle either. Jolted into
wakefulness, Tregare at first felt annoyance: was she trying to
seduce him in his sleep? Then he saw that Erdis Blaine wasn't
fully awake either. Smiling then, he saw to it that she was quite
aware of what was going on.

When he finally decided he couldn't manage still another
time, he sat up and said, "Sure worth the wait. For me,
anyway." She gave him wordless agreement, and with that
reassurance, suddenly his mind turned to the matter of
hunger. "What you like for breakfast?" She told him; he
nodded. "Same here," and he got on the intercom, to the effect
that a few minutes later he accepted delivery of a breakfast tray
from the galley. Since he had shoved all the papers to one side
of his work table, they had a place to eat. "Enough eggs? How's
the sausage?"

After swallowing, Blaine said, "Plenty. And fine."

Bran laughed. "We ought to eat this way more often. If your
watch sked and my routines ever synch better." Then, when
they'd finished the coffee, it was time to get dressed and go to
work.

They kissed first, though and she said, "Tregare? Now we
have to talk a lot, really get to know each other."

"I think we do already—all this time living around the edges
of us. But you're on, Blaine."

181

"Erdis."

"Oh, yeah . . . right. Erdis."

Except for a near absence of axial tilt, Freedom's Ring was quite like Earth—in size, gravity, and mean temperatures as determined by the characteristics and distance of its primary. "Main difference," said Tregare, holding court in Control with all his Hats in attendance, "is lack of seasonal changes. You want summer, head toward the equator. Winter, head away from it. The seasonal climates sort of stay put. Lucky for people, the main island chain slants across the equator, with snow on one end but not quite so cold on the other."

The ship hit what should have been hailing distance, but this Hidden World had no beacon radiating any message. Or not right now, at least. So Tregare decided he should open communications.

Well within detection range if anybody happened to be watching—and with the screen on hi-mag, he could spot settlements but hadn't yet figured which ones might have spaceports—he got on the horn to groundside. "The ship *Inconnu*. Bran Tregare, captain, speaking for *Inconnu*. Calling groundside. Come in, please, Freedom's Ring." No answer yet. "I got your coordinates from Ezra Drake, the Security chief on New Hope. Part of the list he had from Cade Moaker on *Cut Loose Charlie*." Pause. "Freedom's Ring. *Inconnu* here. Come in, please."

After a time the aux screen flickered and lit, as a voice built volume until words came clear. ". . . about the delay, *Inconnu*. We've been reading you, though. We have no listing on the man Drake but Cade Moaker has been here and we do know of New Hope. So if you'll ready a tape input for fast-feed, I will transmit directions for your setdown. Please acknowledge."

Once Tregare's comm operator had complied, Bran said, "Ready." And watched as the digital data ran the screen full of eye-hurting blips—because the operator hadn't disengaged the two functions. Hmmm . . . ex-cadet Hank Cameron would wait a time for his next promotion.

Ideologies, Tregare thought, made nomenclature rather predictable. Located not quite far enough from the equator if you weren't too fond of hot weather, the main spaceport of Freedom's Ring was named Liberty Port. Tregare, handling

the controls himself, landed without incident. Well, just for
the hell of it he came down a little bit slaunchwise, off-target,
and "walked" the ship a hundred meters or so to the
designated landing circle. In response to the port's squawks,
he apologized. When Blaine jumped him about it, and
Gonnelson asked, "Why?" Tregare said, "I needed to know if I
could do that. I found out."

Jonny Payce, in charge of Liberty Port, looked surprisingly
young for the job. On closer inspection Tregare decided the
looks were a little deceiving. The short, sandy-haired man was
simply one of a type that holds age well.

In Payce's office, with Limmer and Erdis Blaine accompany-
ing Tregare, they shared a snack and some drinks with the
administrator and two of his aides. Compared to New Hope,
this place conducted negotiations casually and quickly. In
about half an hour, most of the buying and selling of cargo
items was tentatively settled. "Subject to confirmation check,"
Payce said. He hitched his chair around, so he could stretch
his legs. "Captain? Do you have your next destination picked
yet?"

Tregare set down his empty wine glass, savoring the faintly
spicy aftertaste. The younger aide refilled it. "Not for sure.
Why?"

"You've heard of Number One?" Bran had, so he nodded.
Maybe not the first Hidden World ever established, but one of
the early ones—and now, because of an odd development, the
most heavily populated by far. "You know the story?" Bran did,
but this time he restrained the nod and raised his eyebrows.
Maybe Payce knew more on the subject; it could pay to listen.
The man flexed his knees, pulling his feet back so he could lean
forward. "The damnedest thing. When the *Churchill* made its
Escape, it was carrying among other things a load of frozen
sperm and ova plus an experimental batch of pre-fertilized
zygotes, also in freeze, intended to produce cheap labor for the
mines on Iron Hat. And zoom-wombs to incubate them too,
from zygote to infant in less than two months. You hadn't heard
that?"

"Just rumors," said Derek Limmer. "It's true, then?"

"Right. And when the *Churchill* landed on Number One,
the oligarchs there saw a chance to up population by a couple
of decimal places in a hurry, and they went for it. Insisted on
trading for the entire lot, or no refueling."

Tregare cleared his throat. "Two decimal places? Just how did they handle that many little kids, all at once?"

Payce laughed. "With difficulty, or so I've heard."

"Interesting," said Bran. "But what's the point? With regard to us, I mean?"

"Just that if you're not already set on going someplace else next, I have a standing contract to send certain types of cargo to Number One, any chance I get." He shrugged. "Some rare earth ores they're short on, some food-grain seed to vary their farm output—things like that. And they pay bonus rates, which you and we here would share." Tregare felt his skepticism showing, but Payce said, "Tregare, we never cheat a ship. Some places have tried it, and the word always gets around. And Escaped ships stick up for each other; we know that. Cheating bounces back."

Digesting the new knowledge, Bran said, "On Number One, who would I deal with? These oligarchs, you say. Any names?"

Jonny Payce cleared his throat. "I don't think there's any centralized governing body, as such. The whole thing sounds somewhat like feudalism in the Middle Ages on Earth. At any rate, my contracts are specifically with Hulzein Lodge, and that clan handles the dealings on Number One, from then on."

Hulzein? Bran's entire body went taut; he fought to relax, not to show his reaction. When he thought he could control his voice, he tried to think what to say.

Payce beat him to it: "I don't know how much you've heard about the Hulzein Establishment in Argentina, on Earth. You see—" Tregare halfway quit listening; for one thing, this Payce had his facts more than half wrong. But—". . . not a direct branch out of Argentina, I understand, but a semi-independent operation. A Hulzein 'connection,' I think it's called. Headed by a woman named Liesel Hulzein."

So that's where they went. "Yes. I've heard of that one." He thought about it. Number One, with its larger population, sounded like a place he needed to see. Already he'd found that New Hope and Freedom's Ring didn't have the facilities or the know-how for problems such as repairing the power suit he'd wrecked in retaking the ship from Farnsworth's gang. Though the areas of strength and weakness in expertise were spotty. Entering this Port Admin building, for instance, he'd heard some people discussing, knowledgeably, the problems of stabilizing a Nielson cube, the heart of a starship's Drive. Confusing . . .

Payce still talked. At his next pause, Tregare said, "Number One sounds like a good bet, all right. Sure—let's work out the money angle, and I'll take your load there."

I'll deal with my family. I won't meet with them, is all. Because the hurt, from when they'd abandoned him to UET's Slaughterhouse, was still too great. The conscious rejection he'd had to make there, to free himself from tempting dreams of his home, heartbreaking when he woke, was solid in him. Dammit, they *could* have rescued him: surely Liesel had Underground and New Mafia contacts that could have worked for her even after she and Hawkman and Sparline left Earth. She *could* have done . . .

Reason tried to tell him that maybe Erika's surveillance had been too tight for any such action—but he was having none of reason. The old emotions, the old bitterness, still gripped him too hard.

By effort he shook himself free of it, and paid heed to Jonny Payce and Derek Limmer.

Leaving Admin, the three walked back toward *Inconnu*. There was another ship in port, standing off to one side. Jonny Payce hadn't mentioned it, so Tregare hadn't done any asking. He looked across the landing area, squinting past his own ship at the other one. Its insignia looked faded, but that had to be sheer pummeling from random encounters with interstellar dust; he could still make out the name and graphic emblem: *Spiral Nebula*.

On impulse, Bran stopped. "An idea. You want to look in on this ship, say hello?"

Erdis shook her head. "I'm overdue to relieve Gonnelson on watch. Actually, he took mine." Sure, the man who hated to talk had traded watches, so he wouldn't have to come visiting.

"Sure; okay." Tregare turned. "How about you, Limmer?"

The scarred man gestured assent. "Why not, Tregare?" So Blaine walked off to *Inconnu*, and the men went to the other ship. At the foot of *Spiral Nebula*'s ramp they found no guard. Looking up they saw a woman, uniformed but hatless, and gun set leaning to one side, lounging at the air lock hatch. "Looks sloppy," Limmer said, "but let's not judge too soon."

"Right," Tregare said, but he'd already made judgment

because he couldn't help doing it—and so, he suspected, had Derek Limmer.

They climbed the ramp. The surprising thing was how long it took the woman to notice them. On drugsticks? Probably. When they were only a few stairsteps below her she suddenly gasped, grabbed for her gun and nearly dropped it, then aimed it in a way that made Tregare uneasy. "Stop right there! What the hell do you think you're doing?"

There was no time to argue; the knuckle of her trigger finger was white. Tregare pitched his voice to carry. "Ten-HUT!" And the woman came to attention, holding her gun at a position that resembled Inspection Arms but didn't quite make it. "At ease," Tregare said, and then, "Would you please call your captain, and ask if he will accept a visit from Captain Tregare and Second Hat Limmer of *Inconnu*, just landed today?"

He saw the light disorientation, from the drugsticks, leave her. Her hands relaxed; she put the gun aside. "Oh—? Yes, sir. Sorry, sir. I—just a moment, please." She got on the horn, then, keeping it in hush mode so that Tregare caught not a word of what was said, until she hung up. Then she said, "Welcome aboard, sirs. There'll be an escort down soon, to show you up to Captain Marrigan."

While they waited, Tregare looked around. The plastic underfoot was worn, through in places to the metal deck. The bulkheads, both the plastic-covered sections and the bare anodized metal, bore greasy smudges that looked as if they'd been there a long time. The deck part he could understand; this was an older ship and things do wear out. But the poor maintenance . . . mentally he shrugged. None of his business.

A heavy-set, thirtyish Chief rating clattered down the main stairs and came to greet them. He was ruddy of face and spoke loudly; Bran couldn't decide whether the fellow's manner was joviality or bluster, but gave benefit of the doubt. "My name's Corbett, gentlemen. The skipper's ready to see you now, if you'll follow me."

On the stairs the first handrail was loose; up the well came a faint scent of leaking gases. Refrigerant from the second stage of cryogenic environment for the Nielson cube, Bran recognized. The smell was only a faint trace; maybe someone had been changing a fitting or two.

Still it bothered Tregare: when, on *Spiral Nebula*, was he going to find something in *good* shape?

* * *

Captain's digs seemed cluttered, but comfortable enough. The man inside stood. "Brooks Marrigan, captain of *Spiral Nebula*. Used to be the *Wellington*, but of course that's a long time ago."

As they shook hands, Tregare gave his own name. "—captain of *Inconnu*, which until recently was the *Tamurlaine* and still bears that insignia. And my Second Hat here, Derek Limmer, who jumped ship off the *Attila*, back at Hardnose."

"Pleased, gentlemen. Something to drink, will you have?" They accepted, and at least the booze was good. Sitting, then, the three men traded news—always a preoccupation of spacers, Bran thought, living by the Long View as they did.

It wasn't that Marrigan sounded old, or looked it, but that he sounded like a defeated man. He perked up, though, when Tregare related the destruction of the *Hannibal*. "An armed ship, you have, Tregare? For our side, I think that's a first. Or do you know of others?"

As Limmer shook his head, Bran said "No." Before Marrigan could say more, Tregare got to the subject that was really bothering him. "Marrigan—is this ship in trouble?" He'd dealt with enough cadets to know when someone was trying to figure how to duck a question, so he cut in quickly. "Are you broke, or what?"

"Not—well, I—oh, hell!" Slumping back in his chair, Marrigan said, "Four trips ago. Up to then we'd been doing fine. But I put in at Dixie Belle and did an almost total swap of cargo there, and the bastards skinned us. They knew, and I didn't, that the bottom had dropped out of the market, for most of what they sold me. And since then, it's been like trying to play poker, table stakes, and down to your bare ass."

Tregare's thinking moved fast. "Maybe we could make a deal."

But Marrigan wasn't done telling his grievance. "I should have stayed with safe goods, but they said we could make a killing." He leaned forward. "Do you know—Tregare, Limmer?—on that world they countenance slavery? Just like UET's Total Welfare, except that Dixie Belle doesn't bother to put the fancy name to it. Somebody ought to—Tregare, your armed ship—you should—"

Limmer cut in. "Not necessary, not now. On Hardnose, hiding out, I heard what happened there on Dixie Belle." With a good sense of timing, or so Tregare guessed, the Second Hat waited until he had full attention, then said, "Dominguez, on *Buonatierra*, took offense at that aspect of Dixie Belle's system. He laid down an ultimatum: abolish slavery. He was laughed at, and told that *Bonnie* wouldn't be refueled." He made the smile that looked like a sneer. "Dominguez didn't have fuel for a real trip, but he was by no means dry in the tanks. He gave warning, of a sort—if they wanted to keep their town, they'd do things his way. 'Frig it off,' he was told. So the man lifted *Buonatierra* about fifty meters, held it there, squandering fuel like mad, then tilted and walked his Drive across the major government complex and the rich part of the city where the major slaveowners lived. And landed alongside the refueling facility. Nobody argued."

Marrigan looked pale. "But—didn't he kill a lot of innocent people? How can you condone that?"

"What choice did he have?" Tregare's voice came flat. "All the weapon he had was the Drive. It was use it or don't. Me, I agree with Dominguez."

"Well, actually," said Limmer, "the area he pulverized turned out to be highly underpopulated. The slaveowners thought he was bluffing and stood fast, but others had better sense, and vamoosed."

Tregare laughed. "Derek, you know how to wrap up a story with a ribbon around it!" Then, serious again, "Marrigan, what's your problem here? The bones of it." The man stayed silent. Irritated, Bran went on. "I said already, maybe we could help."

Marrigan sighed. "The Drive's bad—the Nielson cube and its support gear. Maybe it'll last the next trip, maybe not."

"So? I heard they have some here. And repair facilities."

The other man shook his head. "But I can't afford it. If we pay that, we can still buy fuel—just barely—but then at our next stop we'll have no assets left for trade. Or not enough."

Pausing first, Tregare said, "What if I buy you a new Drive?"

Walking back toward *Inconnu*, Bran said, "The trouble is, Limmer, the man's not realistic. I didn't ask much of a handle for our ship's money—just the promise of cooperation, later, on an operation I haven't even figured out yet, all the way. But he wouldn't budge."

"Maybe I wouldn't, either. How far *have* you figured it?"

Bran turned to face his Second Hat. "That one day I twist UET's tail like it's never been done. It'll take a bunch of ships to do it, so I have to start lining 'em up, one way or the other. . . . Use the grapevine, the mail drops, whatever. Buy in, take over, make agreements . . . *I* don't know what all, yet. I—"

"Tregare?" Bran stopped talking, and listened. "For what it's worth, I've changed my mind. In Marrigan's shoes I'd take your offer. But he's wearing them, not me."

Back on *Inconnu*, Tregare couldn't let the idea go. He paced his quarters, wishing Blaine weren't on watch, so he could bounce ideas at her and get feedback. But when he called her up in Control, all he said was, "Can you put me through to Jonny Payce, please?"

"Right, skipper." And in a few minutes Payce came on screen.

"Tregare here, Mr. Payce—or do you hold a rank I should use?"

The man chuckled. "Technically I guess I'm a commodore, though I've never served as a ship's officer. But 'mister' is all right. Call me anything—"

"—except late for dinner!" Both men laughed, then Tregare said, "You have Nielson cubes, and the means to install or repair them. Right?" Payce nodded. "What do the cost figures look like?"

Hearing the numbers, Bran whistled. Payce said, "Yes, I realize that's more than twice what costs would be on Earth. But we're not gouging. We have one new Nielson and one that's used but totally reconditioned here, and equal to new; I'd ride with it any time. And the figures—our markups, figuring parts and trouble-shooting and research, as well as normal labor—runs to slightly under twenty percent. We're heavily invested in these items, and they're scarce. Who knows when we'll get another?"

Tregare grinned. "Right away, maybe. What kind of trade-in can you offer on a cube that landed safe and is still chilled?"

"Forty percent of total job cost." No hesitation; this, then, wasn't an item up for dickering. "But where—? I mean, I didn't realize your Drive needed any major work."

"It doesn't. Thanks, commodore. I'll get back to you."

* * *

The money part would work. *Inconnu* could afford to fix
Spiral Nebula's Drive and to help a little with seed-money to
put the cargo business on a paying basis. What was bothering
Tregare, now, was the Marrigan part.

Over dinner in quarters, he and Erdis Blaine kicked the
problem around. But not right after her watch. First they went
to bed, and there she liked to take her time. Well, so did he.

She said, "The man won't give you any commitment, for his
ship to join in helping you someday?"

Headshake. "It's his ship. Nobody else gets any say in it."

"Then what can you do? If he just lifts anyway, I mean?"

"Who says I have to let him?"

A couple of times Tregare tried to talk with Brooks
Marrigan; finally he realized he wasn't getting anywhere.
When the other ship's cargo was fully loaded, Bran knew he
had to move. Hain Deverel, on the comm board up in Control,
put the call through.

"Marrigan? Tregare here. We need to talk."

On screen the man looked haunted by devils. "Nothing to
say, Captain. Except what we all say: good landings. Because
Spiral Nebula lifts in about two hours."

Tregare beat his fist on his chair. "You *can't*. Marrigan, your
Drive's not up to it. If you take that ship out, two to one you
lose it, and you're all dead."

"That's my business, I think. And—"

"Have you taken a vote, polled your crew? Do *they* want to
gamble on your insane pride?"

He'd gone too far there, Bran saw; Marrigan was ready to
cut the circuit. Quickly Tregare said, "Don't cut! Because
there's one more thing you need to know." Waiting, he said
nothing else.

Until Marrigan answered, "I don't understand. *I* need to
know?"

Tregare sank the hook. "Yeah, you do. And so does your
crew. You wouldn't have the guts, though, to pipe me on your
all-ship broadcast circuit. I might say something you wouldn't
like."

The intercom sounded; Deverel said, "Commodore Payce

on the line, captain. Picked up one side of the argument, I think. He—"

Caught between tension and amusement, Tregare said, "Oh, what the hell, Deverel; patch him in. Conference circuit—the more the merrier." And when Payce appeared as an inset on the screen, Bran said, "Hi, commodore. You're coming in at the middle, so could you please just listen now, and I'll explain later?"

Payce started to speak, then nodded, as from *Spiral Nebula* Brooks Marrigan said, "My crew can hear anything I can. Speak your piece, Tregare."

All right! "Bran Tregare here, on the armed ship *Inconnu*, to all personnel of *Spiral Nebula*. Your Drive's no good; if you lift with it, as it is, you're all dead."

Screaming, Marrigan: "That's your opinion! I—"

"It's an opinion I can enforce."

"What do you mean?" Marrigan, sounding not quite so sure.

"I mean, you lift, you'll never reach vacuum. I'll blow you before you get there. Six turrets; you don't stand a chance."

Payce stuck an oar in. "You can't do that!"

"Try me," said Tregare. Intense now, wound up to busting, he yelled, "Damn you, Marrigan! We're so few, the Escaped Ships! We can't spare any; I can't let you waste yours."

"But you can essay to kill us all?"

Now almost sure of his ground, Tregare said, "Ask your crew, Marrigan. See if you can get your people to do a lift for you. I don't think you can."

"So that's it!" Well, Jonny Payce, at least, had caught on. Marrigan's voice came as a growl. "This is piracy."

And now Tregare could relax. "Not a bit of it, Captain Marrigan. Consider yourself overruled, is all. I'm quite willing—determined, in fact—to buy you out, based on your own computer estimate of the ship's assets. And to buy out any who want to get off with you as well." Fast thinking, now. "Those who want to stay with the ship, and work with the command cadre I'll be installing, are welcome. And when you lift, it'll be with a solid Drive system. I guarantee that."

He was guessing, by this time, the costs and credits, and where the deal would leave *Inconnu* in the assets column. But *he wanted this ship.* Imagining the chaos on it right now, he waited.

In Marrigan's voice when he finally answered, there was no mistaking the sadness. "If it were only me, Tregare, I'd blow

the Drive and you with it, sitting so close, and the hell with
you. But not my people. And . . . and not, I find, my ship,
either. I can't work under you or anyone else, not these days so
I couldn't accept your offer of alliance. But"—well, maybe he
hiccuped—"I'll get off. You can buy me out. *And damn you to
bloody hell, Tregare!*"

No answer at all seemed the kindest thing.

A few more than twenty left *Spiral Nebula* with its captain.
Tregare, along with Gonnelson and Limmer, interviewed
personnel on *Inconnu* to work up the command cadre. At the
same time they recruited replacements from groundside, most
for *Inconnu* but a few for the other ship. It began to seem,
Tregare thought, that any ship was better off running over-
crewed than the other way.

Nebula's Drive was almost ready. Old Mallory stood in to
help that ship's Chief Engineer study the fine tuning after the
new Nielson cube was in place. The groundside techs knew
their stuff, sure—but it wasn't the same as making adjustments
when you were running at a t/t_o of maybe twenty. Or was it the
other way around? Well, symbols or not, Tregare knew what
he meant.

The "trade-in" of *Nebula's* Nielson cube was the item that
put Tregare's dealings in the black. Without it, he'd have run
Inconnu's assets down too thin. As it was, *Nebula* would have
to deal close to the vest for a trip or two, but it was no longer in
real trouble. And *Inconnu* had shed a little surplus, was all.

The main problem, though, Tregare hadn't tackled yet.

When he called Gonnelson down to captain's quarters for
the talk, Erdis Blaine stayed away. Both she and Bran knew
that the First Hat's trouble with talking was even worse with
women present.

Gonnelson came in, nodded, muttered some kind of greeting, and accepted the one drink which was all he would take on
any given occasion. He sat down, and looked at Bran Tregare.

Bran said, "*Spiral Nebula*. It's your command, if you want it.
You're first in line and you're damned good with a ship. I know
you have trouble talking, but your Hats can help with that
stuff. I—"

"*No!*" First time Bran had ever seen the man throw a drink
down in one gulp. Gonnelson shook his head. "Not command.
No."

"Why? Tell me why. You have to." Headshake. Bran said, "This is one time you're taking a second drink, and that's an order." He poured it, and Gonnelson took one sip. "Now tell me."

It took a while and it didn't come easy. Haltingly, a few words at a time, between repeated questions from Tregare, the man told his story.

"Had it."

"Command? You had command?" Nod. "Where? Did you take it willingly?" Headshake. "*Where*, dammit?"

"Slaughterhouse."

"You were in officers' training? I didn't know that. When?"

"No. Combat cadre." Okay—Tregare knew about those. They were a Slaughterhouse sideline, for ratings, not officers, and—suddenly Bran's indrawn breath hissed as he made a gasp. The training maneuvers!

He said, carefully, "They put you into command for a combat exercise?" Nod. "They use live ammo for those, don't they?" Gonnelson's face made any other answer needless. Tregare winced, as he said, "How big a command? A platoon, or what? And what happened? What the hell *happened?*"

"Ambush. Whole cadre." The man's shoulders had begun to shake and heave. "Lost nearly whole *cadre* . . . dead."

Wishing he'd never started this questioning, now Tregare had to follow through with it. "That can happen. But how? *Why?*"

"Orders. Right orders. Knew them. Couldn't *say* in time." Gonnelson didn't seem to notice the tears running down his face. Shaking his head, he looked ready to throw up. "Not command! Please?"

"All right." Tregare went to him, hugging the man's head to his shoulder. "If you can't, you can't. You're one hell of a good First Hat, though; you know that?" Gonnelson's body had been shaking; the movement eased. Tregare said, "I still think you earned your second drink." He sat back and raised his own. "Cheers, First?"

After a moment Gonnelson said, "Cheers," and drank.

So time to call conference, all the Hat's Captain's digs had the most ease, so that's where Tregare gathered his people. With everyone seated and comfortable, comestibles handy, he began.

"*Inconnu* now owns a chunk of *Spiral Nebula*. Well, you all know that. Thing is, we've set up a command cadre to run it for us, but nobody's in charge yet." He looked around the group. "Gonnelson was first in line but he declined, and his reasons are his own business. So I guess you're next, Limmer. Can we deal here?"

The scarred man blinked, and said, "If you mean, will I honor your call on that ship's services—something you mentioned after our first visit with Marrigan—yes, you have my word on that. There's one problem. Working in the Long View, how do you let me know what's wanted, and when?"

To Bran Tregare the question was nothing new. "The grapevine, Limmer. The mail drops. Passing computer info at every landing, and between ships that come into comm range." He shook himself loose from tension. "Look . . . I *know* the odds are bad, hitting enough contacts by way of the Long View to put anything together in one place at one time." Even to him it sounded hopeless. So he laughed. "So if I need to get six ships together, I'll try for sixty. Or more. There'll be ships Escaping, we haven't even heard of. So don't worry, Limmer. If you aren't with me when I pull off the coup I haven't even figured out yet . . . well, somebody will be."

When Derek Limmer laughed, the sneer left his smile. He raised his glass. "Tregare . . . I hope I'll be there."

"One more thing," Bran asked. "You renaming the ship?"

"I hadn't decided. Why? Aside for future IDs, of course."

Tregare held his laughter. "The shape that bucket was in, I thought of calling it '. . . *Like Hogan's Goat.*' But now—"

"No," said Limmer. "Now it's *not* fucked up." He chuckled. "Still, though . . . Tregare, what would you say to *Lefthand Thread?*"

Huh? Pause. "Hey . . . I *like* it!"

For the refurbished ship's lift-off, Tregare threw a good party in *Inconnu*'s galley. He missed the lift itself by sleeping through it. A time later, the intercom brought him awake. "Yeah?"

"Captain?" Some rating on the horn; the name escaped him now. "A ship coming in, close to comm range. You want to speak to it?"

He sat up. "Why? We got a problem?"

"Not that I know of, sir. But I thought I'd ask."

"Thanks. But if we don't know 'em, I expect we can wait 'til they get set down." Another thought came. "You get anything says maybe there *is* a problem, call me five minutes ago. Okay?"

"Yes, Captain." Tregare cut the circuit and started to lie back for a little more sleep. But Erdis Blaine had awakened and was sitting up. It turned out that she had a better idea.

The incoming ship was newly Escaped and now called itself *March Hair*. It came in on awkward trajectory and did not land well. Nothing serious, but Tregare wouldn't have allowed that pilot to set *his* ship down. Expecting the usual exchange of courtesies, he waited in quarters a while, but no message came, so Bran went down to the galley and ate more breakfast than he really needed, because his appetite felt like it. He was dawdling over an excess of coffee when the officers'-table intercom squawked at him. "Is there an officer available in the galley? There is none in Control just now. We have a request, an officer off the *March Hair* who wants to talk with the captain. And says it's urgent. Is there—?"

Tregare hit the switch. "Captain here. Send—I mean, *escort* this other ship's officer to the galley. I'll be here." He didn't need any more coffee but he ordered another pot anyway. Then he waited.

The person the guards brought in wasn't wearing officer's uniform, exactly; it was sort of a mix. But that didn't matter. Bran stood; without thinking, he yelled welcome. Because the man coming in was Jargy Hoad.

"Bran! Tregare! What luck!" They were hugging, shouting, pounding each other around the edges with no intent to hurt.

Tregare it was who first came to caution. "Yeah, good to see you; glad you're here. But what *is* this?" He held them both still. "What's wrong, Jargy?"

Hoad didn't look much older, and seemed still good-humored. "I need off that ship, is all, Bran. The wrong man came up captain—nobody's fault, it just happened. But Grecht and I have hated each other's guts the whole time. I get off, or it'll be a killing."

"Which way?"

"I think I'm faster. But that's not the point, Bran. Escape leaves a lot of strain among the survivors. Well, you'd know about that, wouldn't you? *March Hair*'s people are solid, basically, but the situation won't take any more upheavals and

still hold together. And—" He shrugged. "I think Grecht has
more folks on his side than I have on mine."

"So?" Tregare wanted Jargy to do the saying of it.

"Tregare, do you have a berth for me on here? Or would I
have to ride as supercargo?"

"Is Grecht buying you out? What Hat are you wearing?"

"Third, before Escape. First now. But Grecht only wants to
pay me off as Third, though."

Tregare knew his own grin then wasn't looking amiable. "Is
that right? You mind if I speak with your Captain Grecht? I
think I can change his mind for him."

If something works, use it. Tregare put a call through comm
to *March Hair*, identified himself, and asked for Grecht. He
expected to dislike the man on sight and was surprised to see a
pleasant-looking young man with a blond crewcut and cheerful
smile. The smile went away, though, when Bran said, "I intend
to make sure you deal fairly with my friend Jargy Hoad." He
then explained, much as he had to Brooks Marrigan, the
alternative. "So it's fifteen percent, Captain Grecht, not five. I
won't need to check your figures; Jargy know the totals. So
figure what you want to pay in cargo and how much in
Weltmarks, and if I like it, we've got us a deal."

Grecht chewed his lip. "Let me think a minute."

"Sure. Take your time." Tregare cut his audio transmission
and went to the intercom. "Watch officer. Tregare here. On the
double, get an armed squad to cover the boarding ramp, from
inside." His order acknowledged, he turned back to Jargy and
Erdis Blaine, who had just joined them. "Pure precaution. In
case Grecht got any ideas about direct action."

Blaine said, "He couldn't pull a lift on you, could he?"

Jargy Hoad chuckled. "Not hardly. He's refueling, and Bran
already knew that." Then, "Ready to talk now, Gretch is."

". . . can work it out," the other captain was saying. "Not
more than a third in money, I'm afraid. As to cargo . . ."
Grecht began citing items and quantities. Playing it off the top
of his head, Tregare made his choices, checking his own
computer extension terminal to validate pricings, and saying
yes more often than no. Sooner than Bran expected, the
dickering was done with.

Wrapping it up, he said, "Fine, Captain Grecht. Tomorrow
we can sign papers and take delivery." The call ended, and
Bran said, "I told you, Jargy, I could change his mind."

"Sure," said Hoad. "And thanks. But if I were you, I'd keep those armed guards at the boarding ramp."

"You're not me, lucky for you. But I will."

"That's good." Jargy nodded toward the woman. "I don't think we've met, exactly. Would you introduce us, Tregare?"

"Oh. Oh, sure. Erdis Blaine, my Third Hat. Jargy Hoad, Erdis—he and I were in the same squad room, our snotties year at the Slaughterhouse. He's going to be our new Second."

"Second?" Her face went slack, then made a frown. "But I—"

He reached for her hand, but she pulled it away. "Erdis, I know you expected Second. And if Jargy hadn't turned up, you'd have it. Or if I'd promoted you earlier—just like Gonnelson and Limmer, I wouldn't have set you back, no matter what. But, you see—Jargy's had the full Slaughterhouse, same as me. And while you're doing just fine, training and all, he's simply better qualified." Her face was tight, her expression withdrawn. "Can you accept that?"

Before she could answer, Hoad said, "A moment, here. Bran, what's *Inconnu's* going rate for Second, and for Third?" When Tregare, taking a few seconds to calculate, gave him the figures, Jargy said, "No problem. This is a rich ship; my last one wasn't. Third's all I can afford to buy in for, and glad to do it."

Still angry, Blaine said, "I'm sure the captain is willing to lend the difference to his old roomie, against your future duty credits. Welcome aboard, Second Hat."

This time Bran did capture her hand. She tugged, but he wouldn't let go. "Wrong, Blaine. Welcome our new *Third* Hat. I was sticking to my own rules a minute ago, and I still am."

Narrow-eyed, she looked at him. "You're not just doing this to soothe the spoiled brat's temper tantrum? Bran—"

Jargy Hoad's laugh broke the tension. "I'd think, Blaine, that you'd know Tregare better than that, shipping together. If you want to change his mind, pressure is absolutely the worst possible tactic."

Seeming puzzled, she said, "Then what's the best one?"

"As just now," said Hoad. "Provide new facts." He stood. "I brought a runaway's kit aboard, in case it wasn't feasible to rescue all my gear from *March Hair*. In it is something I think we might use just now. I won't be long."

As he walked away, leaving the galley, Bran leaned closer to the woman. "Don't ever think I undervalue my *new* roomie."

Then she smiled, and squeezed the hand he still had on her own.

Taking longer at his errand than Tregare expected, Hoad came back carrying a bottle of wine. Passing the serving counter he picked up glasses, then came and sat. "While I was at it," he said, "I hauled my kit upship and set it in the corridor, just outside Third's quarters." Somehow he made a ceremony of pulling an ordinary cork, then poured for the three of them. "This comes from Far Corner, a colony noted for tart and tangy wines. Sort of appropriate, I thought"—he raised his glass and waited while the others followed suit—"to toast the promotion of Erdis Blaine to Second Hat on *Inconnu.*"

They drank, and Tregare was surprised to see Blaine bushing at her eyes. She said, "It should be yours, Jargy. I—"

"Don't give it a thought. If I know Bran Tregare, and I think I do, before we're done we'll each have our own ships."

And before the wine was done, with a couple of other people joining in, the occasion became almost a party. At the end of it, Blaine said to Hoad, "You can move your gear right into Third's quarters, if you like. I have a few things in the place, which I'll get out soon, but I don't live there."

Asking no questions, Jargy said, "Sure; thanks," and left. Soon after, Tregare and Blaine went to their own quarters. Once inside, she turned and embraced him.

"Bran? I like your friend. I'm glad he's here."

"Yeah. Jargy's one of the good ones, all right."

Cash and cargo both, Jargy Hoad's shares in *March Hair* were delivered on board *Inconnu*: checked, accepted, and signed for. Grecht himself brought the packet of Weltmark certificates. When the man's entrance was announced, Bran was hosting Jargy a drink. On the intercom he said, "Escort Captain Grecht to my quarters, please."

Hoad gulped his drink, and stood. "I'll leave, if you don't mind. I've seen all I want to of that sonofabitch." He paused. "Unless you might want a little backing, Bran. He's tricky."

Tregare suppressed his laugh. "On *my* ship? Thanks anyway."

So Jargy left, and soon a rating ushered Grecht in, and also departed. The blond man had his smile back; after shaking hands he gave Tregare the heavy envelope. "You'll want to check this."

"That's right. Sit down. You'll have a drink?"

The amenities taken care of, the counting went fast, and Bran looked at this man his friend disliked so much. "The numbers check out. We're free and clear." But he was still curious. *So ask.* "Grecht . . . I've known Jargy Hoad a long time. Easygoing, I'd always thought. How come you two couldn't live on the same ship? Not that it's any of my business, come to that."

Grecht finished his drink, and stood. "Precisely. But I'll tell you, anyway. I *own* my ship, and that includes the people on it. Hoad couldn't accept the principle."

Incredulous, Tregare gazed at the man. "Neither could I."

"So you'd have sneaked off too, tail between your legs?"

No such thing had Jargy done. Two questions here. But only one answer. "No," said Tregare. "I'd have killed you."

Grecht didn't stay much longer.

12

A Job To Do

For lift-off from Freedom't Ring, Tregare gave Erdis Blaine the office. He'd have liked to have done it himself, and drift a little sidewise toward *March Hair* and maybe scare Grecht's guts out into his shorts, but that wouldn't be fair to a lot of other people, so he didn't. And Gonnelson had done a lift, and so had Jargy. It was Blaine's turn. And she did fine with it.

They headed for Number One now. Not a straight shot, because that would pass too close to a UET colony, and the course also needed a bulge to miss a dust cloud expanding from where a star had once erupted as a medium-sized nova. Tregare looked through what records he had from Escaped ships, and hoped he wasn't missing anything essential.

One item caught his notice. His totally random choice of direction in which to bulge his course would take *Inconnu* well within range of a Hidden World listed in his new information. Tregare called a conference; his Control officers plus the Chief Engineer. Holding up a rough sketch, he said, "Shegler's Moon. It's not all that far off our planned course, and close enough that if we go there we'll have a time-ratio of five at Turnover. Question is, should we have a look at the place?"

Mallory didn't care. Jargy said, "Why not?" Erdis Blaine favored the idea. Gonnelson's hand made a sweeping palm-up gesture, sidewise toward Tregare.

"I guess you mean, Gonnelson, it's up to me?" The man nodded. "Okay; consensus says we go there. So—"

"I'm surprised, Bran," said Jargy Hoad. "I'd have expected you to do all your own deciding, not take votes."

Looking, Tregare saw that his old friend was sincere, not needling him. "Well—" He thought about it. "When it comes down to squat, there's no time for voting. And what this ship's going to *do*, someday—anybody doesn't agree, I buy them out. But on stuff like this, the major owning shares should have a say."

"And the minor ones?" Erdis Blaine asked that.

Impatient now, Bran shook his head. "Those are courtesy shares, a system of wages, and you know it. If we have to ask people who don't know what the problem is, we're in deep."

Enough of that; he began telling them about Shegler's Moon. The system's star massed about one-point-five of Sol and ran hotter and whiter. The satellite's primary combined a mass of about three Earths, an atmosphere like that of Venus, and an orbital distance that beat Mars somewhat. "The Moon itself, the Escaped outpost, is maybe eight thousand kilos across—light on gee and thin on air."

Hoad leaned forward. "It hardly sounds like a great place to settle on. All the frequent eclipses, for one thing."

"Not all that many," said Bran. "Good tilt on the orbit." He read them the rest of it straight off the data sheets: temperature range, availability of water, edible vegetation but no vertebrate animal life. "Until their frozen zygote supply grew up to be cows and such, most of the protein came from a meat tank. But this latest report—some years old by now—says they have a stable colony going. And a good fuel-production plant, of course, for refueling ships."

"That part I'd figured," said Mallory. "Or else you wouldn't have suggested we go there at all."

So *Inconnu*, still wearing the *Tamurlaine's* insignia, cut course for Shegler's. With the ship still coming up toward a vee that would halve ship's time compared to that of planets, Jargy Hoad on watch called down to Tregare's quarters. "Bran? Something up ahead. I think we're overhauling somebody. Not straight on. There's some skew between us. You want a look?"

"Be right up." He dressed and went to Control. "What have you spotted?"

In space the passage of a starship left—well, indications. Not a "wake" exactly, but etheric turmoil that jiggled outside viewscreen images and put a bit of hash into communication channels if those were open. If the disturbances were on the increase, it meant you were closing your distance.

"You want to swing over and check this, Bran? Intercept?"

"Couldn't hurt to have a look. Assuming it's not too much

work." Meaning cost in fuel, and they both knew it. For maybe thirty seconds he watched a couple of instruments, then said, "I'd guess we're overhauling, but only by a little. Means he's still on accel, whoever, but running it well below max. Why don't you up ours a smidgen, not too much, and see what happens."

Less than two days later the other ship showed on the detectors, and then, at top mag, as a shimmering dot on viewscreen. Gonnelson had the watch as Tregare said, "I think we've converged enough, for now. Let's run parallel for a while, so that when we pull up with them, their Drive won't garble the comm."

Gonnelson nodded, and corrected course. Tregare went to get some sleep, and it wasn't until he rose and was finishing breakfast that Blaine called him by intercom. "Tregare? We don't have comm yet, but we do have a make on that ship's beacon. It's the *J. E. Hoover*, Captain Durer commanding."

Kickem's on that ship, or was! "I'll be right up."

And it was Kickem's voice, stretched and splattered by distance and wavering magnetic fields, that came from the viewscreen's speaker as Tregare entered Control. The screen itself, at high mag, showed a rear three-quarter view of the ship. ". . . repeat, the *Hoover* here, First Officer Bernardez speaking for Captain Durer who is, unfortunately, unable to give you proper greeting at the moment, though I do take the liberty of sending you his best wishes. And who might yourselves be, out here so far from no place but temporarily sharing course with us?"

Tregare waved the comm tech off and sat in his place. Kickem was up to First on the *Hoover?* This was going to take some thinking. "Third Officer Bran Tregare of the armed ship *Tamurlaine*, speaking for Captain Rigueres who is also indisposed at the moment." *Now what? Oh, yeah . . .* "*Hoover*, you are directed to name your most recent port of call and next destination." That's what the *Hannibal* had pulled, so maybe it was S.O.P. And if Kickem could maybe use a hand . . .

A pause, then, "Tregare, is it? A time it's been. Well now, only Captain Durer himself is authorized, you understand, to put our mission's details onto open circuits. However—"

Bran flipped his switch to Transmit. "Then I hope you're authorized to match course and vee, and stand by for boarding. Because otherwise, *Hoover*, we'll have to fire on you."

Fire on Kickem's ship? But sometimes a man has to bluff. Because here was Bran's chance to help his friend Escape.

From the other end he heard argument: Bernardez and at least two others. Somebody wanted to flip ship, a dangerous form of near-instant Turnover, and lose the *Tamurlaine* by taking max decel at a random angle and then flipping again, to run for it. Sounded as if Kickem disagreed, but Bran couldn't be sure of that.

Well, the hell with it. The way the argument stood, Bran had the wrong people on his side and the right ones against him. So into his mike he blasted a shrill whistle, and when relative quiet came from the *Hoover* he said, "Correction. My orders still stand: heave to! But those orders are from the Escaped ship *Inconnu*, Bran Tregare commanding." He took a deep, shuddering breath. "I'm sorry, Kickem, but this is the best way I can see, to do it."

For a moment he wasn't sure what he was hearing. Then he knew it for Kickem's laughter. Finally, "Oh, Bran! Always so cautious, we have to be. And your ship with those great dangerous projector turrets, to blow us out of space. But no need, no need at all. For in fact I was not, myself, utterly truthful. Because although we've not changed the *Hoover's* name as yet, to make it easier for us to trade advatageously at UET colonies, let me inform you that you now speak with the ship's new captain." Another laugh. "Yes, Tregare . . . it's my ship now!"

Wanting to believe, Bran said, "How many latrines you got on it?"

After a moment, Kickem said, "A great lot more than only one!" And then, totally and necessarily out of synch with each other, what with distance and delay, the two ships' Control crews sang about UET's lack of sanitary facilities.

A few hours of running parallel, the ships' computers indicated, wouldn't cost much in time or fuel, though a physical meeting would—and was tricky work, as well. So talk had to suffice. "Your Captain Durer's indisposition is permanent, then?" Tregare asked. "Same as happened to Rigueres?"

On screen, picture clear now at closer distance, Bernardez shook his head. "No such thing. We had us, you must understand, some great good luck. At Escape we managed to take Durer's woman, and two of his best friends, as hostages. The man announced surrender and enforced it. We had only two Utie loyalists dead, and one of ours. Durer and the other Uties we left safely on Fair Ball." Bran felt his face change, and Kickem must have seen, for he sighed. "Not so lucky in your own case? In usual, I gather, it seldom is." Then Bernardez took on a more cheerful look. "Almost forgetting, I was. We have a great lot of data for you, secret reports from UET's most sequestered files. For this ship, mind you, was on its way as no less than a special courier to the fortress world Stronghold. So if any of our pilfered records should interest you . . ."

"Sure." The aux circuit was set up, and soon the comm panel lights showed digital info coming in on fast-feed. When he'd ever get a chance to scan through it all, Tregare had no idea. Someday, though, and maybe soon enough to make use of it. But right now, he had to ask something. "Kickem? What's your planning? I mean, you have a ship. So now what?"

When the other didn't answer immediately, Bran said, "I'm going to do something about UET. Right yet, I'm not sure what. But whatever, it'll take more ships than one, so I'm trying to line some up. For whenever the idea whips into shape." He told of taking Marrigan's ship for Derek Limmer, and their agreement. "Bernardez, I'll take ships, buy into them, make free alliances, anything—to put a fleet together." Quickly he explained how he was trying to spread word—and later get answers—on the grapevine already begun on the Hidden Worlds by Cade Moaker. He mentioned his plans to arm Escaped ships from his arsenal on New Hope.

"From what I hear, I'll want my main base on Number One. It has the population to support a reasonable grade of production." Bernardez nodded, agreeing with the coordinates Bran gave then. "So what I want to know, Kickem—if I get something set up, and it looks like it might work . . ." He paused. "Are you with me?"

Bernardez smiled. "Had you gone and achieved this thing, Bran Tregare—and having the chance to invite me along, not done so—why, the insult would have been near to mortal."

Two hours later they said goodbyes, and their courses diverged.

Through this volume of space a number of world-to-world routes funneled. Shortly after *Inconnu* passed peak-vee and

Turnover another ship entered detection range. Its beacon, though, was either faulty or deliberately turned off, and no amount of hailing via loop-tapes brought any response. Checking his coordinates against graphic viewscreen simulations, Tregare could make no good guess as to the ship's origin or destination, and the angle between courses was far too great for possible interception. "For all I know," he said to Erdis Blaine, "it could be a Shrakken." And then needed to explain to the woman who had heard nothing but the vaguest of rumors, how UET hadn't invented stardrive at all, but had murdered visiting aliens to steal their ship. He repeated Hawkman's story of Committee Police and cyanide gas.

At the end, she nodded. "Yes, Bran. That's the way they work."

Approaching time for Turnover, Bran called Mallory and discussed the argument he'd partially heard from the *Hoover*. "This quick-flip thing they mentioned. It's been done, I gather—but is it dangerous to the ship?"

After a pause, the Chief Engineer said, "Not if you do it right the first time. Should you end up pinwheeling, though, it could take considerable time and fuel to get straightened out again. But why—"

"Because it sounds like a useful tactic—and I want to be able to do anything that anybody else can."

They compromised. At Turnover, Tregare swung ship about four times as fast as normal, but still only half as quickly as the combat maneuver. At Mallory's suggestion he fed all his moves into Tinhead in real time, then worked to refine the parameters and get rid of minor errors. And finally he put the entire maneuver onto a program requiring only a single key punched to activate it.

Although he warned the crew and asked them to secure all gear, more damage than usual resulted. But he felt it was worth it.

Approaching Shegler's Moon, *Inconnu* detected no call-beacon, and for a time Tregare's own calls, put on a loop-tape when he got tired of repeating himself, brought no answer. Not until about an hour before the ship could have landed did groundside respond. "Shegler's to *Inconnu*. You can land if you want to, but we have nothing to trade just now, and very little spare manpower or facilities for servicing. Fuel is short here,

and—" The whining voice continued explaining its inhospital-
ity.

Inconnu wasn't short of fuel; Tregare figured he could make
Number One, with a little to spare. But still he intended to top
off, any place he landed. "*Inconnu*, Bran Tregare commanding, will land in fifty-four minutes, give or take a couple. We're
not in need of servicing, and require only a moderate amount
of fuel, for which we pay going rates. Who'm I talking to down
there, by the way?"

It was like pulling stumps with a lame mule, but Tregare did
get his answers. The voice was Mace Henry, and, yes, there
was a *little* fuel, but because of unnamed difficulties, a
surcharge was in order, and ships' personnel were quarantined
to the landing area, no fraternizing in the settlement,
and . . .

Disgusted, Tregare said, "We'll talk that small stuff when
we're down. Bran Tregare out." And turned to Gonnelson and
Jargy Hoad, saying, "I don't know what these folks' trouble is,
but let's make sure it stays theirs and not ours." He knew both
scoutships were checked out in top shape. Now he saw to it
that an armed squad would protect ship's security groundside,
at all times. And wound up by adding, "I don't think this outfit
has missiles and I have no idea why they'd want to use them.
But heading down, let's have the scouts manned, just in case."

"Aren't we getting a little paranoid?" said Jargy.

Tregare grinned. "Maybe. Just so we don't get a little dead."

Landing was no problem. Gonnelson took *Inconnu* down.
As with any task that didn't need talking, he did it superbly.
Once groundside, Tregare headed for what had to be the Port
Admin building. With him he took along Erdis Blaine and
three armed guards. Going toward and into Admin he thought
the place seemed normal enough but the people didn't. For
one thing, they weren't much given to saying hello to
strangers.

Entering Mace Henry's office, he and Blaine left the guards
outside; after all, one man wasn't much menace. As Tregare
went to Henry's desk, giving his half of the introductions and
offering a handshake, the other man stood to accept. "Yes.
Captain Tregare. I trust your ship's not staying long?"

"That depends. Let's talk about fuel first." As Henry stalled
and waffled, Bran tried to decide what was *wrong* about him.
He stood and moved like a healthy person. His complexion

was good. But there was something hangdog in his manner. Finally Tregare thought he saw what was haywire here; the man was scared. *Of what?* Still listening with half his attention, he caught a phrase and shook his head. "Forget your surcharge. Straight rates."

"Out of the question. Our problems here—"

Tregare nodded to Erdis Blaine. *Time for the whipsaw.* Blaine said, "We could believe your problems, possibly, if you'd show us some figures to back them up."

"Well, I—" The expression on Henry's face, then, Tregare couldn't figure out. The man stood. "One moment. In the other office . . . I'll have to . . ." He moved to a door, opened it, and went into another room.

Blaine said, "What do you think he's up to?"

"Why not find out?" Tregare walked over to that door, put his ear to it and listened.

Not much at first, then Mace Henry's voice. "Habbeger. Captain Habbeger . . . from Captain Port Henry." Then, more like talking to himself, "I hope that damn satellite relay's working," and again speaking better, "Habbeger, this one's trouble. I think you'd better come around here and be ready to intercept."

Impatient, Tregare waited, back where Henry had last seen him, until the Port Captain brought out a folder of papers and tried to smother everything in figures and confusion. A few minutes, Bran put up with that garbage; then he said, "When can you start refueling?" Tomorrow afternoon, maybe later. "All right; I'll pay the surcharge. Call me at my ship." He motioned to Blaine and they left. Outside the office, the guards followed.

Halfway back to *Inconnu*, Blaine said, "You're paying his squeeze? Ships don't pay blackmail. Tregare—?"

The only squeeze was his hand on hers. "That's tomorrow afternoon. Erdis, we won't be here then."

"I don't understand."

"Neither do I, for sure. But that bastard made a call out to space. And he asked a fella name of Habbeger to come intercept us." He looked at her. "Guess whose uniform *that* one's wearing."

Nobody on *Inconnu* was ready for lift-off to be scheduled so soon; none of the necessary checkoff lists had been done.

Tregare raised his voice some, then, and the jobs went faster. He and Deverel did the comm-system work themselves, and four hours after Bran and Erdis left Henry's office, Tregare called the Port's comm. "*Inconnu* lifting in five minutes. Clear the safety zone."

"You can't do that!" Not Henry this time; the voice was unfamiliar. Not that it made any difference who was yelling.

"I'm doing it. Clear the area. Any dead are *your* fault." He didn't shut down the voice input that kept blithering at him; he simply paid no more heed to it. From down below he heard ringing noises that sounded like projectile weapons hitting *Inconnu's* hull. In that case they might be trying energy bolts, too—so the hell with trying to be nice; he reached over and cracked his Drive-node output. Not enough to raise ship, but plenty to fry the landing circle and a little more. *Fuck around long enough, Henry, you'll win a prize!*

The five-minute notice had been for Mallory, not for the convenience of groundside. Bran used the rest of the time to make sure his assigned gunners had the turrets ready. Missiles he didn't know, but he asked who did and Gonnelson said "Me," so the silent man held down that seat, with the fate of four fusion heads under his splayed fingers. Erdis Blaine had the counter-missiles, though neither she nor Bran knew much about those. And Jargy Hoad was riding sidekick.

Good enough. On mark, Tregare took *Inconnu* up like a bat.

Just under redline max but not by much, Bran kept his indicators. Not straight up but heading around Shegler's toward its primary, he went. Because that was where any interceptor would have to come from, and he wanted the sonofabitch in front of him, not behind.

Coming in, he hadn't had time or occasion to take a good look at that oversized version of Venus; now he did. Awesome, the thing was; bright slanting light from the system's white star showed the heavy, roiling atmosphere, hundreds of kilos deep.

Not much time for looking, though, for at one side of the planet and straight at him came not one but three intercepting ships. And they had to be UET's, and if they were all unarmed, the Easter bunny came on Christmas.

Tregare hit his talk-switch. Forget viewscreen contact, just say it. What was the name? Oh, yeah—"Habbeger! Get your ass out of my way! Bran Tregare here, speaking for *Inconnu*."

". . . surrender, and amnesty will be considered. I repeat, Captain Habbeger offers amnesty if you surrender. If not—"

It was all bullshit so Tregare didn't bother talking. Three oncoming ships, and his hi-mag view showed that only one was armed, were coming in straight side-by-side triangle formation.

Well, that left the middle, didn't it?

Ahead of any viewscreen indication, Tinhead piped up the oncoming missiles and spotted the ship that threw them. And as programmed, the computer took control of all six turrets and blew those missiles before any human gunner had a chance to act. No time, in that situation, for any niceties about range or convergence—it was, Tregare knew, a case of blast *right now*.

There was time, though, for Bran to say, "Gonnelson! Hold your missiles! You'll get another chance." Couldn't say any more because he was punching to gain control of turrets and now Tinhead let loose and Tregare got one good rake across a UET ship. Not the armed one, the missile thrower: it wasn't closest in line, so Tinhead didn't let him have it. But he holed the other one pretty good; its Drive didn't blow and it didn't tumble, but if that one got home at all, he figured it would limp a lot.

Then he had *Inconnu* through the middle of them, past and free and clear. Except, he couldn't be satisfied with that.

He called the Drive room. "Mallory! Prepare to flip."

"If we have to, captain." The voice had a sigh in it.

"Do we want to nail an armed Utie, or don't we?"

"Yes, *sir!*" Pause. "Wait for the count, though."

So Tregare did, and when it came he swung ship so fast that the centrifugal and then the stopping forces left him dazed. Only fixed purpose let him hit max accel to chase the retreating, separating triangle of UET ships and aim for the one he wanted.

They lost us; they don't know where we are. And the hell with sportsmanship; too much came back to him: the forced death fights, the gauntlet-running, the Special Cell, the panic fear of Butcher Korbeith. He said, "Gonnelson? Can you put me a missile into that armed ship up ahead?" With no word, the man nodded. Tregare said, "Then do it."

The missile was fast but Habbeger's ship was still spreading debris as *Inconnu* flashed past it; some hit and clanged against the hull. But not all of that ship was dead. Going away, Tregare felt *Inconnu* jerk and shudder; its thrust fell away to less than half of max. "Mallory? What's wrong?"

The older man's voice sounded tired. "Their turrets didn't quit soon enough. Got us across the Drive nodes. I think we can land once, if that damned tricky settlement will let us. But I wouldn't bet more than even odds on that landing."

It took some tricky juggling, trying to balance the burned nodes against the aux ones. Long gone now, the two surviving UET ships—one probably damaged a lot, and the other away free. Both unarmed, they were no danger to *Inconnu*—but now UET would know of Shegler's Moon, and someday claim it. So that, Bran now realized, was why Mace Henry and the whole place had been running scared; they'd been retaken, was all, and trying to cover their own ass.

Not good enough, that excuse, or so Tregare saw it. If they'd trusted him, helped him, things could have gone better.

Well. Relying on Mallory's advice, Bran eased *Inconnu* back toward Shegler's and called the Port. Mace Henry answered, and told *Inconnu*, "We can't allow you back here. The trouble—"

Blaine had been doing the talking; Tregare took over. "You haven't seen trouble yet. You try to stop me landing, you give me any problems on Drive repairs, *then* you'll see trouble." He was fuming, mad as hell and glad of it. He said, "Gonnelson? Mallory? Can you two land this thing if I clear it at groundside?"

He got qualified assents, and turned to Jargy Hoad. "What you say, once this bucket hits a good place to orbit, we take the scouts downside and show these closet Uties how the cow ate the cabbage?"

Jargy grinned. "Sounds good to me."

Shegler's had no missiles worth worrying about. The scout-ships dodged them easily enough, and Tregare saw them explode harmlessly, upstairs. "Jargy? Two launching sites, I spotted. You see any more?"

"Just the two. I'll take the one nearest me."

The scout's projectors weren't in the same league with the ones ships carried, but they did the job. Both missile sites went up, taking quite a lot of Shegler's soil with them. Circling, waiting for the dust to settle or drift downwind,

Tregare spotted the ionization trails of projectors reaching up from groundside. Big ones, too—But not geared for traverse fast enough to nail a scout. Bran yelled to Jargy, and the two methodically wiped out the gun emplacements. Then Tregare made three fast passes over the settlement, at speeds intended to break every window in the place and maybe a few other things, and then two slow ones, to draw fire from anyone who still had some. Nothing happened. "Looks like Shegler's has shot its wad," said Jargy.

"Seems as if." He called up to *Inconnu*. "Gonnelson? I think it's safe to land now. Let's see if you and Mallory can set yourselves down like a crate of eggs." No answer, but after a while the ship's ID-beacon came in, signal strengthening, so he knew it was on the way down.

Anything more, now? He first rejected the idea that came to him, then reconsidered it. Item one: *that Henry could've warned us*. Item two: *maybe these people need a little more convincing*.

So before he landed his scoutship, Tregare made one more pass, and blew the Port Admin building purely all to hell.

The Port itself, it turned out, had been the government of Shegler's Moon. Now there wasn't any. So while *Inconnu* sat, undergoing repairs, the only government was Bran Tregare. The main item of business was refueling and repair of *Inconnu*, but he did take time to ask who among the survivors had held down what kind of semi-executive job previously, and made some appointments. To the woman he assigned to replace the late Mace Henry, he said, "After I leave, you're in charge for just as long as you can keep things under control. Can you?"

She pushed short, greying hair back from her thin face. "After the way you shot hell out of us, what do *you* care? And what's the point? Now UET knows about us. When they come back—"

"By groundside time, that'll be years from now. If they bother, even. Still—" He thought about it. "In your shoes, I'd think in terms of evacuating. A few at a time, whenever a ship comes in and has room to take some extra aboard." Pause. "Guarantee me no Uties in the lot, I could take on maybe a dozen. More, if they're real friendly and don't mind sleeping crowded." He shrugged. "Food, things like that . . . they're no problem."

She looked at him. "Suppose we did that. The last few left here . . . what do *they* do?"

He knew what she meant, but that wasn't what he answered. "They blow the fuel plant, so UET doesn't get the use of it."

She shook her head. "Tregare, you're a real monster. You know that?"

He couldn't let his hurt show. "Well, I had some help."

Before Mallory pronounced *Inconnu's* Drive solid again, Tregare did a little trading, after all—remembering Number One's reputation for being interested in new food plants, he swapped some electronic components for a few bags of seed. He took aboard seventeen evacuees from Shegler's: mostly tech people, but also a mother with two children. He wasn't too crazy about having kids loose in a ship, but they behaved themselves all right. And finally, quite a bit later than he'd expected at the time of landing, Bran lifted *Inconnu* off Shegler's Moon. Just out of atmo, Gonnelson docked one scout and Jargy the other.

He picked his time so as to use the Venus-like primary for a vee-enhancing sling turn that put him dead on for Number One—no need, on this leg, to take any detours. The first couple of days he worried about the Drive and hung around Control a lot. Then, deciding that Mallory knew his stuff, he went back to his normal routine.

He didn't know why things weren't so good between him and Erdis Blaine, but they were not. Down on Shegler's he'd been too busy and harassed to have much time with her—time that did either of them a lot of good, anyway. Now, when he could relax with her, it wasn't working. She'd miss one rendezvous after another and make some kind of excuse. He never checked up on her, because if he had to do that, the whole thing wasn't worth it.

And then about once a week or a little less often, she'd meet with him in quarters and be totally passionate, sometimes so much so that it put him off his stride and he bungled it.

The trouble was, he had so much on his mind that he couldn't really concentrate on his problems with Erdis. Maybe if he could have (and he realized as much), things might get straightened out. But he couldn't . . .

When she'd taken to leaving him a lot of spare time he didn't want, he started using some of it to scan through the mass of

UET data that Kickem Bernardez had fast-fed to Tinhead. And found some things he knew were probably significant, but not *why*. Or how he might be able to use them.

There was the list of UET colonies, with their coordinates and descriptions. Some of them he could keep in mind—Terranova, the Twin Worlds (well, he'd *been* there, and at Penfoyle Gate and Hardnose), Iron Hat the mining world, Far Corner, Franklin's Jump—and some he couldn't remember. Well, he'd better think more solidly along those lines. Because one way to help give UET the trots was to raid their colonies. Even unarmed ships did that sometimes—and anything they could do, *Inconnu* could do better!

Then there was the rather cryptic description of UET's fortress world, Stronghold. Not a fortified *planet*, of course, but an armed outpost on a world to the far side of Earth from all other UET explorations. And Bran could find no other reason for the venture, except Hawkman Moray's theory: that Stronghold was UET's guardpoint against any approach by the alien Shrakken.

Appended to that block of data was a listing of ships and dates. Future dates, if Bran hadn't lost track of planets' time. For a time the codings, not cryptographic but mere abbreviations, had him puzzled; then he figured it out. Maybe. If he had it right, every two years UET on Earth sent to Stronghold a group of ships to add to that world's arsenal. Not all of those, he gathered, stayed at Stronghold. Some returned as messengers to Earth and others went out patrolling or on missions to other colonies, for reasons not at all clear in the text at hand.

But every two years, something like six or eight ships, one out of three armed (on the average), went to Stronghold.

Somewhere in this load of facts there had to be an angle. But right now Tregare couldn't see what it was.

Turnover came and went. The planet Number One was about three or four months in *Inconnu*'s future—and in Bran Tregare's. He thought about it. His family was there—or so he'd been given to believe. He'd have to deal with them; anywhere a Hulzein was, that person would be a major factor in the local setup. But he did not want to see them, and he wouldn't. Well, there were ways. . . .

Everything he'd seen, heard or read said that Number One was his best bet for a permanent base, to set up whatever offensive he would someday mount against UET. That might take some doing. *Inconnu*, though, carried leverage with it wherever it went.

All right. When he got to Number One he'd play it by ear, because, when had he ever had the chance to do it any other way?

Between Tregare and Erdis Blaine the tension grew. He was mostly too busy to pay attention, but sometimes it got to him. Then, only a few hours short of detection range from Number One, that planet spotted and identified by Tinhead, Bran went to quarters for a quick shower and change of clothes, and found Erdis drying herself from her own bath. He said, "You heading for watch, or chow, or what?" He didn't care much.

"If you're not busy just now, how about bed?"

"I—" *I can't shift my head so fast, just like that,* was what he had in mind to say. But it had been a time, and for a change his annoyance worked for him instead of against him when it came to arousal, so he peeled his clothes off. "Wait a bit. I need a shower first."

Neither of them clothed, she came and hugged him. "After." So they did everything they ever had done, and to his mind very well indeed, and then lay together, half-embracing. And she said, "Buy me out, Bran. At Number One, I'm leaving the ship."

How many ways can you say "I don't understand"? Bran tried several; none worked. Finally he said, "Just *tell* me." She nodded and tried to explain.

"I can't stay with you, and on this ship I can't live away from you." *It made no sense.* He asked more. "I know your past," she said. "For a long time, to me it justified your actions." She shook her head. "But not what you did on Shegler's. The woman there, that you told me about—she pegged you, Bran. You *have* become a monster. And I can't live with that."

Memory hit him. Fighting inside himself, determined *not* to strike this woman and stop the hurt she was giving him, he said, "You're the third to call me that. The one on Shegler's was the second."

"And the first?"

If you smile, they don't know they got to you. "Me. Back at the Slaughterhouse."

* * *

There was more to it, and long before Tregare could admit it out loud, he accepted her need to be off the ship, away from him. If that's how she felt—*how many hours 'til we land and she gets the hell off?* She was talking and talking, off into the kind of diatribe that never says what it's *about*. By the chin, not hard, he grabbed her. "Erdis? You got more on your mind, for peace's sake get to it!"

Not pulling away at all, she tilted her face up to the angle he'd always found the most lovely. "I'm not leaving you behind entirely, Bran. Part of you stays with me."

To cover his puzzlement, he said, "Nothing I'll really need, I hope?"

She shook her head. "Hardly. Just your child."

But how—? "But how—?"

"Coming out from Shegler's I didn't renew my contra implant. Because I've loved and valued you, Bran—for some qualities you may not even know you have, by now. But you've let yourself be warped; Shegler's showed me that."

Let? Butcher Korbeith? The Slaughterhouse? LET?

But he held silence as she said, "So I can't be with you any longer. But your child, Bran, won't carry your hate." Trying to smile, she almost made it. "You understand?"

Almost gently, he said, "No. No, I don't." Suddenly thirsty he poured bourbon and gulped half of it too fast, but kept himself from coughing. "But you don't understand, either."

How to say it? "It's nice you and my kid can live peaceful on a Hidden World and not hate. Nice. But I can't do that. I had it from Arbogast and Channery and Korbeith and—" He shook his head. "Never mind that. What it is, somebody has to *do* something about those bastards, and it's not going to be any nice bunny rabbit. It's going to be people like Derek Limmer and Jargy Hoad and Kickem Bernardez—and like *me*. From here it doesn't look like what you say, but I guess I have to live with that. If I'm a monster, as you call me, I had a lot of help getting there."

His gaze unfocused. Looking back in time he said, "I thought when I got away from Korbeith, and then from UET itself . . . but I expect you're right. The longer it goes, the meaner it gets."

He stood. "You better move into Second's quarters. I'll have your stuff brought over." He had another thought. "The ship can't pay your shares off all in cash, but I'll see you get good marketable cargo for the rest—and maybe I know a connection on the planet that can help you handle it the best way." Yes, his family owed him that much, even though they'd deal through intermediaries. If they didn't think so, he'd show them different.

Offering no kiss or handshake, she said, "Goodbye, Bran."

He nodded. "That's right. Except on business, we won't see each other again." He watched the door close behind her.

He felt he should want another drink, but lay down without one. After a while, Jargy called on intercom. Tregare answered, "I'm busy. I expect to be that way for some time. You and Gonnelson do the hails and landing; don't call me unless there's a problem. All right?" All right, so he lay back again.

I'll take Stronghold, that's what. Don't know how yet, but I will. Kickem's data, that's the key. . . .

What was it with him and women? Murphy, now—with the raw-scarred face and the eyepatch—catch *her* bleeding tears over any dead Uties? Not hardly. Or Janith Reggs on the scoutship? Well, maybe. Salome Harker . . . and where was she, by now? Escaped, Bran hoped. Either way, they were probably years out of synch with each other. But she'd been a fighter, and likely still was.

Without volition his mind scanned ahead, and his gut clenched. Phyls Dolan, tumbling frozen between stars, forever. No matter what he did to Uties, he'd never pay them back for Phyls. But Erdis couldn't see it that way; she hadn't been there. On the ship itself, yes, but not where it happened.

Headshake. *After Stronghold*—there'd be more of a move he could make, some way.

My family. Well, they'd dumped him, so that was that.

With the lights softened, he squinted into dimness. The way things were, no point in worrying about people who couldn't see what the problem was. The way things were . . .

The hell with it. I've got a job to do.

ABOUT THE AUTHOR

F. M. BUSBY's published science fiction novels include *Rissa Kerguelen*, the related *Zelde M'Tana*, *All These Earths*, and the now-combined volume *The Demu Trilogy* (*Cage a Man*, *The Proud Enemy*, and *End of the Line*). Numerous shorter works, ranging from short-short to novella length, have appeared in various SF magazines and in both original and reprint anthologies, including *Best of Year* collections edited by Terry Carr, by Lester Del Rey, and by Donald A. Wollheim. Some of Busby's works have been published in England and (in translation) Germany, France, Holland and Japan.

The Star Rebel, the first of two books concerning the early life of Bran Tregare, is set in *Rissa's* universe, as is *The Alien Debt*, a direct sequel to *Rissa* (forthcoming from Bantam).

Buz grew up in eastern Washington near the Idaho border, is twice an Army veteran, and holds degrees in physics and electrical engineering. He has worked at the "obligatory list of incongruous jobs" but settled for an initial career as communications engineer, from which he is now happily retired in favor of writing. He is married, has a daughter in medical school, and lives in Seattle. During Army service and afterward he spent considerable time in Alaska and the Aleutians. His interests include aerospace, unusual cars, dogs, cats, and people, not necessarily in that order. He once built, briefly flew and thoroughly crashed a hang glider, but comments that fifteen-year-olds usually bounce pretty well.

COMING IN MAY 1984 . . .
THE REMARKABLE SEQUEL
TO THE CLASSIC *RISSA KERGUELEN*

THE
ALIEN
DEBT

BY F. M. BUSBY

F. M. Busby's RISSA KERGUELEN is widely considered to be a classic science fiction saga. Now, after many years, he follows-up on this brilliant novel with the story of Rissa, Bran, and their daughter Lisele as they confront the vicious mind-fury of a powerful alien race.

"THE ALIEN DEBT will delight the readers of RISSA KERGUELEN. It's a great space adventure in a richly imagined future world."

—Jack Williamson

"Busby writes fine adventure stories, the kind that made us love science fiction in the first place."

—Jerry Pournelle

Read THE ALIEN DEBT, on sale May 15, 1984, wherever Bantam paperbacks are sold.

OUT OF THIS WORLD!

That's the only way to describe Bantam's great series of science fiction classics. These space-age thrillers are filled with terror, fancy and adventure and written by America's most renowned writers of science fiction. Welcome to outer space and have a good trip!